STATE OF DOGS

A NOVEL BY

TURU KHAN

Blue Ocean Press

Copyright © 2025 Blue Ocean Press All Rights Reserved.

This publication may not be reproduced, stored in a retrieval system or transmitted in any form or by any means, electronic, mechanical, photocopying, recording, or otherwise, without prior written permission of the publisher, except by a reviewer who may quote brief passages in a review to be printed in a periodical.

Published by:

Blue Ocean Press

U.S. Office

P.O. Box 510818

Punta Gorda, Florida 33950

URL: http://www.blueoceanpublications.com

Email: books@blueoceanpublications.com

Translator from Mongolian into English: AMARSAIKHAN Batsaikhan

Cover design: BATBILEG Dagvadorj and photo by Jan Locus

Graphic art | Illustration: GUNGAA Dashtseren.

Editor: Colleen O'Brien

ISBN: 9784902837667

Table of Contents

Part 1   5

Part 2   57

Part 3   135

Part 4   193

Part 5   221

Part 6   255

Glossary of Mongolian and Cultural Terms   275

Note: Italicized words in text can be found in the glossary.

PART 1

One, two, three, four, five, six, seven
I need seven reasons to die
If I'm not inspired to write an original verse
If I can't sense the beauty of low hills
If I turn my head to the red light at dawn
If I don't feel like tasting lips and breasts
If I hear alien sounds disturbing my dreams
If I'm seduced by someone else's false paradise
Or if I want to escape from this foolish life
Then I wouldn't hesitate to choose death

One, two, three, four, five, six, seven
I need seven reasons to live
If I'm inspired to write an original verse
If I sense the beauty of low hills
If I enjoy the red light at dawn
If I feel like tasting lips and breasts
If there are no alien sounds disturbing my dreams
If I'm not seduced by someone else's false paradise
Or if I want to live this foolish life
One, two, three, four, five, six, seven hundred years
You can see me anywhere, anytime
I am now here
I am nowhere

— Galsaa Axt

1

Dawn was breaking on the morning of *March 8*, 1997. The red light of dawn could be seen over the five yellow brick buildings called the twelfth *mikroraion* (the Russian word for a small neighborhood). The neighborhood was barely spotted from afar among the thick smoke coming from the *Tsagaan Davaa* (White Hill) slums in the north. There was only one lighted window from a first-floor household of one of those mundanely similar buildings.

Avid woke up at four in the morning and looked at his wristwatch. He got up, dressed quickly, and made himself a mug of black tea, spread butter on a slice of bread, forked sprats in oil from the can, and added them; then he sat down behind the kitchen table to have his breakfast. He enjoyed the whole thing with such appetite. As soon as he got up, *Avid* quickly lit one of his Bulgarian "Stewardess" cigarettes, picked up a Vintov rifle from behind the curtain, and got underway cleaning it.

Soon, a small truck drove up the paved road in front of the building, its light flickering through the thick gray smoke, and stopped by the first entrance. The truck was heaving with even more smoke when the driver gave three honks and stepped on the gas pedal relentlessly to keep the motor running. *Avid* tilted his head, as if the loud honks were suddenly audible, and swiftly bagged his rifle, standing up with the cigarette still in his mouth.

Almost in his thirties, *Avid* had started working part-time for a sinister company called The Reserve, the main function of which was killing dogs. After graduating from the tenth grade, he took an exam to study at the School of Internal Defense of the Soviet Union in Volgograd under the auspices of the Ministry of Social Security. His father was a military man, but he had allowed his son to grow up in a disorderly and somewhat spoiled manner, so to make amends, he sought to have him sent to military school. The city of Volgograd, where *Avid* was closest to Western Europe, was where he first heard Western music from Russian students. He became obsessed with rock. At that time, the momentum was on Boney M. and ABBA. *Avid* formed a rock band—*Gvozd* (Nails)—with the Russians and began playing solo guitar.

He studied international espionage in the Soviet Union and performed in the band. After the performances, he hooked up with Russian girls and drank heavily. Everything fell into disarray, and confusion reigned when the new form of economics, Perestroika, began. His schooling was no longer the same, and he dropped out in his final year.

Because he had attended school under the Ministry of Social Security, when he returned to Mongolia, he got a job at the Ministry, translating and writing articles for a small magazine for official in-house use. He grew his hair long and wore jeans to work, so he became an object of criticism. As an employee of the Ministry, he was looked down upon despite his good work.

During his studies at the intelligence school in Volgograd, *Avid* excelled in sniper shooting. He was awarded the badge of Best Hunter in the country, so he was recruited to a special service in the ward of the *Ikh Tenger State Residence*. With his father's support, he served high-level national and international guests with their hunts: he gunned down the prey simultaneously as the hunter released a shot. The ward, consisting of about 30 people, belonged to the Ministry of Social Security, and he was the only hunter on staff. Hunting was a common hobby for socialist leaders back then, and *Avid* led the team of deer herders whenever there was a hunt on *Bogd Mountain*. The honorable guests brought the best rifles with them; however, their hunting abilities were not advanced by blasting away with their expensive weapons. The only thing that mattered was if the prey was killed, no matter by whose bullet. So, the professional hunter made simultaneous shots for the guests, and most of the time, the prey was shot and killed. The high-class hunt would end well, with those politicians proudly posing for photos next to the dead deer killed for them by Avid.

Meanwhile, *Avid* never stopped writing and translating for the magazine for intelligence activities.

In 1990, when the democratic revolution took place in Mongolia, the Ministry of Social Security was transformed into the General Directorate of State Security, and Avid, being the most criticized employee, was laid off in the first retrenchment.

With the advent of a society called democracy and a free-market economy, the number of stray dogs in Ulaanbaatar suddenly increased. In ancient times, Mongolians used only male dogs to guard the livestock, and the female puppies were usually thrown into the wilderness. People would also buy only male puppies, especially those born strong. This and other reasons contributed to the increase of stray dogs around urban settlements. To make it worse, when the families of Russian army men stationed in Mongolia from the Soviet Union started leaving the countryside in the 1990s, their dogs were left behind. With the elimination of herdsmen's cooperatives and farm foundations, herding families could not make ends meet any longer, and they sold the animals as they sold their herds and migrated to the cities; they abandoned their dogs.

In the cities, the factories were closing down for good, and the number of unemployed suddenly increased; so, not only dogs were straying, but people, too.

On top of barking all night, the now-abandoned dogs were despised for carrying infectious diseases. For those reasons, the Reserve company under the Ulaanbaatar city government started killing off the strays through contracted professional hunters with gun licenses. The company allowed 30 bullets a day for each hunter and tasked them with killing at least 20 dogs. The hunters cut off the snouts of the dogs they killed and brought them in once a week to calculate their salaries. As soon as he heard about the job, he went to the company to offer his services. As he was the best hunter in the country, the company immediately hired him. The locals came to know of this vicious hunter who butchered stray dogs in the early hours of the morning.

But nobody knew it was *Avid* who made a living butchering dogs because he told no one. As a young man, he made acquaintances with a few women, none of whom he ever thought of marrying and, therefore, to whom he told little about himself. The time itself was not suited for marrying, let alone for beginning a family. So, he remained living in the one-bedroom apartment inherited from his father. *Avid* could not dare to think of building a family on killing dogs as dawn broke. Killing one dog made him 200 *tugrugs*, so he made roughly 2,000 to 3,000 *tugrugs* each morning. Because a public servant's monthly salary was around 30,000 *tugrugs* at that time, the dog-killing job made him good money, but marrying did not seem to go with killing animals. Whether he liked it or not, he got up each morning and hunted.

Avid accepted the fact that his reputation would be destroyed if people knew he killed dogs. From ancient times, Mongolians believed that dogs were reincarnated as humans. Killing dogs was considered as unforgivable a sin as murdering humans, partly because of the myths and partly because of the obvious reason that dogs were man's best friend. Most people were familiar with the tradition that when a pet dog dies, the masters cut off the tail and put it under their pillow, wishing the dog to be reincarnated as a good person. Mongolians usually took their dead dogs to the mountainside to bury them and erected a stone cairn to mark them.

There was an old man who killed a dog under the same contract as Avid. The old fellow once spilled his own story about dog-killing to a man he drank with, who immediately burst into anger, knocked the old man on the head with his gun, and set his home on fire with the dog and him inside. The rumors spread among dog hunters, and those who killed dogs were even more careful never to tell others about their work. Although the murderer was arrested eventually, the police and the court ignored the case, deciding that the dog hunter had died in the fire, thus spreading the assumption that "the sinful creature who killed dogs had died in the same disgraceful way as the dogs he had killed." That is why all dog hunters spent their days in fear of exposure.

Avid wiped the barrel of his gun one more time, lit a cigarette, put on his hunting jacket, and turned up the radio, which had been whispering against the wall as he walked toward the door.

"Dear listeners!" the radio commentator spoke. "Tomorrow, on March 9, 1997, a special phenomenon known as the total solar eclipse will be observed in our country. A solar eclipse is a phenomenon in which the moon enters into a position between the sun and earth, and the whole or some part of the sun is blocked by the moon, depending on your location. This phenomenon occurs only during the new moon. Two to five solar eclipses are observed on earth each year, but no more than two total eclipses.

"Our ancient scriptures suggest that the solar eclipse was the result of a giant dragon called *Rakh* that swallowed the sun and that during a total eclipse, people would beat their dogs to make them whine and howl, would pound pots and pans, and do everything to make loud noises to repel *Rakh*. Nowadays, people need not be so superstitious during the eclipse. Needless to say, a solar eclipse will bring temporary darkness during the daytime and return to normal in a few minutes. Foreign and domestic tourists flocked to *Edenet*."

2

The beginning of this story was traced back to the twilight of the autumn of 1989, where a woman listened to the radio in a small village store in New Jersey, adjacent to New York City.

No two things are more different from each other...

The lonesome woman listening to the radio was named Daisy Maria (as many women are not fond of their names, she was no exception. She knew so many dogs that were called Daisy, which rhymed with the word 'lazy.' Whenever someone called her, she heard Lazy Maria).

At the time of her birth in 1948, the town's traditional steel factory, dating back to the 1700s, had expanded into an arms factory during the Second World War. Her mother told stories of how the village was a bustling place. But there was no soul left today to prove the former liveliness; it had turned into one of those desolate villages so often found in America. She was conceived three years after her father returned from the war.

At 41 years old, she never started a family. But she fell in love once. The man was a drunk and a junky and was infamous for getting in trouble. One day, he came home soused and hit Daisy Maria out of jealousy, blackening her eye. He left and never returned home because, still in a rage, he fought with several men that night, chasing one of them with his car and running him over. He was sentenced to twenty years in prison.

Daisy never fell in love again.

She had been in a few relationships, though.

As the city became less and less populated each year, Daisy continued to make a living as the shopkeeper at the store. The owner was a Jewish man who had become close to her mother soon after her father died. The man treated Daisy as his daughter.

Her father's wounds from the war worsened steadily, and he was hospitalized for osteomyelitis. He died the year she turned three, and she had no memory of her father other than reminders in the black-and-white photos in the family album. Daisy grew up with her mother, but in 1966, when she was only eighteen, her mother died suddenly of a heart attack.

The village lost its population year after year due to the 1973 oil crisis, after the Nixon shock, which followed the fall of the Bretton Woods system when the metal and steel industries crashed. The crisis peaked during Ronald Reagan's presidency, making the village a ghost town.

In January 1989, when George W. Bush became the new president, the hope that the city would recover was long gone, and most of the residents had moved to other cities.

That day, as Daisy listened to music on the radio while sitting behind the counter of her usual customer-less store, a tall and bright-eyed man showed up out of nowhere. The villagers knew each other so well, it was clear that the man wasn't one of them. He came in, bought a few small flashlight batteries, and then stopped to take a look at the lottery tickets laid out on the once green-painted wooden shelf.

"Well, my small-town beauty, let me test my luck," he said. "Please grab five tickets for me with your pretty hands. If I pick one, I will give you ten percent of my win."

His voice resonated in a deep, masculine way, as though he were a nighttime radio commentator.

The woman was so lonely, she would flirt with anyone, especially a handsome stranger. "Okay, sure," she said, as she let her hand momentarily rub against his masculine and hairy hand as she gave him the five tickets.

The man smiled. "My name is Bradley Doan. I am an artist, thinking of making a documentary about this deserted town of yours. A woman as pretty as you might as well play the lead. I am calling the film 'A Lost Ballad.'"

As they looked at each other with acute interest, he picked a pink-colored ticket without looking away from her. Finally, he looked down and began scratching the shiny blue part with a quarter from his pocket. Bradley liked the art on the card—a woman wearing a hoodie with "Free hugs" printed on it.

He asked, "How much if I hit the jackpot?"

"Probably a hundred bucks? Most of them are empty. Twenty at best."

He finished scratching, hid the ticket between his palms, and said, "Okay, a hundred bucks. You open my hands; I'll have my eyes closed." Watching him close his eyes made Daisy feel dizzy, and she almost had to close her own eyes. She gazed at his eyelids for a moment and then leaned in to pick up the ticket under his hand.

She looked at it with narrowed eyes as though she had bad eyesight. "Jesus fucking Christ! One hundred here!" she shouted.

Thinking she was joking, Bradley Doan reached inside his backpack and pulled out his black wallet chained to the bag. "Five bucks, is it?"

Daisy held the ticket in her hand and shook it at him. "Why aren't you happy? Don't you believe me?" she asked teasingly, passing him the ticket.

Without even looking at it, Bradley Doan put five dollars on the counter and turned away.

"Hey, you're not leaving without giving me my share." Daisy opened the nickel drawer and threw four twenties along with the ticket. "I'm taking twenty. You have eighty," she declared.

Bradley looked at the ticket finally, his eyes going big in surprise. "Oh, my God! You have golden hands. Give me one more ticket, which means you get fifteen. But I'll wait until later to scratch it off with you. What are you doing after work?"

Handing out another lottery ticket, Daisy smiled. "I'm closing at ten. The bar will not be open that late, my dear filmmaker. Are you really making a film?" she asked with an even more playful voice.

"Of course, I am." He pulled out a small camera from his backpack.

"With such a little thing?"

"Little camera for a little town. I'm staying at David Insley's, spending three nights there. How about I come back here before ten? Let's grab some beer or something. Let's talk movies. I can even interview you!"

He showed her a small microphone, looking into her pretty face. "By the way, lucky girl, do you have a name?"

"Daisy."

"Jaisy?"

"Daisy Maria."

"Oh, Daisy? I have a film to shoot." He turned around and held his fingers to his lips. "Good luck, Daisy Maria," he said and blew her a kiss.

As Daisy winked at him with a hint of a smile on her face, she was thinking, He's never coming back.

Bradley spent hours shooting inside and outside the deserted factory; he forgot his promise to return to Daisy's store before ten. For him, the sight of the giant gears and machines from the last century amazed him so much he felt like he was on some other planet or in a time warp. He ran around shooting videos, even after dark with the help of his lighting. Finally, his batteries died. It was too late in the evening, and he put the cameras back inside the backpack, unwillingly.

I'll continue tomorrow, Bradley thought with a little sorrow and finally got out of the factory that had made him forget about everything else. He headed north along the empty nighttime street.

As he strolled along with much satisfaction from his day's work, Bradley spotted a little red brick place that resembled a cat's house from a fairy tale. After looking at it for a while, he noticed an old man with a long, white beard sitting inside, enjoying a sandwich. Bradley Doan could not resist knocking on the glass door.

The old man pointed at the clock, hesitated for a moment stroking his beard, and came to the door. With a bit of surprise on his face, the old man half-opened the door. "How can I help you? Our bank is closed. It's past ten."

"If you don't mind, can I sit with you for a moment? I am staying at David Eastley's, the one who lives by the post office. Do you know him?"

"Know him? He's an old friend! Come in."

The old man unhooked the door chain, and Bradley entered the room and took a good look around.

"You're not scared to spend the night in here alone?"

"What's there to be scared of? We know everyone in this town. This bank used to be huge. That's when I started working security, when the bank was at the building out back. The bank bought this one from John Smith and moved here two years ago. This is an ancient building, from sometime in the 1700s. You've probably never heard, but John Smith Family & Company was the richest family around here. John's son used to live here by himself, and he finally sold it and moved to New York. When did you come to David's? I worked with his father. He was a banker."

"I arrived today. Is the store in the back closed now? The shopkeeper, Daisy Maria, must have left now, hasn't she?"

"Probably closed now. Daisy Maria is single. She was a real beauty in her time, but this hopeless place has worn her out. What's your business, anyway, in this lost town? Are you some kind of an adventurer with those hunting clothes on?" The bearded old man observingly interrogated the tall man wearing army fatigues.

"No. I am a videographer. I promised Daisy I would drop by before she closed down. Well, look at how late I am for that. Is there a place around here where I can buy a beer or two?"

"Yes, there is one, but it's far north from here. If you would bother hanging out with an old man like me, we can grab beers from the gas station down the road and drink together. Or should I call Daisy up? She lives very close, not even a mile."

"Really, she does? You're so friendly. So, if I go grab some beers, we can drink here?"

"Yes, we can. Things are different out here. Nothing happens. Tomorrow's Sunday besides, and everything will be closed. While you're out to buy beers, why don't I call Daisy and ask her to come down here? Chatting with someone from outside the town is a breath of fresh air to us."

The old man chuckled as Bradley slung his backpack over his shoulder. "What's your name, by the way? Mine's Bradley Doan."

"People call me ZZ Top," the old man said, picking up the receiver from its cradle. Without breaking his glance at the tall, army-clad man heading to the gas station, he dialed Daisy. "Miss Daisy, I have news for you. A man who was supposed to meet you came here and just went out to buy beer. If you could come, both old and young gentlemen would be so happy. All in all, it's Saturday night; what's the harm in having a chat over drinks? Won't take you a minute to get here, will it?"

3

The dim light of morning arrived. A blue truck parked in front of *Avid*'s apartment, engulfed in thick black smoke, as the driver restlessly stepped on the gas pedal to keep the engine running. *Avid* moved swiftly with the rifle in his hand and quickly got inside the truck. The Russian driver named *Orosoo* (The Russian) glared at *Avid* sleepily.

"Had a good night's sleep? Where shall we go today?" he murmured.

"Well, how about we start with *Tsagaan Davaa* since it's close and has its fair share of strays? We haven't been there since last year, have we? We'd better stick to the slums, anyway; otherwise, we'll be messing with pets by mistake."

"People let their dogs run free and then complain when we kill 'em." *Avid* spoke as the truck picked up speed, heading north. He unbuttoned his military jacket, adjusted his sweater, and turned to the driver:

"Your daughter's still going to school, eh?"

"Yeah, with her mom, early in the mornings. Poor little thing …"

"Yes, they're now talking about taking six-year-olds to school. Even testing this new system next year or something. Have you heard?"

"Ugh. The idea of making a mockery of education! Making a carbon copy of the Western sedentary culture is no good here. Six-year-olds can't even wipe their asses, let alone study. Worse in the countryside. The mothers are going with the children to the centers, and the fathers are going to struggle alone with the animals. It's gonna be a mess. Everything has gone south since the 1990s came along."

"We were taught in the academy about this. They always pass a law first, and then the change begins."

With this, *Avid* wrapped up the uneasy topic.

The blue UAZ truck pulled over at the gas station to fill up, and *Avid* went off to the side of the road to have a smoke.

When a young woman hurried along the sidewalk toward where *Avid* was standing, sucking greedily on his cigarette, he wondered why a pretty girl would be walking alone in such early, dark hours of the morning, without even wearing a hat against the chill of the air. She was probably his age and had a beautiful face, and her overwhelmingly sad thoughts and tears inside revealed themselves in her expression. She looked like a student and shied away a bit as she noticed his eyes on her.

Her eyes shone with a mix of spark and hatred. She was worried if the man noticed her hatred from the strange look she had just given him but, at the same time, felt as though this man had a connection with her for some reason, although they had never met.

She suddenly thought he appeared like a messenger of death, as if resurrected from when she had seen him in a previous life, a familiar and powerful man who could give both fear and joy. But no. She had seen this man in her dreams, even though she had never dreamt of a man in a checkered jacket and a black hat like this man. In her dreams, men very much resembled Che Guevara. This man, if his anger burned — she shivered — lives would be lost; if he laughed, lives would be created. He was now puffing on his cigarette right in front of her. The woman could not slow her pace and passed by him with fear and resentment.

4

"My dear, today is a great deal. I know David Eastly fairly well. From what I hear, this man is visiting him," the long-bearded man told the woman.

Daisy Maria had changed into a fancier cotton dress from the mundane shopkeeper's uniform and pulled her hair up into a casual bun, so she looked younger and more beautiful than the woman she was in the afternoon.

Daisy chuckled with her friend as she plunked herself into a revolving chair and stared at her red stilettos on her little feet. *Well, let's see what happens now, she thought. The man says he makes movies, and that he even wants to cast me...* Daisy saw a shadow behind the glass door. It was Bradley.

Bradley Doan stared at Daisy with such surprise. "Please forgive me, miss. It was I who was supposed to come to you, but I had someone else call you out here. My heartfelt apologies. I was so caught up in my work, I didn't notice the time passing..." He looked fully at her. "You look beautiful," he said and thought to himself: Prettier than this afternoon. And one sultry woman! Her body, oh! So slender. Her skin is so dazzlingly white. Her thighs just right to have a grip. Why didn't I notice when I first saw her?

He jerked his head away from the enticing woman and said loudly to the old fellow, "Why are you called ZZ Top? Is it because you have a long beard?"

ZZ stroked his silky beard. "A long time has passed since people started calling me that. My name is Theodore Jeremiah."

"I intend to make a movie," said Bradley. "I live in New York." Bradley's deep voice mesmerized Daisy as she watched him open the brown bottles of Sierra Nevada Pale Ale.

"What movie did you come here to make?"

"No decision has been made yet. This is my first day. I was lucky to meet you because I'm very curious. I bet no one will believe me when I tell them I would be drinking beer with a beautiful woman and ZZ Top inside a bank. By the way, do you know how many dollars are in this bank safe right now?"

"Of course, I know, but only roughly. Four million dollars, at least."

Bradley was walking back and forth with his bottle of beer now. "Which safe has those four million bucks?" he asked.

The old man laughed and pointed his finger at the silvery-white door of the bank vault in the back of the hall. "It's in there. Our bank has only one vault now. Before, when we were in the back building, this bank was a big one with seven vaults like that."

Bradley had already taken out his small Sony camera and started recording the old man's speech. Daisy laughed out loud, "Bradley has started shooting. So, the documentary starts with the bank?"

Bradley raised his eyes from behind the camera. "Daisy, why don't you introduce yourself in front of this four-million-dollar vault?" She posed in her swivel chair, waving her arm languidly toward the back of the room. "My name is Daisy Maria. Behind this giant safe is the four million dollars I saved. I was born in this small town, and now I am the queen here. This old man is ZZ Top. He says he played in a band when he was young." She smiled up at Bradley. "What's left to say here?" Daisy stuck her tongue out and laughed heartily.

Bradley Doan remained holding his camera, shooting. "This city is as peaceful as heaven. Unbelievably calm. It's midnight, and we're having a beer together in a four-million-dollar bank. It's like a fairy tale." He walked over to the window, placing the lens of his camera against the glass. "It's pitch black with no one outside. The road out there—where does it go?"

"Highway to hell. Not many use it. The road is long abandoned now except for the occasional car speeding by, maybe once a week. Lost country ... lost town ... lost way... "

By the time the three ran out of beer, they were quite tipsy. The table they sat around was next to the window in the south of the small bank hall, and under the table were all the empty beer bottles.

The old man perked up and laughed, stroking his beard. "I went to ZZ Top's concerts several times when I was young. It was a band from Houston in 1969. They said I looked a lot like Dusty Hill. So, I grew my beard to look even more like him. My father also had a long beard." He stroked his beard, lost for a moment. "Did you know, Mister, that beard culture is almost an independent form of art?" Max didn't answer, so he went on. "You are a very funny guy. You won't show everything on TV that you take with that little camera, will you? It's not appropriate to drink beer in a bank at night. Or at all, for that matter. It doesn't amount to much in this godforsaken place, but it's still not allowed in other parts of the world."

"No. This camera is my eye. Everything I see, I shoot."

"Hey, we're out of beer, Bradley," Daisy said loudly. She burped.

The old man, startled, almost spilled the beer from his mouth. "Go get something strong, you two. Daisy, go with him, breathe in the wind!"

He turned on the radio to music. "I've gotten drunk on your conversation, Bradley. You're a chatty one. Let's have a bit more, and I'll lock the doors and go to bed. This is a bank, for god's sake. The bank is called Chase Manhattan Bank." The old man chuckled and tossed his bottle onto the collection under the table.

5

After watching the woman for a while, *Avid* got in the waiting truck so he could shoot more female dogs. *For Women's Day*, he thought with a grimace.

He started shooting stray dogs as soon as the truck entered the narrow streets of the *Tsagaan Davaa* neighborhood. As an experienced sniper, *Avid* would not waste a single bullet, each one of which took a stray life. His rifle was a good one. However, the dogs were smart enough to feel a killer coming to murder them; they started fleeing in all directions. Regardless, it was *Avid*'s expertise to shoot them down. If a dog was cornered and about to be shot, it would cry, begging for mercy. But *Avid* thought of the dogs as a bounty; he would fire a single shot, drag the dog by one leg, throw it in the trunk of the truck, and move on for more. No mercy.

A stray he named Sharik noticed the blue truck approaching, and from whatever natural instinct, the dog slunk quickly into a sewer hole. Although it was a relief that the riders in the truck passed without spotting him, the dog waited a long time after the truck disappeared.

Sharik was born and raised in the countryside, and he could smell a bad thing coming his way from so far, the thing could barely be seen. His life was owed many times to his splendid eyesight and acute sense of smell.

6

Bradley grabbed his backpack, hugged Daisy Maria around the waist, and walked out the door with her. The wind was blowing, and a bright light shone on the empty streets—the moon bursting out from the cloud cover to greet them on the now clear autumn night. For the past few years, Bradley Doan had been estranged from women, but he was completely intoxicated by Daisy's desire for him. The loss of desire meant the loss of love, devotion, a common spirit, and the absence of a source of nourishing energy. Daisy's passionate gaze boiled his blood.

As soon as they were out, Daisy Maria held him to her. "Where have you been hiding anyway? Am I really going to be in your movie? Or are you just teasing? Well, if it's true, you'd give me my lines, right?"

"Sure, I would. You're too pretty for a town like this. So hot, I can't even take my eyes off you. I'm literally in love."

"Ha ha. In love? What are you in love with? This?" She bent over slightly and slapped herself on the butt.

"You're so simple, Daisy—pure, unlike the complex New York chicks," he said as he went for the bare rump exposed by Daisy's lifting her dress. "Yeah, of course I am."

Daisy Maria swayed a bit when Bradley gently caressed her butt, then jerked up. "Oh, I forgot to pee. My bladder's about to burst."

In full heat, Bradley nearly fell over. "You can probably go anywhere you like here," he choked out, breathing heavily. "It's not like anyone's around."

He pointed to a barbed-wire fence next to a short building that looked like it once was a garage. Laughing, Daisy entered the front door of the cage of barbed wire, squatted down against the wall of the building, lifted her skirt, spread her thighs, and began to urinate until she squirmed. Bradley Doan turned his face away, but in the corner of his eye, he could see Daisy's thighs glowing in the moonlight.

When Daisy was done, she deliberately lifted her skirt. "Wanna see a pussy?" She showed her private parts shamelessly.

Bradley burst out laughing. "Let's find the store first. Shall we get something strong and go back to the old man? Or shall we go somewhere else, where your pussy can meet my big boy down there?"

Daisy stared at the man with hungry eyes, suddenly grabbed him, and started kissing him passionately. "We can do anything here. It's free America! You can do me right here in the street, on the dirt, in the garbage, like a dog, like a bitch," she said between short breaths.

The street was quiet except for a couple of dogs barking. She continued, talking between short breaths. "Why is it that we conceal the act of love, anyway? Why is it that cruel military men are decorated for the count of their killings, but we cannot love each other in peace? What's there to hide for the two of us?"

Bradley watched Daisy's eyes tear up as she spoke. Her passion and honesty and the silence of the night and the full moon made him think that Presley's Blue Moon was playing out loud just for them.

He held his body against Daisy's and asked her to come with him. "For the rest of my life, okay?"

She broke away and laughed as a car came up fast from the south on the empty road. Bradley grabbed Daisy's hand and ran her to the gas station. They both felt infinite freedom. *Happiness was only possible when there was freedom, Daisy thought. Our souls ask each other why it is this way instead of the other way around.* They raced like schoolchildren toward the gas station. *Love has no body nor shadow, just like a whirlwind, but it has the power to feed the soul. It is an energy that can burst out whenever and leave without telling, like the wind!* As they entered the door, her mind quickly shifted to the idea that the act of love had to be hidden from the public eye as if it were a sin. Sadly, she thought how sexual love was propagated as a vile and hateful thing. *This is discrimination and hatred for love*, she thought, her ire rising. *Everyone races to read the books and watch the movies that show sex as the evil in this world, where love has such short refuge in flicks.*

The screen door banged shut behind them as a Chevrolet El Camino passed them at high speed.

7

The Reserve Company wanted only the killed dogs' snouts, so *Avid* traded off the dogs' corpses to an old Inner Mongolian woman, who made medicinal oils from dog meat. She was the only one in town who knew how to handle the dog corpses, and she paid 500 *tugrugs* for each dog skin. *Avid* divided the bounty with the driver.

The weary, sky-blue old truck ran down the street and stopped by a fence at the foot of the *Tsagaan Davaa*. *Avid* pounded on the gate, stopping the guard dog from barking relentlessly. A young boy came out running and asked who it was.

"It's Avid, Khurlee. I've brought dog skins for your grandmother."

The boy opened the big gate to let the truck inside the fence, grinning happily at Avid, who pulled over and threw the dead dogs on the ground, their blood splashing in front of the old lady's guard dog, who was now barking and jumping to the point it seemed like he would surely break loose from his chains.

"Khurlee, my boy! I think there's no need to tell you, since you can count, but we brought twelve of those nice fat dogs. You will help your granny to skin them, won't you?" He took off his gloves and shoved them into his pocket and went into the clay house at the very back of the yard with his driver *Orosoo*.

As soon as they came into the house, he noticed a man—strongly built, brownish skin and big eyes—drinking tea at the battered table.

The old woman took a look at *Avid* and exclaimed, "Well, well, the messenger of death! How many lives did you take today? I was worried you were not coming."

She turned to the stranger and said, "Please meet Doctor Sainnamar. This is the man who cures headaches by spilling boiling *tangs* on people's heads. It's an honor for an old woman such as myself to welcome such a talented acupuncture professional. He is a doctor at a military hospital in *Hohhot*. He's been on our TV." She looked proudly at the man sipping his tea.

Avid checked him out with curiosity and sat down. After taking a sip of the cup of tea the old woman made for him, *Avid* took out his snuff bottle and offered it to the man, who sniffed the snuff and returned the bottle. "How is your spring? The granny has exaggerated my abilities. I owe my skills to Chinese medicine and try to help out our fellow Mongolians. Also, I discovered a secret, ancient medicinal recipe, had some Americans do research on it, and had it certified. You might know this singer called Gerelt-Od, who came to me for treatment. After one treatment, anyone can forget about headaches for three years."

The man seemed like he was not going to stop talking for a while, but *Avid* cut in when the fellow took a breath. "What a perfect coincidence! Ever since I became this sinful animal that kills other animals for a living, I have been deprived of sleep. To add fuel to the fire, unlucky as I am, I nearly died of slipping on rocks a few years ago while hunting bighorns and wild goats for wealthy, fat men. For that and whatever other reasons, I have a constant headache."

"If you don't mind, Sir, I still have some *tang* with me. I can spill hot *tang* on your head and rid you of the pain." The Inner Mongolian man looked at *Avid* expectantly. *Orosoo* winked at his friend as though in support of the man's suggestion.

"That sounds great. I will pay you," said *Avid* and stretched his arm out with a handful of cash.

The man grinned, revealing shining white teeth. "No." He proceeded to get up to boil a *tang* on the stove. Soon, the house filled with the smell of medicine. The big man continued talking as he stirred the boiling *tang* with a small spoon.

"The madam told me she purchases dog skin and the body from you. She also picks Northern Mongolian medicinal herbs for me, as well as some dog oil. Dogs are hot-blooded animals. Dog oil is good for treating respiratory illnesses, even tuberculosis."

The man kept on non-stop. He talked about how his father was brutally murdered by an iron nail to his head, how his mother mourned the loss of her husband and eventually died of a broken heart, and how he was orphaned after that and began learning acupuncture in medical school. The man also narrated in detail years of service to an elderly Chinese healer to grasp the knowledge and skills that he now possesses.

It seemed like the *tang* took forever to heat. Finally, when it was ready to be spilled on *Avid's* head, the doctor quit yammering and poured a bowl of lukewarm *tang* over *Avid*'s head. The old woman ordered her grandson outside with *Orosoo* to start skinning the dogs. Then, the doctor wrapped *Avid*'s head very tightly in a drape of cloth.

Once *Doctor Sainnamar* poured his *tang*, he began a diatribe, which continued with an elaborate insight into how to defeat the Chinese people: "The main thing is to become wiser than the Chinese," he opined to *Avid* as he patted the cloth on *Avid*'s head. "Rather than hating them bluntly," Sainnamar said, lifting the head-wrapping and pouring more of the *tang*, closing the wrapping, and ordering *Avid* to nap. *Avid* was knocked out soon enough, eager to get away from the droning voice.

Orosoo and the boy came back into the house, reporting the completion of the dog skinning. The old woman glanced at the warm dog skins spread outside, giving off steam.

"Son, you are getting better at skinning. I hope you did not pierce the skins. *Avid* here takes good care not to damage their skin by shooting them dead with one shot either in the throat or the head. Evil job. Still, someone has to do it. I call him the messenger of death." She chuckled, enjoying the idea.

A while later, *Avid* woke up from his nap, energized. "This *tang* really is something! My head became lighter right away and I just nodded off. If only I could fall asleep so easily at night."

Doctor Sainnamar gave *Avid* a few bundles of medicines. "You will have such a good night's sleep starting tonight. You won't have dreams. The bunch in the brown silk should be taken with warm vodka with at least 60% alcohol before bed. And these in the red bundle should be taken on an empty stomach every morning for one week in a bowl of hot soup."

"Oh, now I have to get my hands on that vodka! It was found everywhere a few years back, but it's a rarity now," *Avid* sighed.

"I have a bottle. You can have that," the old woman offered.

"How kind of you, friend. Let's compensate with the dog skins I brought today. Please don't say no this time. I have to pay somehow for at least the treatment."

"No need. No need. We already have good business running with you. This time is just a favor for a business partner." She insisted on paying. *Avid* happily headed outside with the Chinese vodka in his jacket.

8

In 1981, he attended a large meditation commune in Oregon headed by Rajnesh, short for Rajneeshpuram, better known in the States as Osho. Of course, he took his camera (that he took everywhere) and filmed everything he saw. He was able to record the story of a man who had been with thousands of women, but all of the films (including this one) were destroyed, along with his home. He returned to the ashram in 1985, but it was around the time when Osho's followers had been accused of a series of serious crimes, including salmonella poisoning and a plot to assassinate U.S. Attorney Charles H. Turner; and when Rajnesh revealed his true identity, his secretary Ma Anand Sheela and his close supporters could not be filmed again at the time of the prosecution.

Bradley was carrying a bottle of *Nikolai* in his backpack and a few cans of soda. He led Daisy out of the store and into the driveway. They passed by the place where they'd just shared hot and heavy moments of satisfaction, which seemed like a place in heaven, no longer an eerie abandoned alley. At the same moment, they spotted a car parked outside the bank. It was the same El Camino that had passed through the road earlier.

It is a lie that nothing happens here, Bradley thought. A million things have happened since I arrived in the morning. It's also a lie that nobody comes to visit. "Do you know whose car it is?" he asked.

"No idea. Just a passerby, probably. Maybe someone who knows our old man."

The two glanced at the car and went through the bank's glass door.

From the bank hall, "New Kid in Town" by the Eagles was playing on the radio that ZZ Top was listening to.

Bradley couldn't contain his excitement.

"... Johnny come late, the new kid in town. Everybody loves you, so don't let them down..."

He continued to smile as he sang along.

They entered the bank, saw no one, and Bradley yelled out, "Where are you, ZZ Top?"

No one replied. Daisy hurried to the bathroom through the dark hallway. Bradley set the vodka on the table.

Remembering the lottery he had won that afternoon, he turned on his camera resting on the table, spun around, and walked toward the vault the old man had shown him earlier to make a video log about his winning. But a few steps down the hall, he came across a strange man holding a gun, and ZZ Top with his mouth gagged.

The stranger aimed his gun at Bradley, put his finger to his lips, and nodded to him as a greeting.

Bradley was shocked again to see that another man was turning the number of the large vault with his right hand, holding a baseball bat in his left. Bradley simply froze with his mouth open.

Finally, he sputtered out, "D-Don't do anything stupid, guys. He's an old man. There's also a woman in here." He swallowed and regained his aplomb. "Well, well. It really is a lie that nothing happens in this town," he said in a calmer tone, his voice low, as usual. The man who was matching the vault code grabbed the baseball bat with both hands and looked at him.

"If you don't do anything stupid, we won't," the first stranger warned. "The old man gave us the code. We'll just leave when we're done. This is not a movie. We don't need drama." He smiled knowingly at Bradley, camera in hand.

When the man logged the code, the huge, round, steel door clicked and sat silent. When the man with the pistol, still pointing his gun at Bradley, turned the wheel, the door heaved open as if it was grasping a deep breath. The door was very thick, and behind it was a brightly lit room.

At that moment, the old man moved his eyes as if he was trying to say something.

So, the man with the gun took off the tape from the old man's mouth.

"You can't go in now." He choked and finally spit out that the room had a camera.

The two looked at each other in confusion. One of them took a packet of Marlboros out of the pocket of his red shirt, which looked like a Canadian fireman's outfit, and lit up a cigarette.

"Now what? You just said there was four million dollars in here, didn't you? How do we get it?" He pulled up a chair and sat down.

Just then, from the basement, footsteps were approaching. It was Daisy.

"The girl. Don't scare her," Max whispered.

"Are you two alive?" Daisy came in as she followed the sound of the radio, and when she saw them, she froze.

The man who sat in a chair and smoked went pale when he saw Daisy.

"What are you doing here?" Daisy looked at him mockingly. "What are you doing here, Frank? You're a bank robber now? I guess I haven't told you enough not to watch too many movies. You get out now! I know you better than you think I do. Who is this stranger? Also a movie star?" she laughed heartily.

It was as if the man with a baseball bat in one hand was seeing Daisy for the first time, and her mocking laughter ignited his anger. He sprinted toward Daisy and, without a moment's notice, knocked her to the floor with the bat.

Max found himself lifting Daisy's head up on his lap, drenched in her blood.

"I told you to just leave it," Bradley screamed.

The strange man took the pistol out of Frank's hand.

Bradley Doan was staunching the blood with his shirt. He shouted, "Get away! Get away!"

Daisy suddenly gathered herself up, stood shakily, and walked straight toward the man holding a bat in one hand and a gun in the other. The man, caught by surprise, pulled the trigger.

The room was filled with the smell of gunpowder and smoke. Bradley unconsciously jumped on the man and fell to the floor with him. The lottery ticket he purchased from Daisy that afternoon fell on the floor next to Daisy's dead body.

9

Avid got in his truck. "Now the headache will go away like a thorn pulled out," he said while taking out the bottle of Chinese vodka.

"Oh, I don't know about that," said the driver. "All I know is that the boy's gotten really good at skinning the dogs."

"I've given the dog skins for free today. I'll spare the cash for you, I promise," *Avid* said. "Today is the day they collect the snouts and calculate our salaries. Remember, it's a 'snouty' ? day. We'll swing by my apartment first and collect the snouts of the dogs we killed in the last two weeks. Today is *March 8*. Buy something for your wife."

The driver was leaning toward the windshield, seeming to have spotted something in the distance.

"A dog is walking up the ravine," he said. There was no one around. *Avid* grabbed his rifle, slowly opened the car door, slipped out, and pointed at the dog.

That dog was Sharik, who had previously hidden from them and survived. *Avid* sat down, pointed his rifle, held his breath, and pressed the trigger. When the bullet hit the yellow dog's chest, it howled and ran at full speed through the ravine, crashing into the green-and-yellow fence. *Avid* hurried toward the dead dog. For him, Sharik was just another snout to add to the calculation. If only he knew that the dog was being shot by him for the second time. And this time, the shot killed the dog.

10

The old man named ZZ Top came running and hugged her, but she was bleeding profusely from the bullet in her chest.

Bradley hit the man with all his might, grabbed his pistol, and stood up. He pointed the gun at the two men, one of whom was still glued to the chair he was sitting in—such a shock he could not finish his smoke.

"What have you done! You killed a woman!" Daisy heard, whose life was ebbing away. As the echo faded, it became clear that someone was counting. "One, two, three, four, five, six, seven. I need seven reasons to die."

At first, she could clearly see the lottery ticket that had landed next to her. She was overjoyed to see it for some reason.

But not long after, Daisy saw two men holding wooden bats coming through the front door, saying, "Where's that crazy dog?" When the two men came to the door, the dog, completely unaware of the men's intention of killing her, thought they were burglars, so she started barking to protect her home.

But she was helpless.

"Beat! Pound! Yeah!" they shouted. The poor dog came to an end, and at last, he was dragged by the side of the house with a wire trap around his neck and dumped.

Daisy was surprised to see Bradley sobbing. Bradley was below her, and she was lying down, looking down, and she thought the tears of the crying person were supposed to fall on the floor, but they dripped down her face. The energy of love shone through Bradley's weeping eyes, and it seemed to ignite her spirit.

Then, as the light behind Bradley's face shone brightly, and his soul became enormous as if it were connected to the energy of the universe, there was a great sense of relief, a boundless space, and everything became lighter.

Random images began flashing in front of her eyes—her mother laughing and, for the first time, her father appearing. Daisy felt that she was floating in the sky above all while dying on the ground.

Suddenly, an unfamiliar red-faced Asian man replaced her father's image and preached. "May you, the dog, find the body of the sacred light of the human race and help all beings with the supreme magic of *Mahamudra*. Now you can feel the momentary light and let it go. You listen carefully: Let it be clear to you that it is the nature of God *Samandabadra* that you feel you are not born and do not die."

Her chest filled with air, and she was screaming at the top of her lungs.

The next morning, breaking news was being reported on TVs around the small town.

"Yesterday, around 3 o'clock in the morning of October 3, 1989, an armed attack took place on the Chase Manhattan Bank branch in our city."

"While Daisy Maria, Bradley Doan, and bank guard Theodore Jeria were drinking beer inside the bank, a young man named Frank Milton, who had once lived with Daisy in a neighboring village, tried to rob the bank with his friend Anthony Schneider.

"Bradley Doan shot and killed the perpetrators. Daisy Maria was also killed by a gunshot wound.

"Sheriff Michael Douglas is investigating the incident and said he could not comment further. Freelander's camera was on the desk at the time of the incident, so it recorded everything.

"We will report back on this incident."

11

Shortly after Daisy's death, in the middle of the fall of 1989, two people were riding a motorcycle on a dirt road near Choir, a small town in Govisumber Province, Mongolia, on the other side of the globe.

When *Gerelsaikhan*'s puppy's chest was filled with fresh air, he remembered that he had once smelled it before—the scent—flowers. *Wow.* He sighed in delight.

"What a beautiful puppy," said the boy on the back of the motorcycle, cuddling the puppy in the hem of his coat. "I'll make it a hunting dog." He stroked the wet snout of the pup, and the canine youngster's mouth started watering from the smell of the boy's sleeves; they smelled of fat and meat.

"Oh, I don't know, you're the one who picked a stray puppy," said his companion.

"What do you think I should name it?"

"Name it yourself. Whatever… Hasar or Basar…"

"I'd name him Sharik, like in the movie 'Four Tank-Men and a Dog.'" The boy started singing: *Yanek the sniper, Sharik the messenger, Mariusya the sweet girl, and Guslik the insatiable.*

The singing boy on the back of the motorcycle was about ten years old, and the man driving was in his early twenties. As they hurried past the village where the Russian soldiers lived, the young man suddenly turned the steering wheel and sped toward the prefabricated gray houses in the distance.

"What are you doing? Let's go straight home."

"I'll meet an officer—a Russian officer," the older boy said, roaring toward the village on a paved road.

The puppy, who was enjoying the song of a Polish TV series in Mongolian at the time, suddenly began to smell the bitter smoke of the diesel engines and barked in disgust. As the motorcycle approached, the fence of the Russian military barracks began to appear.

"Oh, brother, there are a lot of tanks. Sharik!" the boy shouted. "Hey, like the four tank-men in your movie!"

Bayarsaikhan rode his motorcycle past the parade of tanks and came to a fence with an iron gate, a five-pointed star on top. He braked sharply, got off his motorcycle, and approached a Russian army officer who was commanding the tanks with a yellow signal in his hand.

"Comrade! I'm visiting a friend's home. May I?"

The Russian soldiers, dressed in black and white, waved their yellow flags up and down at the tanks lined up outside the fence. They barely acknowledged the fact that these children were even human beings. All in all, *Bayarsaikhan*'s words could not be heard in the deafening noise of the diesel-gassed tanks.

At that moment, a green *UAZ 69* came out of the town gate, stopped right next to *Bayarsaikhan* and *Gerelsaikhan*, and then two ranked soldiers came out.

"Well, let's go!" one of the tankmen shouted. "*Vperyod s pesnei!*" The other two ran and got into a tank.

In the midst of the noise, the dust, and the smoke, *Bayarsaikhan* stood and watched them as he lit an *Ohotnichyi* cigarette he'd been given by a Russian soldier.

A man in a gray overcoat came out after the two men. "Take all the nonperishable food first. These buildings must be handed over to the *Choir* city administration. A chief named Ravdan is supposed to come and set things in order. We pulled an all-nighter last night. An order is an order. Now, go!"

"Sir. Yes, sir!" yelled a soldier who ran toward the truck in the distance.

The Major in the gray overcoat waved his leather gloves behind the truck and walked to the tanks.

Bayarsaikhan pushed his motorcycle into town. *Gerelsaikhan* followed him, sticking his puppy's snout out of his lap. From everyone around him, the dog could smell something he knew. The smell of the houses was faint but as familiar as it had ever been.

When he entered the yard, *Gerelsaikhan* was surprised that only dogs were running here and there; no person could be seen.

"Brother, why are there so many dogs here?" he asked, puzzled.

"I don't know. Probably, the families moved out and left their dogs. And yet, you're carrying another dog." He kicked the stand of his bike down and got off the bike. "Well, I had a Russian friend here. Let's go into his house."

The two of them went up the stairs to the entrance, which was littered with garbage, and up to the fifth floor to a door covered with reddish-brown linoleum. The door was half-open; they entered and stopped.

The family had moved out, and there was no order; it was as if an army had raided the home. *Bayarsaikhan* paused for a moment and entered the kitchen next to the door, where he saw a large yellow enamel bowl on the table full of *borscht*, a fish on an elegant white plate with a black lining, a bottle of vodka with a gooseneck, and several glasses around it; in the center of the table was an apricot jam. *Gerelsaikhan* stirred it with the spoon lying next to it.

"Taste it." The puppy's nose smelled good food, and saliva flowed down his jowls. He began to bark. "Grr… woof, woof."

"Sharik, what are you barking at? Do you wanna eat this fish? For Mongolians, fish is a sacred animal of the sea heaven. So, eating it is taboo. Only Russians eat fish. It stinks anyway."

Bayarsaikhan looked through the clutter in the kitchen, walked down the hall, and into the living room. At that moment, *Gerelsaikhan* took his puppy out of his lap and let her run free. The puppy was immediately up on the table eating delicious fish. He jumped down, sniffing the floor, wagging his tail, and sat.

It was obvious that the family had moved out on short notice and left almost everything behind. *Bayarsaikhan* looked around in amazement as he walked through the mess and opened the window to see that no one was out on the street. Dogs were running everywhere, barking crazily.

"All these families have moved. Let's both run and bring Dad with the trailer. These families left everything. Last year, I visited Mr. Bolooj's house and sold fox skin. Auntie Zina made this delicious apricot jam. This is very strange. Each and every one of them is gone. Let's come with a tractor and trailer and load the stuff."

Gerelsaikhan called for his puppy. He found him comfortably lying on the velvet sofa in the living room. "Oh, you've cozied up, huh? This is not your home. Your home is in the countryside with me, so let's go!"

The two brothers passed a burning trash can, came to the gate, and started their motorcycle. A truck pulled up on the road and drove into the town. The car, in which several Mongolians were riding, came to a stop on a tarmac road between prefabricated gray houses, and two men from the chief's office got out of the cabin.

"Hurry up! You go and start from the first entrance of the first building and collect what is left. A cart is coming from behind. I already talked to Vladimir Ivanovich. How the hell would we know they're moving out in under a day?" a man blabbered.

Bayarsaikhan and *Gerelsaikhan* jumped on their motorcycle and rode down the tarmac after the tanks.

"If we don't hurry, the *Choir* people will come and haul everything out. And yet you've gotten yourself in a weird jam now. At least, we should have taken the carpet in the living room. You and I are a couple of idiots. But it's still weird because I knew the family. I feel like a burglar. Uncle

Bolooj said he wanted to give me his nice set of tools. Did you notice that the TV was still on?"

Gerelsaikhan tried to feed the puppy jam. The puppy licked the jam and was trying to give his master a thankful look. He stared up at the sky with his two small eyes and yawned pleasantly. It was a wonderful day for him. Only several days after being born, he had a master and a home.

12

Avid was going to get paid for the snouts that day, so he went home and added what he had, then turned in the bag of snouts, got his money, and met up with some people on the way home. He let them go on ahead of him, though, because he had gone to work at dawn that day, and he also had this treatment for a headache going on; he decided to go to bed as early as possible.

His phone rang. "Hello?"

"Hello. I'm calling from Erdenet. The city's swarming with visitors. Another Japanese TV group came to shoot the eclipse."

"So, you're traveling with them as their guide and driver as usual?"

"Yes, and I have a favor to ask. They say they want to go to *Bulgan*. Apparently, the eclipse is better observed in *Bulgan* or something, I don't know. Do you know anyone that can host us for just one night at their home? It's even better if that person has livestock because households with livestock are very hospitable. Of course, they'll pay for the stay. Do you have any relatives who will vacate their home for guests for one day? Guests who have a shitload of luggage, though?"

"Well, I am originally from *Bulgan*, but I'm long gone from there. I lived all my life in the city. But let's look at what I can do. There must be a man named *Baldantseren* who was an agent of the ministry. He said he was working in the *aimag* administration and probably still is. How many people?"

"Only six. But their luggage is amazingly large. Okay. Anyway, I at least have a name. It's still dark. Let's just go there and see what we can manage. Thank you."

Avid went to bed, but the call had chased away his sleep. He lit a cigarette, took a few drags, covered himself in a dark gray coat, and went outside.

The mild spring wind was blowing with a bit of a bite in it. He saw a lot of black cars coming from outside the Chinggis Hotel, stopped for a moment to smoke, and went up the narrow stone steps behind the building to grab a beer from the store.

What a pathetic excuse for a life it is, he thought to himself. No matter how much I want to stop doing this sinful work of killing dogs in the early hours of the morning, I have nothing else to pay my bills with. No matter how much I want to chase a career in writing, the only thing I'm passionate about, who would hire a person who doesn't have an appropriate diploma? After all, no one cares about a vicious dog killer like me because now everyone is hustling to make a living. Wouldn't it be better to find a good woman to live with?

Out of the blue, *Avid* ran into the same girl who had passed by him early in the morning. She stared at the ground with the same sad look on her face. She looked even more beautiful. *Avid* girded his courage and said, "Hello! Happy *March 8*!"

She seemed to recognize Avid. Suddenly, she fell on the stairs as though she was about to faint. *Avid* panicked and lifted her by her elbow. He shook her slightly and asked if she was okay.

"I'm not well. I think it's the baby," she said.

Avid carried her down the stone stairs to the road. He lifted his hand to catch a cab, and a white car pulled up. *Avid* took a few bills from his pocket and gave them to the driver.

"Young man," the cabbie said. "This woman's health is deteriorating. Let's take her to a hospital."

Avid put her in the back seat of the car and sat next to her, propping her up. When they reached the hospital, a female doctor, who seemed to have had a little drink celebrating *March 8*th, saw the woman, gave her a small injection, and said it was okay to leave.

"It's all about stress," the doctor said as the girl stood up, wobbly. The doctor looked at her more closely. "Did anyone hurt you? Even on Women's Day, men manage to find a way to hurt girls."

Avid took the poor girl home that night. For some reason, the apartment felt so close that it seemed like he had visited the place many times before or even lived there. *Oyunchimeg* fell asleep while watching the Women's Day concert on TV. *Avid* looked at her face in the moonlight and sat next to her watching her sleep. She looked as beautiful as an angel, and he felt attracted to her, as if he had met her a long time ago.

The next morning, *Avid* got up early to make soup. He poured a bowl of potato broth for the girl. They spent the whole day together. It was an eclipse day, but neither of them noticed.

Later that night, however, she became ill again, and *Avid* called an ambulance. In the middle of the night, *Oyunaa* had a miscarriage. After three days, she was discharged from the hospital. *Avid* picked her up as if he were picking up his wife and brought her home for good.

A hunter named *Avid* and a woman named *Oyunchimeg*, who liked to be called *Oyunaa*, lived together for many years since that day of the solar eclipse.

13

It was one spring afternoon in the 1990s. *Gerelsaikhan* stroked his dog lying outside the *ger* while his father gazed through the binoculars.

"Well, Sharik, my father is selling his livestock and moving to the city. The so-called democracy in the city overthrew the government, and all the people began to chase after papers called money. What to do with you now? In the city, we will live in a house where families live on top of each other. There is no place for a dog. You remember visiting such places where the Russians lived in *Choir* a few years back, don't you?"

Sharik remembered just about everything: the houses he had first visited and the events of those days. *Gerelsaikhan*, his brother, and the rest of the family started up the tractor with a trailer. The tractor made a loud noise as the engine heaved along. Sharik was left alone outside his home. He sniffed around and soon fell fast asleep.

He had a strange dream in which he was called Daisy. It felt as if he had been called that before. Everything around him smelled like gunpowder, and he suddenly woke up from the dream. Sharik looked inside the *ger* and gazed at the poster of a Soviet magazine called *Sovetsky Ekran* with a blonde woman's photo on the cover. The blonde woman, too, seemed familiar to Sharik. As the dog got up and stretched, he heard the loud noise of a tractor outside. The family was coming back from the abandoned barracks of the Russian army.

They returned with a trunk full of luggage, and now they were climbing on top of it, having confiscated everything in the shed. The wooden furniture from the Russian village smelled of fish and other unrecognizable scents. Sharik remembered very well that they had taken some things home that night, laid the carpet, used the cups and buckets, and left the rest untouched in the outhouse.

Three years ago, when he first came to this home, Sharik stayed inside to pass the winter. From the next spring onward, Sharik became a watchdog and started living outside.

It was pleasant for him to live here in the countryside. He enjoyed herding the sheep with *Gerelsaikhan* and running after the flock in the open spaces. Each sheep had its own unique scent, and when wolves sneaked in at night, they stank of an indescribable viciousness. *Gerelsaikhan* rode a horse and tended his sheep, sitting in the field and looking through the magazines he found in the garbage of the Russian military unit. Although he was only eleven years old, he did not attend school, but he had learned to read a little from his brother. He would tear out the photos of women from the Russian magazines and save them. After following the sheep all day, Sharik would come home in the evening to watch and guard the flock. A dog's duty really starts at night. Sharik had an excellent sense of smell and a protective instinct, so everyone in the family treated him well. Among the family members, *Gerelsaikhan* was the dearest to Sharik. He was the one who found him in the *aimag* center. *Gerelsaikhan*'s scent would stay in Sharik's mind forever.

Sharik mused about humans: *Why would they want to live in a building? Why do they have to move to that city when their life here is this happy? My family is full of good people. In the morning, everyone gets up and drinks milk tea and eats meat. They always throw me a slice of meat. Then they also eat some boortsog to fill up and go out. I don't eat much during the day. But my masters cook a delicious dinner with even more meat every evening. When I look at Gerelsaikhan, licking my mouth, he gives me a bit of his dinner. Then he serves a large bowl of food when I stay outside for the night to look after the sheep.* He knew everything about humans but did not understand them.

From a distance, there was a bitter smell of technical oil. Sharik guessed it was just another piece of steel called a car. Sharik lay on his back and stretched his legs. *Gerelsaikhan* petted him on the belly.

"When I get to the city, I will have to attend school now that I'm twelve. My brother will work. Dad will get a job, too. Even my mother. Dad said we would sell our livestock and buy an apartment in the city with the money. Dad will become a driver, I guess. We will be riding in a car every day. Now that we've had breakfast, we will move. I'll take you and show you the city. We decided to stay in the yard of a family we know in the first few weeks. There are no wolves there. You will probably stay with that family."

Gerelsaikhan unbuttoned his deel, a long robe-like piece of traditional clothing, and ran home.

Sharik didn't quite understand what his master was saying, but he followed and wagged his tail. The door was open, and the smell of boiled intestines wafted from inside the house.

"Well, I don't see a car. But *Demchigdonrov* is a man of his word. I bet he'll be here soon enough." The man of the house took out a long knife, cut a little piece of boiled sheep intestines from the pile in front of him, then cut equal pieces and put them in everyone's bowl. He saw Sharik lying on the doorstep.

"Well, should we take the poor dog with us now and leave him at Tsoodol's? Now we have to be very tight with the money, Khandaa, my dear.

The housewife was sitting by the stove and pouring intestine soup into a bowl.

"What choice do I have? What's all the fuss about the city, anyway? I don't know. We were happy with what we had. Food on the table, clothes on our backs. Everything was fine herding the livestock. I guess our moving will only be justified by the sacrifice for the two kids, eh? But I still can't understand how we would make a living without animals there. I'm not sure if I can even get a job. Can Khaltar get a job? Everyone seems to be going to Russia to bargain."

Bayarsaikhan, who was sitting in the back, broke his silence. "What do others have that we don't? I'll go into that business. What have I collected all those marmot skins for? I used to trade with the Russians, and I can speak a little Russian, too. I'll see Russia and check out what kind of place that is."

"Oh, I don't know," Khandaa said. "I hear it's no good. I hear people are being robbed and looted. Russia is not like the few soldiers who were here."

"Well, we've already decided, haven't we? Got a pretty reasonable price for the livestock, too. Let's follow the trend. Since the Russians moved out, this place became stranded. The rest of the buildings are empty. The first winter since the fuel oil ran out, the boiler stopped working and began to freeze. Everyone emptied the houses, even stripped the window frames and burned them for heat. A place that was beautiful when the Russians were here became a garbage dump. Our people are helpless. Waste…"

"Dad, you are such a bluff. If I had made our move quickly enough three years ago, we would have collected all the necessary furniture to move to a city apartment," *Bayarsaikhan* said.

"Robbing someone's house is an act of fools. Do you know how Gulgur the blue got his truck ZIL 130? He bought it with a bottle of vodka."

"That's nothing. The governor found almost a couple dozen vehicles in the garage in the unit and sold them all for his own profit."

"That's right," the housewife said. "Fat Baldan is a greedy but very clever man. Soon he moved his family to the city. People say he founded a firm there, selling iron to China or something. I don't know. I heard that he became crazy rich. During the privatization, he bought a Chevron factory, or so they say."

"Fat Baldan's wife is very greedy. She's a Buryat, also a very hardworking woman. But as greedy as a witch. Why, before she got married to the Fat, she lived with Luvsansharav, who used to spend the winter in the north. At the time of their divorce, she split with all the livestock. Poor Luvsansharav was left alone with his daughter; he got drunk and later died of typhoid fever. When he died, she came and took her daughter. She only married into Baldan's wealth. They say she was some kind of a secretary to him. I think that's horseshit. She probably clung to him like a tick, had him carried away and orphaned his three children."

"Well, well, enough with the naysaying," Khaltar said. "Let's just get moving. Now the car will come, and everything will be packed, you know. We've wasted so much time, about a week, to reinvent the wheel! So, just eat up well. Let's move." He went out the door.

Sharik followed her master, wagging her tail. *They're definitely not leaving me behind. What kind of place is this city?* Sharik thought as a truck approached them from behind the hill in the morning sun.

The family moved to the city and left Sharik with a family in *Tsagaan Davaa*. The owner of the house chained Sharik to the front door of his yard, but Sharik, as she was not used to being chained, cried and jumped nonstop. The man of the house got tired of her whining, so one day he freed Sharik to the streets.

Thus, Sharik became a stray dog, roamed the area, and on *March 8*, 1997, she was shot to death by Avid. Sharik would have been reborn as a baby to *Oyunaa*, but she had a miscarriage on the day of the eclipse. So, Sharik's spirit is still floating in a temporary universe between life and death.

It is said that there is no such thing as a coincidence in this world and that only through the karma of the past do people meet each other by destiny, and things happen as they are destined to.

PART 2

"Keep a diary, and someday it'll keep you."

- Mae West

"A reflection of longing and companionship amidst stillness."

1

A man nearing his fifties, wearing a gray shirt with blue jeans and a suitcase in his right hand, stood watching a shiny silver plane spotted through the dark clouds reigning over the majestic Himalayan mountains. If one stood a bit taller, the snow-clad peaks, magnificent with the reddish tone they adopted from the setting sun, could be seen through the grayish dark clouds that blanketed the sky. Orange lights flaring through the clouds gave a feeling of a great fire sprung up in heaven, a fearful feeling that the great fire might descend to the earth any minute.

After spending a while gazing at the sky, the man entered a lodge called Green Hotel. This man, by the name Avid, was supposed to be on his way home from Delhi after his attendance at the Cross Words Awards annual book fair, popular not only in India but in the whole world. Because this year he was turning 49, an important age in any Buddhist's life, he decided to go to Dharamsala and offer his respects to the Dalai Lama. Unfortunately for him, a taxi driver was the one to break the news to *Avid* that the *Dalai Lama* was away in some foreign country.

But he had another reason to come to Dharamsala, and he did not return from the Cross Words Awards empty-handed. He had won the award and prize money of 100,000 U.S. dollars for his novel *The Last Seven Days of The Emperor*. It was obvious this award would have a substantial impact on his book sales. He should be happy that his wish had come true, but instead, his heart surged with bad feelings of overwhelming anxiety. Maybe this was what happened when wishes came true. He put his old suitcase, graffitied by stickers from all the airports he'd ever gone through, on the wooden bed of the cramped hotel room, and someone knocked hesitantly on the door.

"Yes?" he asked and turned to the door, opening it. There stood a young Tibetan monk in a faded crimson robe topped with a red *kasaya*, bringing him worn-out linens and a gray cotton cover.

Avid accepted them and carelessly threw them on the wooden bed as the young man left. He took off his glasses, gave them a few wipes with a sleeve, and put them back on to take a careful look around his hotel room.

A *Xanadu-colored* footbath sat on the floor, a mirror with its zinc coat coming off hung on a wall, and a brass teapot and two glazed bowls were placed on an old wooden table as though they were prepared for a *naturmort*. Except for a few English magazines.

Lying on the same table, there was no entertainment—no TV set, not even a radio. A piece of cabinet-like furniture that had hangers in it resembled an old Soviet safe rather than a wardrobe. There was also a door on the other side, but it looked as though it must be locked shut because the bed was placed across it.

The only perk was the view of the Himalayas through a window by the door, a view that seemed like a Chinese *guo hua* painting put in a *Xanadu-colored* frame. "Well, at least I shouldn't get bored as long as I'm here for only a few nights," he said aloud, then thought, *The rumor that the Dalai Lama is away in a foreign country might as well be a lie.* He tried to relieve himself of the negative ideas. A phone rang as he pulled his belongings out of the suitcase. He looked around and spotted it, a shabby old phone ringing reluctantly in an awkward corner of the room.

"Huh, a phone!" he exclaimed as he walked over to it. "Strange… who the hell might be calling me here?" He hesitated as the English phone kept ringing in a muffled tone.

After waiting a while for the caller to give up, he picked up the receiver. "Hello?" he answered. He was confronted by a woman speaking in a foreign language—he could not guess which, but assumed it was local. *Avid* patiently listened to the lady until the point he thought was the end of a sentence: "Can you please speak English?" he asked. "I don't know Tibetan."

"Oh, sorry, sorry." The woman ended the call.

Avid avoided putting his clothes away and picked up one of the magazines. Flipping through, he found an article about the awards.

"The Book Awards, one of the series of awards initiated by Cross Words, an Indian book retailer, in 1998, are upgrading their rank to keep up with prestigious Western literature awards, such as the Booker and the Pulitzer. Since 2006, more nominations for literary excellence have been added to the awards as proposed by the public. The 2011 Book Awards were sponsored by The Economist Magazine; therefore, the prize bore the name: The Economist Crossword Book Awards."

Prize money is included in the awards, and each nomination is judged by a team of authors and academics. This year the award also went to Vikram Seth, Kiran Desai, and Salman Rushdie.

Avid continued through the magazine:

"The Green Hotel establishment belongs to one of the renowned lamas of Dharamsala, Rinpoche Dashdavaa, who is said to live on the top floor." The hotel was rumored to accommodate not only the faithful but also American and European medical tourists who stay for months on end because it's cheap. That's why Avid, in fact, chose to stay there.

Avid briefly regretted his decision as he read that the Green Hotel was the cheapest of all five or six hotels that exist in Dharamsala. He felt like a cheapskate.

But the hotel looked upon the city from a hill so high he gazed over treetops. This time, *Avid* spotted an old woman in a sackcloth dress carrying firewood through the fog. He let out a long sigh as he lit a cigarette and left to find the public restrooms and showers.

The hotel's four-story building was under repair from the looks of the scaffolding made of long streaks of bamboo. The sight of the scaffolding—long streaks of bamboo—left him marveling at the courage and trust of those who had built a structure on such a rocky hill, but his thoughts were suddenly interrupted by the sound of sticks and leaves crackling. Looking up, he spotted two monkeys glaring at him as though they were surprised to see a man with a lighter skin tone.

In a split second, one of the monkeys fell dead from the tree.

Avid hesitated for a moment. *Can it be that the monkey just died right here and now?* He looked to the ground below the balcony to find the monkey. There was no sight of the creature. The other one kept staring at him, which was immediately eerie. He strode down the stairs as fast as he could until he got on a narrow stone walkway, where he continued swiftly, as if he were running away from the monkey. *Avid*'s stomach turned as he felt that the monkey was still staring at his back. He saw no dead monkey.

In a few moments, he was going along an alleyway so narrow that a single car would not fit through. Along the pedestrian way, there were shambles of dwellings. *In such a country where temperatures do not drop, anyone could build a home using just pieces of cotton sacks. Seems so!*

Most of the dilapidated buildings were home to owners of teahouses and small shops. In a peek, one of the booths looked to have a fire burning and a stall stocked with cigarettes, snacks, and drinks. A small gang of unruly kids was dragging themselves home, reluctantly preparing to call it a night. *Avid's* observation was interrupted by the owner of this shop; an Indian man with an uncomfortably large grin on his face asked, "How can I help you?"

Avid was caught off guard as he realized he'd inadvertently stepped inside. "How much?" he asked, pointing at the packs of cigarettes.

"Marlboro, 4 rupees," said the Indian. Avid no longer had rupees on him, so he held out a dollar bill. "Will it do?" he asked as the shop owner nodded, quickly clutched the dollar, and stuffed it in his sleeve.

After taking a long walk down the dark alley, *Avid* saw a two-story, American-style wooden house giving off radiant light, a sudden blessed relief from the dimness he'd just walked through. Several Caucasians, most likely Americans, lounged on the veranda. The deafening sound of clanging Indian music was replaced by the pulsating melody of Paul McCartney's "No More Lonely Nights."

Avid had barely seated himself at one of the empty tables on the veranda when a skinny waiter appeared, handed him a menu, and lit the candle. *Avid* hurriedly ordered a pint of Gold Star, the first beer that came to his mind because he remembered drinking it in Delhi.

"No problem." The espresso-skinned Indian waiter strode away. *Tibetan dishes look a lot like ours, Avid* thought, but he could not find anything familiar on the menu except for European dishes. Moments later, the waiter brought a large glass mug full of beer. He asked *Avid* what he wanted for dinner, and after a prolonged discussion, they decided between them that a Tibetan dish of some kind would be perfect.

The sun suddenly set. In that country of mountains, it happened without even a moment's notice. A loud French crowd entered the hotel lobby just as the nightlight set in. A tubby man with a straw hat was immediately checking the boxes stacked up by the check-in against a paper in his hand and shouting here and there. *Might be the chieftain of the crowd, seemingly a film crew, Avid* decided as he took wonderful sips of his beer.

The same tubby man who might be the director came right to *Avid* with a cigar in his mouth and asked in English if he could sit with him.

Avid nodded.

"Merci," the Frenchman said as if everyone understood French. The man shouted to the crew again. *Avid* imagined he said something like "Enough with the boxes! Come eat!"

By the time he finished his beer, the sunlight had completely left the place, *Avid*'s dinner was in front of him, and he had exchanged a few words with the French director.

Fuck. This shitty hotel with no antechamber, he thought to himself as he entered his hotel room.

He switched on the bed light, flopped down, and stared at the ceiling for as long as he could manage before getting bored. Then he picked up the bottle of vodka from the table, poured himself a glazed bowl full, and quaffed. He heard a couple of women whispering in English in the next room behind the green door by the bed.

There he saw the peephole on the door.

Huh, people are all the same wherever one is, poking a hole through a door! he thought and began watching the women with idle curiosity. The next room was a reflection of his room in the mirror, except that it had two beds.

Avid guessed the women might be students. They lay in their beds and conversed in mild tones. Judging from the disheveled hair on them, he guessed they might be what was left of the hippies. The smoke was coming through the peephole on a beam of light. The smoke gave off a hint of wormwood and manure. *Smoking weed, these two*, he thought.

Just hours after arriving, he realized the place he once thought was the home of gods felt suddenly different than he had long imagined it.

He felt guilty for drinking the first night of being in God's land. Nevertheless, he poured the vodka again. This time, he drank only half a cup.

No matter the vodka, he could not fall asleep. All these years seemed like he had spent living for others. Whatever time he might have left, whether it be a decade or two, or a day, he decided to dedicate his life to himself, doing what he liked.

But the reality was he could not truly live for himself. Writing helped him a lot through the solitude. So, that's the only thing he kept on doing. In his observations over the years, each and every person seemed to be a hypocrite. People tried to make the impression that they were active members of society when, in fact, their inner selves were entirely different from the roles they took on in public. The inner person was the only person any author was supposed to be talking to. Writing was merely the transcription of those conversations.

Such thoughts had chased away his sleep, and *Avid* remembered he'd received a few copies of his book from the awards ceremony. He retrieved one from the suitcase and opened *The Last Seven Days of the Emperor*, engraved in golden letters on a burgundy-colored cover.

"A sacred energy emanates as meditators transcend the earthly ties."

2

Through the window on the opposite side of the bed, the moon rose over the ridge of the Himalayas, and a faint blue light illuminated the room. He got up, lit a cigarette, and went back to bed, but he could not understand why earlier in the day, all of a sudden, one of the two monkeys suddenly fell from a tree and disappeared. He opened the book and read:

"One night in the first month of the summer of the thirty-sixth year of the reign of *Togon- temur the Great Emperor of the Dai Yuan Dynasty*, a sudden downpour from black clouds fell from the dark sky like a fiery light.

"The temple was built in 1271, eight years after the founding of the Yuan Dynasty, and in 1279, the year of the unification of all of China, Khubilai Khan personally visited the new temple and named it '*Bogd Nasten Tumen Amgalant.*'

"'The white hair that came down from the sky was a cubit long and was the hair of a dragon,' he told the king.

"As he lay in his bedroom in the dormitory of the Academic Preaching Center, he remembered, as a child, that he had been exiled to the Da Yuan Xi Temple in Jinjiang Fu, Guangxi Province.

"At that time, Harbish, the wing minister of the Ministry of Justice, was on a boat to take the little king to exile.

"*Togon-temur* asked, 'How many other monkeys are there?' The minister pointed to the riverbank. He was surprised to see hundreds of monkeys swarming there, and he thought it must be for some reason.

"Two years later, when *Togon-temur* returned to the throne of the Dai Yuan Dynasty, many more monkeys came out of the area and followed the ship, and thirty-six of them suddenly died.

"On that rainy night, King *Togon-temur* thought that the death of this monkey was a prophecy of the Yuan dynasty for thirty-six years.

"Seven days after the alarming news that Zhu Yuan Zhang, the leader of the Red Handkerchief Rebellion, had taken *Guangping leave*, he left the throne of the Yuan Dynasty."

Avid did not know for sure if one of the two monkeys he met fell off a tree and died. It's strange nonsense. *Am I one year old?* He laughed out loud. *I laughed and thought that I was an unfortunate lonely writer who had been abandoned by an ordinary wife, not Togon-temur Khan.*

Two years before, *Avid* emailed a man. The first letter he received in return:

> "My name is Aajim Purevjal. I was born in 1966 in The Labor Ward Chelsea and Westminster Hospital in London when my father worked as a Consul at the Mongolian Embassy to Britain.
>
> My father, Purevjal Punsal, worked for the Foreign Ministry of Mongolia his whole life.
>
> Interest in literature was instilled in me from a very young age, mostly because of my teacher Eddie Florence, who taught his classes through simple, yet captivating discussions.
>
> I have been keeping diaries for as long as I can remember. I trust my writings with you because it is my sincere wish that you compile my writings into a book.
>
> I live in Bruges, Belgium. My mother passed away in London 20 years ago, and my father died 5 years before her.
>
> Aside from the fact that there is barely anyone left in Mongolia to remember my father, I have taken notes of my mother's stories about my father's roots and other fascinating stories worth being told. These reasons have led me to the idea of creating a book with my diaries.
>
> My first spoken words were in Mongolian, and I continued to speak Mongolian with my mother throughout my childhood. In seventh grade, I started taking notes and keeping my diaries in

English. Recently, I have been taking up Mongolian again, but I have to warn you, my Mongolian language skills are nothing to brag about. I was even a bit embarrassed to show you my memoirs. I understand you are an English speaker, so I believe you will be able to translate some parts from English to our mellifluous mother tongue. If my notes are not worth becoming a book as they are, you are trusted to use them in your own books. The stories can be sent to your email, one after another if I get your consent. I reckon my memoirs are not so bad, although they could use some proper editing.

As I was born in London and am leading a life here in Bruges, I have grown greatly apart from Mongolia. My sole purpose is that my stories reach Mongolians, and I dearly hope for and look forward to your acceptance of my request.

Respectfully yours, Aajim Purevjal,

a.k.a. Jim Edmund

3

May 12, 1983

I am 18 years old today.

I got up early in the morning and looked out the window, and it was raining from a very low gray cloud. For some reason, it seemed <u>to me</u> that someone was standing on the balcony waiting to read my mind, so I turned on the radio to distract myself.

There was a lot of mundane news all over the radio, and even though it was mostly said in a very calm and smooth voice, I switched the waves until I found music.

"Moore's debut studio album by American alternative band R.E.M. was ranked 36th on the Billboard as soon as it was released in April 1983." I liked the release so much that I had the foolish thought that someone was standing on the balcony playing it.

I don't remember my childhood very well, but from time to time many different thoughts come to me, as if someone other than I had appeared inside me, or as if it were a previous life event or a very convincing dream. Yes, that's when I often took notes.

As I made my way to the kitchen to make coffee and eggs, I picked up my silver-gray Japanese radio, Sanyo, and placed it on the old wooden table in the middle of the kitchen, where I was sniffing like someone fighting off a lingering cold.

I've taken notes for a long time, but I don't show them to anyone. I don't even show a thing to my only loving mother. I don't even know why or for whom I'm writing this notebook. I don't speak only Mongolian with my mother; I also speak English, and I dream in English. My mother loves me very much; she misses her homeland very much, too, and she has no connection here but me. My mother and I have not been in contact with almost any Mongolians here, and for us, we have been our own small Mongolian island for a long time.

The announcer later spoke on the radio about Bob Marley's death.

During this time, it became clear that there were grounds to assassinate the U.S. CIA Section Chief in connection with his political position in Jamaica. Carl Colby, the son of CIA Director William Colby, wore shoes on both of his feet, and many sources confirm that he was stabbed in the toes with radioactive copper wire placed inside the shoes.

"It's 8 o'clock in the morning in London. You are listening to London's number one radio station Capital 95.8 FM."

Even though I've been here since I was a child, the memories of my childhood in Mongolia are as vivid in my mind as a color film.

Compared to Mongolia, England is like a black-and-white movie in the fog, as I can see through this window, and the thought that I was born here overwhelms me.

However, when I ask myself which country I was born in, I have no doubt that despite having physically been born in London, my true birthplace is Mongolia; but I have no one to say it to but in this book. It seemed to be a vast, windswept place. My father gave me the name *Aajim*, but now I go by Jim. I feel like the same person, just missing a vowel. I often tell my mother that I go to Mongolia every year, though for some reason, today is the day I turned 18. When I was with my father, I always saw a bright yellow in my mind. I felt like I was living a fairy tale as I rode across the prairie on the back of his motorcycle.

I can still picture my father riding his motorcycle, the wind whipping around us as I clung to him. The sound of the engine roared like a whale's blow, and the scent of my father filled the air when he wiped my nose with a towel. That towel carried the comforting smell of him, a scent that always made me feel safe.

Because my mother is next to me, Mongolia, far away and associated with my father, is more like a fatherland than a motherland. It seems very odd to me that the Germans do not talk about the motherland but about the fatherland. But even though there is a Nazi ideology behind the word Vaterland, I still think Vaterland. I always wanted to go because it felt like Dad was there.

Today my classmates come home to celebrate their birthdays. People here celebrate their birthdays in restaurants and bars, but they come to my house because my stepfather emphasizes celebrating at home.

From today, I will write these notes for a Mongolian who will read them someday. For the first time, I thought I might be writing this for my dad's Vaterland.

Yes, this is the only window into my heart, the door to such a calm, peaceful world. This notebook is the inner peace that inspires me. I wonder why my father gave me the name *Aajim*, but I think it's a symbol of slowness and calmness. That slowness is deep in my heart with my father. It's as if I'm slowly entering that peaceful land with notes.

Well, I can hear my mother approaching. I'm an Englishman named Jim Edmund, but this book will be written by a Mongolian named *Aajim*; he lives inside me.

June 13, 1983

It's two in the morning right now. I am visiting my friend Mary Osmond from school at her home, sitting at a desk with this notebook.

The red neon lights of the tavern outside the window are flickering silently, and the sky is overcast, making it an ordinary London night where the moon is not visible.

The headboard of the iron bed in the center of Mary's room and the brass faucet by the wall twinkle in the red neon lights. On the oil-painted brick wall hangs a Pink Floyd poster from his Wall concert; it is a person with a wide-open mouth. Shouting? Angry? Frightened? The poster takes on an eerie vibe in the flickering lights. On the bedside table are a few books and notebooks, and next to them is a German record player called Thorens, plus a column of records vertically aligned.

The Japanese Pioneer amplifier and two speakers are clearly visible on the opposite wall, and there are a lot of unruly books lying on the shelves. These are just about all the furnishings her room can offer, although there is a mirror on the other side of the bed. Sitting at the small desk against the wall, I pull out my notebook and am writing these lines down with a black pen. *Aajim, you were a bit reckless today*, I tell myself.

Let me explain to you what happened. I had just gotten home from Pink Floyd's Wall concert at Earl's Court with a wide grin on my face when I found my mother weeping in the kitchen.

I asked her what was wrong, and she started sobbing even worse.

"What happened? Who hurt you?"

I asked a number of times, but I could not get a response because she was sobbing ceaselessly. Mr. Thomson, whom I call my father now, walked in on us, picked up a glass of water, and turned to me angrily as he drank it.

"Your mother has been acting out of character lately. She does not keep a record of her expenses from the debit card. Money requires love, care, and attention. Only then can one have stable finances. Of course, I have not scolded your mother, but unfortunately, I tell her to be frugal and set an example for you, her son, and she started quarreling.

"In order to get you into the London School of Economics and Political Science (LSE) and get your higher education, we need the money. I am not saying she wasted all her money. But you will graduate this year."

He said education is a great wealth in this country that cannot be measured by anything.

His words ignited my anger. "Who are you to oppress my poor mother? My mother really can't live without you. But I can!" I slammed the door open against the wall and ran out.

Mother kept shouting "Edmund!" behind me, but I didn't look back; I only felt her running through the dark streets, lagging farther and farther behind me.

With Pink Floyd's *Another Brick in the Wall* ringing in my ears, I ran down the street at full speed, running the lines through my brain:

We don't need no education
We don't need no thought control
No dark sarcasm in the classroom
Teacher, leave the kids alone
Hey! Teacher, leave us kids alone
All in all, you're just another brick in the wall
All in all, you're just another brick in the wall...

I came to a stop outside Mary Osmond's house; she and I watched the Pink Floyd concert together. For some reason, I wanted to vent my anger on her. I knocked on her door, which swung open by itself.

"Who is it?" she asked. I was startled.

"Mary, it's me, Jim Edmund," I replied weakly, and the old oak door creaked all the way open, and Mary pulled me through.

She was already on my side, but I didn't like her at all; a smart girl, but with a red face with freckles, a snub nose, and green eyes. Nonetheless, she is very good at her studies. I sighed as I silently followed her up the narrow stairs to her room.

"Mary, I'm sorry. I got in a fight with my stepfather. I am reluctant to ask if I could stay with you today and go to school with you tomorrow." I said all this in embarrassment.

When I ran out of my house, I came with my yellow leather backpack that I hadn't taken off my shoulder, and I began to think I had left it hanging from me on purpose.

"Of course. You sleep in my room. I will go downstairs and sleep in the living room," she said, and there was an element about her as if she were about to ask me something, but she did not.

It was awkward for me, sleeping in a girl's bed, so I sat down for a while and opened my notebook.

Aajim, your actions today did not live up to your name, I scolded myself in my journal. *My mom probably can't sleep now; even worse, she might be in pain.* And I ran away.

4

July 11, 1983

I passed the LSE entrance exam on July 2.

My father did everything to make sure I enrolled in the business administration program at the prestigious school.

I saw on TV that Mongolia is celebrating *Naadam* these days. I know that the *Naadam* revolves around three competitions—wrestling, horse racing, and archery, which they call the three masculine games.

I recently read a book that was very moving. It was published in 1974 by Robert M. Pirsig: *Zen and The Art of Motorcycle Maintenance*.

In this book, a father and son travel together for ten weeks on a motorcycle from Minnesota to Northern California. The story is narrated from a third-person perspective and has interesting philosophical insights.

I have a lot of work to do to prepare for my new school, so I don't think I'll be able to keep up with my notes to myself in the near future.

It's very doubtful whether I can become a politician or an economist after graduating from this university. In this place, everyone is bound by their desires. This is a place where everyone lives by the rules of a prison they've built to contain themselves, which they call the future. There's no guarantee that those goals or desires will ever be realized.

September 21, 1983

My stepfather is a devout Catholic.

I thought he was very rich because he regularly went to church and regularly donated to the fund to help the poor, which was run by a monk.

Regardless of the heap of money he donates to his faith, he gives so little to my mother. This ignited a rage toward my stepfather from time to time, even as I tried my best to conceal it. Nevertheless, I have to say that from the moment I came to my senses, I felt that he was good to me and that he loved me in a very deep sense of love, even though he appeared to be cold. But I can't shake the feeling that my stepfather is a despicable person.

He was a military man when he was young, and it seemed to have molded him firmly, so he demanded a lot from my mother to keep things neat and tidy; he treated me a little differently. I still don't know why he liked my mother, how they became close, or how they cheated on my real father. I asked my mother about it once, but she said it was destiny and changed the topic.

Well, my mother would tell me when she decided to. My stepdad would never tell me. The English word "bastard" is just right for him. In Mongolian, "baas" means "shit," so it seems like "bastard" means "turd." There is also a Mongolian saying: "The shit never stops stinking even if it's dry." I always wondered if my father had killed many people when he was in the military. He has an office that he doesn't let anyone in, but I've peeked in, and he has his uniform and guns exalted there. Apparently, he was a high-ranking officer with a shoulder strap and a helmet that distinguished the officers from ordinary soldiers. He never told me about his days in the military.

Once, on a holiday, a group of old soldiers from the army who had served with him came and drank expensive cognac together. They got very drunk. I sat outside his office, and I overheard their conversation and found out he had served in some kind of intelligence.

And what he did after leaving the army is also a mystery. For a moment, I thought he was like James Bond, but I stopped thinking that because there was no such thing as a James Bond with a big belly and a bald head. I figured that the root of his strict Catholic faith settled guilt in him; in other words, he probably committed a great sin at a young age or in the military, and now he was repenting and praying.

But he was a man of his word. That night, while my mother was crying, my stepfather swore he would send me to a prestigious university; this proved to be true.

He had no real friends. Few people visited us, and I didn't see anyone who seemed to be an old friend except for that one time, so I think his only friend is my mother, who is going to spend the rest of her life stuck with him. But the way he approached other people was generous and open. He greeted shop assistants with goodwill and treated them as if he were very close to them; when he turned around, his face suddenly had the blunt look of the ruthless soldier he once was.

My mother claims to be a Buddhist, but her devotion is not much visible except for the image of a god hanging on the wall in her room, the prayer wheel, and the ash bowl on the shelf in front of it.

Because Mongolia is a communist country, religion does not seem to be truly believed because it is forbidden, although it is clear that it is worshiped secretly by burning juniper and incense. However, it is still curious why my mother has to hide her worship. My stepdad had a lot of respect for her Buddhism, but he was also surprised that she was hiding it from other people. I quietly observed my mother on the weekends when she went outside and recited prayer mantras. I wondered why she splashed milk toward the empty sky; it only fell to the ground. It sounded like she was saying my name in her mantras while offering milk, seemingly saying something like, "Please protect my son and have mercy on him."

Although I did not believe in the Catholic god, I followed my stepfather to church each Sunday. At school, I was taught the history of

Christianity, my least favorite subject. It seemed like a strange dogma and a very cruel history of the Crusaders, among other things. From *the burning of Jordan Bruno to the story of the horrible bliss*, it made no sense to worship Jesus, the corpse of a man who shed his blood because he was nailed to a cross.

Today is Sunday, and I had agreed to meet my stepfather at church, so I took my yellow backpack and stopped at a tea shop for something to eat before I walked on to the Catholic Church in Westminster. From my table, I watched two nuns sitting in a dark corner where there were no other people.

One of the nuns stood up, lifted her skirt, and leaned down to adjust her pantyhose along her thighs.

I couldn't take my eyes off her. It seemed as if she were deliberately holding up her black dress, flashing me, so to speak.

So enticingly weird was this that I got up to take a closer look, pretending to go to the counter ahead, and came right up to her, staring at her pale thighs. The nun took so long to fix the pantyhose; it aroused me. The young nun noticed me peeping and smiled shamelessly at me. She then dropped her skirt down very slowly and walked straight toward me.

"Do you always come here to do that, young man?" she said. "What does that mean? I came here to eat."

She laughed salaciously.

"We're done eating," she said. "Unfortunately."

"I'm sorry. If only we could have eaten together," the other one said.

These are not nuns, I thought, and wondered what they were as the two of them suddenly headed for the door as if pulled out by a demon.

I watched them, and once outside, they turned back into ordinary nuns. Had I imagined those thighs that seemed to come straight from the bosom so strongly to seduce me?

I ordered an orange juice and a ground beef, grilled cheese sandwich, and I wrote it all down while waiting for my meal.

I still have classes to attend. In addition to economics, we are given very boring lectures on world history, as well as lengthy and tiresome lectures on the political situations throughout the world.

The only interesting lecture was about the end of socialism in Eastern Europe. The professor who gave the lecture was a man who had worked as an economic consultant in developing countries, and I was most interested when he spoke about himself:

"I've worked as a chief economist for some of America's most influential financial corporations. My main task was to form agreements with poor and weak economies. In other words, we would provide those countries with large amounts of financial loans that they could not repay; in poor countries, such as Indonesia and Ecuador, for example, about $1 billion. They could not repay 10 percent on a dollar. For the remaining 90 percent, the American corporations obtain the rights to construct facilities, such as roads and power plants that have direct significance to the economies. Today, Ecuador spends at least 50 percent of its budget on debt relief. For the unpaid debt, the creditors demand that the country give our oil companies the right to own the forest-steppe zone of the oil-rich Amazon forests. Even if they agree to do so and pay off most of their debt, a certain percentage will still remain. As a result, to a certain extent, they become dependent on our country, and roughly speaking, they become our slaves.

This is how a modern empire is built. Such a scam, like these development projects, is likely to be repeated in the countries that are now entering the free economy. The People's Republic of Mongolia is one of the countries he mentioned, so I found this topic very interesting and scary. Right now, the former socialist countries, including Mongolia, are building a structure called Democracy and Freedom, which is weakening their statehood. The great powers have designed a system in which the people choose a government that has an expiration date of four years. It is in our nature that we live in apartments we rent in some way, and in our own home in another. Just like this, no one in that temporary government will truly prioritize the interests of the people better than his own.

I finish eating and am off to Westminster Catholic Church.

5

It had been a month since *Avid* returned from India. He had almost no work, so he began to read the diary of a young Mongolian living in England. He woke up at seven o'clock every morning. He always awoke a few seconds before or after and had stopped wondering why the shorthand of the clock would point at seven and the long one at twelve. He had had a strange dream in which his lower body ached, which had him reaching inside his pants to his penis to make sure it was there.

The meaning of the dream fit in a single sentence: "Love is giving up."

In his dream, he saw that he was tormented in a fiery hell after death, the cost of living inappropriately all his life. He dreamed that he had lived immorally, that he had been ordered by a messenger of death to run a hot iron wire through his urethra up to his bladder and all the way up through the stomach and lungs to come out of the crown of his head. He didn't even have to look because he could feel the pain in all the cells in his body. He was being roasted like a pig on a stick.

The demons that sat and watched him around the fire had very odd, slimy bodies, different from how demons were usually represented, such as with horns and tails. These demons had transparent skin, their internal organs visible. He could see the red-masked demons' blood rushing through their veins every time they spoke a word.

"Because you were burning with passion in the past life, you are damned to burn in the fire of hell in the afterlife," one of the demons said, turning him over above the fire and roasting him on his other side.

I have committed no sin, other than loving abundantly. I have not sinned. Is it wrong to love others? Avid said in his dream. The demons laughed coldly, roasting him for hundreds of years. As he struggled to get rid of this endless pain, he thought, *Only love can overcome this pain. I loved others. It's okay to love these demons, too.* He was relieved of the pain as soon as he started loving the demons around him unconditionally.

That is why he woke up with the notion that loving is giving up.

Isn't love just giving up? When people love their children, they acknowledge those children's wrongdoings and, in a word, surrender to those they love. If I can give up my arrogance and give in to others, can't I love others? In my previous life, I felt sorry for others. Now, who would love me in a body with visible organs like these demons have? There is something disgusting in our bodies.

Avid lay there thinking about his dream, knowing that a human being is a very beautiful animal. *Dreams are vague and incomprehensible because they are dreams, he thought, not real life. And I am unable to get rid of them because the words seem to contain a great deal of philosophy.*

He slept with the curtains closed, and the room was dark, but when he sat up, he was surprised to see a strange bright pink light disappearing from the ceiling. Apparently, a string of sunlight had sneaked through the blinds, reflected on the Christian Dior perfume on his wife's dressing table, and shone on the ceiling. He lay on his stomach for a while, then got up and went to the bathroom, shutting the door behind him.

It's strange how human lives derive from this small organ in the human body.

Avid washed his face and hands, brushed his teeth, and looked at himself in the bathroom mirror. Someone with sharp features, thick eyebrows, and a long, tall nose stared at him.

Avid had lost his charm because he had been drinking every day during the month since he returned from India. He had even rented an apartment for a while just to drink alone, and he returned home only recently. His wife despised him, but she reluctantly opened the door and let him in. He worked at the Institute for Strategic Studies and continued to write and translate on the side. For the last decade, he mediated businesspeople with the National Security Council, and that's how he managed to reap additional income and buy his nice four-bedroom apartment. His life was more comfortable than that of any of his peers.

Yes, I betrayed Oyunaa. This did not happen suddenly. No one is at ultimate fault, he thought.

They had drifted apart, and there was cold space between them now. The obvious fact was that they could not have children. But in the lives of his friends, *Avid* knew that even the couples who had children also became estranged. Women often stop caring about their husbands once they have a child.

Life does not always go the same way, and the first few years of marriage often seem to be full of love and care, and then it suddenly changes as the man and woman begin to think of themselves. Realizing they were both physically and emotionally lonely, *Avid* secretly began looking for another woman. He had always been looking for someone to understand and indulge in his writings, but it is rare to find such a woman or even a man. But when a woman who read and encouraged him came into his life, he immediately accepted. From his point of view, he believed that it was usually the woman who started the relationship.

Avid came out of the bathroom and opened the heavy curtain that covered the window. The sun shone through, and the golden roof of the nearby Buddhist temple glistened in the sun, illuminating his sad heart. He sighed heavily and stared for a moment at the silvery green piles that covered the roof of the temple, which stood oddly in the middle of the gloomy gray apartment buildings. The golden top of the roof stood erect like the top of a Mongolian traditional hat, which looks like an erect penis.

He still loved his wife like that golden top of the temple roof, but she seemed to have lost the ability to see that light. Or her love had truly faded; the darkest night had overtaken her heart forever. They were on the brink of a divorce.

The coldness of their relationship began with a note. *Oyunaa* was stricken by the note *Avid* wrote about the girl he had met many years ago: "Why should a man love only one woman? Mothers and fathers can love their many children equally, but why can't a man love a woman equally other than his wife? Isn't it too cruel not to?" *Avid* had written this; *Oyunaa* had read it.

He walked slowly through the living room to the kitchen, where he put ground coffee in the coffee maker and set it on the stove. He went back to the living room, where he picked up a blues record by Robin Traver from among the many records on the wall shelf, put it on his player, and pressed the amplifier button. It took a long time for the lamp's amplifier to warm up, but after a few moments, Robin Traver's guitar was heard throughout the whole house. He loved music, and he thought briefly about his introduction to it when he was studying in the Soviet Union.

"I actually played in a band that I helped start," he thought.

Avid grew up an only child and a city kid, whereas *Oyunaa* came to the city from the countryside well after graduating from high school. So, the two had their differences that influenced their lifestyle and interests. This could be one of the reasons they were estranged. One has to live in harmony with others, and conflict arises only when people try to make others suitable for themselves. Divorce is the separation of the mind first. As the depression deepens, they can no longer bear being together. When a man and a woman no longer want to have sex with each other, they have no energy to share at home, and there is a cold, invisible wall. If they had a child, their cooling would have been replaced by warming. But when he first met his wife, she became infertile after having a miscarriage. Now *Oyunaa* is just a barren woman in her forties. It's a rather harsh justification, but *Avid*'s sin for killing all those dogs can be coming to haunt his life in such a strange way, as if the fault were his.

Shortly after, the bubbling sound and the pleasant smell of the boiling coffee filled the house. At that moment, *Avid*'s cell phone rang. He picked it up and walked away from the music.

"Hello?" a woman's voice asked. "How are you? I'm parked in the driveway in front of your building. You know yesterday was my birthday?"

She asked *Avid* to come out and fix the zipper on her dress.

Avid left his cup of coffee on the table, dressed quietly, sneaked out the door, went down by elevator, and walked out the front entrance of the building.

The yellow autumn sun had fully risen. This was an enjoyable morning. He walked down a narrow street to the south, under the arch of the previous five-story building, onto the main road, and he saw the white Renault jeep parked to the side.

When *Avid* got to the car, she pointed to the driver's seat and laughed, so he got in the driver's seat. Everyone called her Janna, short for her real name, *Javzandulam*. She was in her mid-thirties. *Avid* hugged and kissed her. And then he said, "Happy birthday! Why don't you have anything on under your coat?"

"I told you. The zipper on the back of the dress doesn't work. So, I just took it off and put on my coat."

Avid looked in the back seat and saw a black dress lying next to a few bottles with the dregs of wine and several bouquets of flowers. He tried to fix the zipper but to no avail.

"It's impossible without tools," he said. "You haven't been drinking and driving, have you?"

"Of course I haven't. After spending the night at my friend's, she drove me here and went back home. I called an on-call driver to drive me. Hope he's getting here soon." She reached to the back seat of her car, grabbed a bottle of Gato Negro, and started chugging it straight from the bottle.

She laughed happily. He wanted to shout, I love you! Life is good! But she said, "You have a wife; I'm single. And love is love, no matter the kind."

She opened the car window and shouted as loudly as she could. *Avid* gave her an adoring look. Then, a police officer approached the car.

"Why are you shouting? Are you drunk? Is the driver sober?" The cop peeked through the window.

Janna stared at him, and when he finally looked at her, she asked, "Is it a crime to shout from my own car? I'm going home after my early morning birthday party?"

The young policeman looked at them coldly.

"Get away from here. Now. You've parked under a no-parking sign, and you're shouting. The whole city can hear you. Now, move!"

That morning was the day of the 2012 parliamentary elections. One by one and in couples, voters were heading to the polling stations. The elections were held on June 28, and all 76 members were elected that day. The campaign, the first of its kind in the proportionate system, focused on the fight against corruption and the equitable distribution of mining revenues.

Elections, Avid *thought glumly. I also seem to have come at a time when I have to make another choice in life. I love my wife more than this woman. And she doesn't seem to love me anymore. We haven't slept together in three months. Before I left, she wouldn't touch me. When I got home from India, she wouldn't let me touch her. But sleeping together is not even that important. I can have this woman next to me right now. But no one can accept the truth if they don't like it.*

6

October 18, 1983

The autumn of 1984 was cold and rusty.

It rained almost every day, and my mood was gloomy, like on all cloudy days. That autumn, I rented an apartment near the school and lived alone. Although it was on a hill, the north-facing window of the only room outside the kitchen was so close to the back wall that I could only see the damned wall through the window. In the pouring rain, the stone wall looked even sadder; it resembled the face of a sobbing woman.

Why I rented such a dark room was because of one of my stepfather's actions, but my stupid actions had more to do with it if I'm going to be honest.

I did very well in school and became one of the top students.

Gradually, I became more and more accustomed to my professional studies.

In 1982, my stepfather retired, and to escape the humdrum life of an elderly person, he got a job at a telecommunications company. My mother and I didn't know what kind of occupation it was, though it seemed like something to do with the security guard type of job. He left for work at five o'clock in the morning, so at eight o'clock in the evening, no matter what happened, he quietly went to bed after some reading. We would spend only an hour of our evenings together. It seemed like he was constantly absent and that only my mother and I lived there.

He still went to church every Sunday.

That year, my stepfather not only bought a new Motorola Dina TAK 8000X from the United States for £3,995 to gift to a bishop named Talula Carris (leader of the seven regional monks who were appointed to take care of the poor), but he also gave him an additional £2,000 to pay the annual cellphone bill and another £17,000 for him to purchase a car. My father made the donations in a public ceremony, where everyone at the gathering applauded his virtues and cheered for his generosity. What's more vulgar is that he never said a word about these donations to Mom and me before the gathering. Cardinal Talula Carris was the beloved one here.

As usual, my father gave my mother only a small amount of money. After almost a year of this, my mother fell seriously ill.

I was deeply troubled by this sudden, sharp action. Why the urgency? When my mother's tuberculosis was worsening, and she was on the verge of becoming bedridden, why did he choose to make such donations to his faith instead of caring for her?

When I asked my mother about it, she smiled and said, "Well, your father is a very religious person. I still don't know how much money he has. His father was one of the shareholders of a large company, so he probably inherited property. But they do not tell anyone about their personal wealth. You are being educated in an expensive school, and we are living as comfortably as anyone. I have gotten old.

There's nothing to wish for, but to see you do well."

"What is the wisdom in giving so much money to a monk instead of paying attention to you when you are ill? Then in the evenings, he hides in his room!"

"My treatment is going well. I am getting very good medical attention. LLL-131 is the first and best hospital of the Kentucky TB Movement, which began in 1907. Your father is not a doctor; he has paid generously for my treatment. All you need to do is study hard so you don't have to worry about such nonsense. It looks like you're going to be involved in a big project when you graduate from university. I have noticed you have been cold to him recently. Your father is 11 years older than me. He's a pensioner. He must be tired after working that job of his. There's nothing wrong with going to bed early."

It was at this time that I became involved with a girl named Priya, who was of mixed origin—Indian and Irish. I felt a strong connection with her in many ways. But for some reason, I could not open up completely to her because it felt that once I did, we'd become too close. We first met on the dance floor of a large club near the school.

Dire Straits' *Love Over Gold* concert was performed on July 22, 1983, at the Hammersmith Odeon in London. In March of this year, we bought the album *Alchemy Live* from the concert and started listening to it together.

During an event, I met a strange man, Julian Lennon, son of Cynthia, the first wife of the famous Beatle John Lennon. Julian is a singer and photographer, and this year he released the album Valotte, which became a documentary.

Julian Lennon wore sunglasses and a hooded sweatshirt, but Priya recognized him. After we exchanged a few words, the bodyguards next to him managed to take him away from us. He was the same age as me, but news that his father had been shot dead by a freak called Mark Chapman in 1980 was still circulating in the press, so he was accompanied by several bodyguards. That night, I took Priya to her apartment and then left for the bar to have a drink with a friend.

Priya had pitch-black hair and brown skin. As a British citizen born in Manchester, she seemed to have a lot in common with me, but in fact, I was the one who spoke, and she was the one who listened in silence. But she and I were more attracted to each other physically than mentally. Going to bed with her was the happiest time of day.

I still find it strange that what I'm about to write happened just like the night I came home from the Pink Floyd concert.

When I got home late, my stepfather was in bed, and my mother, who looked pale and weak, was sitting alone in the kitchen as usual. I had a lot to drink that night, so I was emotional, and I couldn't bear to see my mother sitting alone in the dark suffering from her pain.

"Where's Dad?" I asked. "Why are you sitting here alone? You don't seem well."

My mother looked at me sadly. "Your father has to go to work early tomorrow, as you know. I'm just getting up to take my medications. I feel very lonely. I want to return to my homeland. But even if I manage to get there, who would I turn to?"

I thought she was about to burst into tears, but she kept staring at me with dry eyes as if she had run out of tears. I got up in a rage and went to my stepfather's bedroom.

He was lying with his spectacles on his nose, reading John Jakes' best-selling book *Love and War*. When I saw him, I became more disgusted. And I was drunk, so I said stupid things that probably were meant for me.

"You stupid soldier, do you want to kill my mother? You poisoned my father to death, and now you're killing my mother! How can you lie in bed reading a war book when no one is around to take care of your wife? You give so many presents to monks, but who's giving to Mom?"

He just lay there.

"Get up!"

My stepfather stared at me as if he had seen a demon, but he put the book he was reading on his bed and got up.

"You bastard, get out of my house once and for all!" said the soldier in his commanding tone.

Without saying one more word, I left the room, kissed my mother, grabbed my yellow backpack, and hurried out the door. Only later did I regret my drunken behavior.

The words, "You poisoned my father to death" must have shocked him. I can only imagine how horrible it must have been for my stepfather to hear such foolish words from a boy whom he had loved as his own for many years.

Not only did that hurt my stepfather, but it hurt my mother even more, and the next evening she called me and said, "Don't come back, you're not my son anymore."

My mother's health deteriorated day by day.

I especially remember that dark night when I ran out of the house. I went to a bar near the school with a friend named Baldie Johnson and drank till I blacked out for the first time ever.

From that night on, my independent life began.

Priya and I became even closer as she was spending more and more nights at my rented apartment. I became more and more accustomed to being with her and unknowingly wanted to spend more time with her.

It was nice to be able to call her whenever I wanted. In those few months, I felt what freedom was all about. But I'd been talking to my mom on the phone every now and then. Of course, when I think about how my mother felt being alone at home all day, I wanted to go running to her, but something weird held me from doing so. My mother was angry with me at first, but at the end of the day, she was merely lonely.

"When you were here, son, I had someone to look after and spend time with. But now, when your stepfather comes home in the evening, we watch TV for two hours together and go to bed," she said. "But you said something very stupid. Why would your father poison your birth father and kill him? I want to tell you how we first met. I want to tell you something else, too. Your stepfather is still talking about getting you involved in a big project. He said that the project would be implemented in socialist countries like Mongolia."

So, the next day, I went to my mother. It had been three months since I left her.

When I came home and pulled open the metal door of the small garden near the door, I had a strange feeling that I had never lived in this house before.

My mother was waiting for me at the dining table. She had prepared a nice dinner. Although we talked on the phone two to three times a week, it had been so long since I'd seen her that I could readily see the changes in her appearance: she had lost weight, and her voice in person sounded like she was speaking from inside a glass bottle.

When my mother hugged and kissed me, I could feel her skinny ribs under my hands. I sniffed again the warm scent of the flower my mother always smelled like, tears welling up in my eyes, and the sad thought that I was going to be without her soon had me in tears.

My mother hugged me as if guessing my thoughts, put her thin and fragile hand on my face, wiped away my tears, and sighed deeply.

"My son, a big man like you must not cry."

She sat down at the table and smiled lovingly, right then looking like she would not give in to the illness. To ward off the sadness in my heart, I told her a few things about my school. I also talked about Priya. My mother took out her baked dumplings, put them on a plate in front of me, listened to me, and stared at me as if she were looking at me for the last time. She told me:

"You were interested in how I met Thomas Edmund. It wasn't a simple encounter," my mother began. "In the fall of 1956, I worked as a typist in the Dundgovi *Aimag* administration. At that time, I was a beautiful girl who could sing well and recite poems. I participated in competitions, too. After working there for almost two years, I moved to the city in 1958 to work as a typist for the trade union and later as a clerk.

"At that time, many people were trying to learn Esperanto, so I did, too. Later, I started learning Russian and English. I was becoming an active member of my community, constantly attending conferences and taking up every challenge.

"Then, from July 26 to August 4, 1959, the 7th World Student Games were going to be held in Vienna, Austria. Mongolia had participated in the 6th World Youth Student Games in Moscow in 1957 with a large delegation, so they decided to send a smaller group of delegates to the 7th Austrian Games.

"My trade union sent me along with the delegation.

"Even though I studied Esperanto, since it is a made-up language, not many people could speak it. So, I studied Russian and English even harder. They enrolled me in intensive English language training with some young people from the Ministry of Foreign Affairs.

"We would attend English language classes in the circular hall of the Ministry, where I met your father. He was a tall, handsome young man with shiny black hair combed back, a gray suit, and a pair of pointed, shiny black shoes. They called him Tall Pujee.

"As soon as your father first met me, he asked me out for the next day.

"His friends were also elegant intellectuals. There was a young motorcyclist named Grish and an artist named Tserenpil (who later designed our banknotes). Most of them are still around. Grish, on the other hand, although he was a master of racing motorcycles, died in a traffic accident riding a simple Java, like a sailor dying in a swimming pool. The others later became famous intellectuals and contributed greatly to Mongolia's development.

"Your father lived alone with his mother, a Russian named Marusya, there on Consul's Hill. He was such a tall man, like you are now. Almost all of the young men who graduated from the training went to the 7th World Student Games in Vienna.

"Two years later, I married your father, and shortly afterward, he was appointed as consul here, and you were born here in 1966."

"You saw the picture we took together at the festival in the album, didn't you?" Her face filled with happiness. She noticed my look and knew I was going to ask her, "Then why did you meet Thomas Edmund, and how did you become friends?"

My mother let out a long sigh. "My son, why don't you eat some more *buuz* that I made for you?" She patted my head and continued.

"In 1964, the year we got married, your father was appointed consul in London, and we came here, as I just said. In 1961, our country became a member of the United Nations and established diplomatic relations with Western countries. However, since the mid-1960s, when relations between the Soviet Union and China became strained, Mongolia aligned more closely with the Soviet Union. At this time, Soviet troops were once again stationed in the People's Republic of Mongolia. As a result, Soviet influence increased. Mongolia's economy grew rapidly during the 1960s, making it the first country in Asia to achieve complete literacy. Although it had diplomatic relations with the West at the time, Soviet influence continued to grow, and the Ministry of Foreign Affairs became more active. It was also a time when Chinese residents in Mongolia were expelled, and relations with China became marginalized. There was talk that China might invade Mongolia at any time.

"The most amazing thing is that your father and I first met Thomas at the World Youth Student Games in Vienna. When we first arrived in London, it was a bit difficult to cope with such a humid place, but I gradually got used to the climate, and your father got used to his new job as consul. One day, your father came home with Thomas. Well, you know that a consul is responsible for issuing visas to foreigners visiting Mongolia. That morning, your stepfather had applied for a visa to go to Mongolia.

"The three of us went for a walk that evening, ate together, and had a good time. Thomas Edmund went to Mongolia, and we didn't hear from him until he came back about two months later.

"Our home was within the Embassy premises because I worked for the embassy, too. When Thomas came back from Mongolia, he brought us lots of presents. From then on, he visited us from time to time.

"Meanwhile, your father was summoned to Mongolia. When I asked what the matter was, he just said the Ministry of Home Affairs had called. Your father was not a man of many words, especially when there was a problem. During such times, he'd become silent. He only said it was something about his origins and about issuing a visa for a Chinese citizen.

"In the meantime, Thomas came in and out of our house after your father left for Mongolia. We didn't know what kind of work Thomas went to Mongolia for. He was a very ambitious man, but apparently, he was a military man.

"Then I received a call from your father from Ulaanbaatar again. You were only a baby. Whatever happened, your father told me that he was ill in Ulaanbaatar. Moreover, the Ambassador's treatment of us had degraded. It had been over two months, and there was no news about your father. It was a time when we could not talk on the phone whenever we wanted to. So, I decided to take you with me to Ulaanbaatar to check on your father, even considering returning to Mongolia for good.

"Just as we were about to leave, Thomas came in. 'Your country is in a very difficult state. I have just been there for more than three months. I don't want you living there,' he said. Nevertheless, I boarded the plane with you in my arms.

"When we arrived, you and I were greeted by the news that your father was very ill and hospitalized in the 2nd Hospital for Ministers. The doctors said he was diagnosed with stomach cancer.

"Well, the unbearable sufferings began, one after another.

"When I left you with my mother and went straight to the hospital, your father was so thin I barely recognized him. He did not say why he suddenly got worse, but later, when he fell even sicker, he told me that he suspected someone had poisoned his food while he was jailed for a month. Apparently, he was imprisoned, accused of issuing a visa to a Chinese national.

"That's why Thomas was hurt when you said, 'You poisoned my father.' Of course, he'd think I had told you that your father had died of poisoning. My son, I have no strength to speak beyond this. Your father's condition did not get better, and he died that year. The diagnosis was acute gastric cancer. I could not believe my life had fallen apart so completely."

My mother fell silent again. She seemed to be crying inside, but outwardly, she swallowed her tears. "And then Thomas came to Mongolia and helped me through my difficult times and brought us here. After three years, I stopped searching for reasons why your father was treated so badly by the country he had served so loyally. So, you need to apologize to Thomas immediately. Your stepfather is in emotional pain. I can't fathom the fact that you really said the word 'poisoned' to him."

Finally, my mother started bawling her eyes out. Even as I write this, I feel as if I'm writing with my mother's tears. I have not told this story to anyone, and now I'm just telling myself, the person called *Aajim*.

7

November 23, 1983

It was a Sunday, so I waited to see my father when he arrived from church. We went out and drank beer together, for the first time ever, in a nearby bar, and I apologized that I had realized what foolish things I had said and done.

My father listened to me until the end, and with tears in his eyes, he pulled me into his arms and sniffed my head like a Mongolian parent does.

"Thank you, son. Yes, it looked like your father was poisoned. But that's also unproven. The diagnosis was completely different; it said nothing about it. If your mother had been left with you in Mongolia then, you would probably not be here by now. That's called destiny, son. You are a good boy. I have only one child, and that is you. Your mother and I later learned that I had become sterile while serving in the army. I thought I would marry your mother and give you a sibling, but it didn't happen. Now your mother and I are both old. But if I'm lucky enough, I hope we can see your children."

"I won't stop you from living by yourself. You don't have to worry about your mother. Your mother is from a country with a dry climate, and it is very common for people like her to go for many years without knowing that she has TB. But it's not going to be easy, son. If your mother leaves this world, I'll follow her.

"I have bequeathed all my possessions to you. When the time comes, it's the money that will go to you according to the law. I ask you to think about doing something in Mongolia with that money. Your country has potential. I think you'd better marry a Mongolian woman, a beautiful girl like your mother. The British women just don't give you the attention you need. They won't cook dinner; they'll just tell you to grab a hamburger.

"Now you have a good education. Economics is the most sought-after profession, especially in your country."

That night we went to another bar and drank a stronger beer called Guinness, and my father got up and took me to the dance floor, and the father and son danced together until we were exhausted.

Then, day after day, I did great with my studies, graduated with honors, and joined the European Council in Edinburgh. The European Council is a collective body that sets the general political direction and priorities of the European Union. Founded in 1975 at an informal summit, the European Council was originally headquartered in Strasbourg but later moved to Brussels, Belgium.

My stepfather, who had danced with me that night, was the first to recommend me for a job.

8

The scholars at the Institute for Strategic Studies under the National Security Council, where *Avid* works, travel abroad almost every year for research. The director told him that he was going on a week-long trip to Amsterdam and Brussels, the capital of Belgium, funded by the organization. He was in correspondence with *Aajim* in Belgium, and he was glad to have the opportunity to meet him.

Every time *Avid* got home, his wife opened the door for him and left his sight to escape to the other room. Although his wife was quiet, did not quarrel, and cared a little bit more, such as by cooking and leaving dinner on the table for Avid, the spirit of the family was gone. The thought grew stronger that she would never return to what she was, a sweet innocent woman who loved him more than anything in this world. All the frustration started three years ago when *Oyunaa* read *Avid*'s notes, which he called a "sad diary," where he wrote about his experiences and troubles to relieve stress.

Avid initially gave all his earnings to his wife, but for the past two years, he kept some of it hidden and opened a savings account. He worked side jobs, such as receiving royalties from the book he translated from English, so he had enough money to take someone to Amsterdam without telling his wife. Something inside him whispered that it's better to take his wife to Amsterdam. But he had not slept with her for months. Would things change? So, he decided to take someone who listened to him and enjoyed being with him. Janna was fluent in English. She made a living doing freelance translations for mining companies. She had free time on her hands. Also, the conversation with her felt nice and warm. But *Avid* hesitated, thinking that his invitation wouldn't make her that happy because she had already studied abroad and traveled from time to time. On the other hand, *Uyangaa* was the kind of woman who could cry for joy if invited.

Avid first met Janna five years prior and met an artist named *Uyangaa* three years ago. *Avid* was not a typical playboy; not at all. He was not even that handsome. Also, he had never been like a dog in mating season. In fact, he met one of the girls only once a month or every three months and hadn't spent three days in a row with any of them.

He decided to tell Janna first, and as he pulled his phone out of his pocket and tried to call, his phone rang.

"Hello? It's Janna."

"What a coincidence! I was just about to call you, and you called me!"

"Avi! I'm just going to ask you a little favor. I really need the money. Can you lend me 900,000 *MNT* for a month? Don't be surprised. I never ask you for anything. My brother is in urgent need of money, and I don't have any money at the moment. I'll transfer it back soon."

"Okay. Just a moment."

Avid ended the call and went to his account to get a loan from his savings. He first thought to withdraw one million *MNT* and wrote six zeros after one, then changed his mind and decided to transfer the exact amount she asked for. He deleted the number one and wrote nine instead.

Suddenly he thought it would be better to take *Uyangaa* to Amsterdam because *Uyangaa* is an artist, and *Van Gogh's* land of Amsterdam is full of things for her to see and do. When they got to Brussels, they would also see the museum of *Uyangaa's* favorite artist, Rene Magritte. She would be very happy. Also, just when he picked up the phone to invite Janna, her asking for money out of the blue felt unpleasant. So, he called *Uyangaa*.

"Hello, darling," she said. "Are you getting along with your wife? Maintaining a family is work that requires skill. I'm worried for you."

Avid smiled and listened to her slender voice.

"*Uyangaa*, I want to see you today."

"No. You reconcile with your wife. It's hard for me, too. I feel guilty. We can see each other later."

"No, I want to tell you something else. Well, my wife is a little thawed, but she still sleeps separately."

"Let me tell you now. It would be useless to meet at such a time. A woman has a hidden instinct."

"No. What about now? I am going to Europe for work for a few days."

"Oh, congratulations. That's a good thing. Isn't it a good opportunity to reconcile with your wife?"

"I want to take you. I have enough money to pay for one extra person. It's Amsterdam. The land of artists. *Van Gogh* and Gauguin."

"What? Why me?"

"Yes. I want to bring you! Also, I want to talk about this and more."

"Wow! Of course, it's beautiful, but it seems weird."

"Come on! It's not weird at all. I'll be at your studio soon. Okay?"

"It's weird, like ants are running up my spine. I'll see you later."

Avid felt very happy. *Uyangaa* is a sweet girl who lives up to her name. Such innocence can be seen in her paintings, too. He doesn't give her many presents, but he does occasionally give them on special holidays. For the first time on her birthday, when she was given a secondhand laptop, *Uyangaa* was happier than he had ever imagined her to be. She was kind of short, had fair skin, and a voluptuous figure. *Uyangaa* is a happy artist, always optimistic.

Avid imagined how happy she would be when they walked the streets of Amsterdam, how happy she would be when she saw *Van Gogh's* original paintings.

9

December 12, 1994

When I heard that my mother's condition was worse, I hurried out of Brussels to London, checked in at a hotel near my home, and met my stepfather as he came home. As he removed his coat, he told me he had seen all the good doctors, but that it was nearly impossible for them to find a treatment when the pulmonary tuberculosis was so severe.

However, my mother seemed so bright and healthy, so hope was restored in me, even though I couldn't help but remember people saying that right before death, sick people can rally and become cheerful and healthy-looking. My mother was sixty-two, but she looked much younger that day. However, as her TB worsened before my eyes, she lost weight and began looking older than her age. When I made tea for her, she sat me on the edge of the bed and stroked my head. Then she began to talk.

"You're thirty now, son. Even though you don't remember your father very well, you've been told a little bit about him. But there is one more thing I must tell you. You might remember your father's mother, Marusya. When your father was a consul here, he suddenly found that his birth mother was a woman named *Khanddolgor*. It was then that some consulate people began to get suspicious and pursued your father.

"I never approached the woman called *Khanddolgor*. I hear she's still alive. When your father was a baby, he was adopted by a relative of your grandfather, the woman named Marusya. The reason was that *Khanddolgor*'s late father was *Ayurzana*, one of the leaders of the 1932 Tariat uprising. I finally talked to your grandmother *Khanddolgor*, and I want to tell you now.

"*Ayurzana* was born in 1892 in Sain Noyon *aimag*, now *Ikh Tamir*, Arkhangai *aimag*, and was executed in 1933. He came from a wealthy family with a lot of livestock. One morning, a man on horseback came and warned *Ayurzana* that he was to be arrested. *Ayurzana* went into hiding in the woods, riding a horse. Soon after, the Tariat uprising came about, and one of the generals who led the uprising turned out to be *Ayurzana*. He was head of a large detachment, and later the Mongolian People's Revolutionary Party (MPRP) suppressed the uprising with troops in armored tanks.

"At that time, *Khanddolgor*'s grandmother and mother were also arrested and imprisoned. Between April 19 and May 10, 1933, the Supreme Court sentenced General B. *Ayurzana* and 16 others to death.

"His mother and sister were later released. After the release, one morning a group of union leaders came to their home to have a feast, they said. They prepared food and treated them to alcohol. In one of their *gers*, *Khanddolgor*'s mother and sister slept, but when *Khanddolgor* awoke in the morning, her mother and sister were lying on top of each other, dead. She guessed they were given poisoned food. They appeared to have vomited on each other and died. Soon, party members came and confiscated their livestock. Your father's mother fled to the city with some of her orphaned siblings.

Grandmother *Khanddolgor* married a man named Punsal. The reason I'm telling you this is that you may have the opportunity to meet your father's mother."

While my mother and I were speaking in Mongolian, Thomas was on the phone with the doctor. At the time, my mother seemed to be holding her own, and death seemed no longer imminent. I promised my mother that I would return, but that I had to get back to Belgium for a few days because I had work to do.

I soon left and went to my hotel near Mother's house to write it all down.

I found out a week later when I returned from Brussels that that was our last conversation.

My mother died on December 19, 1994.

I was left without a birth father or mother.

10

After reading the notes, *Avid* drank a cup of coffee, took a copy of *The Shambhala War and the Khalkha River War* from a bookshelf in the basement, turned on his computer, and read the chapter about the rioters.

The 1932 uprising in the four western provinces was an armed revolt by Mongols against the policies of confiscation and Sovietization, which targeted nobles, monks, and the wealthy, and forced herders to collectivize. This uprising spread across the four western provinces of what was then the Mongolian People's Republic (MPR).

At the time, there were efforts to establish contact with the Tibetan Panchen Bogd Lama in Inner Mongolia. During the uprising, various rumors circulated about the Panchen Bogd Lama's involvement. However, claims that the 1932 uprising was a rebellion instigated by foreign monks and feudal lords, supported by the Tibetan people and the Japanese, remain unsubstantiated. Later, an author named Lodoidamba wrote a novel about the uprising called Tungalag Tamir, which depicted it as a period of horrific terror. The novel was eventually adapted into a film. The rebels maintained that they did not receive any foreign aid and relied solely on their own strength.

The rebels were led not only by monks and feudal lords but also by various influential figures, including government officials. The soldiers were mostly ordinary people. In Arkhangai, 70% of the rebels were civilians, including members of the MPRP and youth unions, some of whom had attended military school or had been arrested and released. The rebels ranged in age from 19 to 68, with most in their 20s and 30s. At the local level, rebel forces were led by generals. In the spring of 1932, when a group of more than 20 locals formed, Ayurzana volunteered to join. Due to his literary and management skills, Ayurzana was appointed as a general with Baasan as his assistant. This account is detailed in B. Zinamidar's book The Shambala War.

Several books have been published about the battles led by generals such as Ayurzana, Tugj, Jur, Darin, Badrakh, Badamjav, Tumenbayar, Tarva, Sambadev, Sumiya, and Magnai, each commanding forces of 150; Shagdar Duvchin, Tarav, and Tsogoo, each leading 100; Ayurzana with 250; and Magnai with 50. The leaders were not acquitted at the time.

Tragically, more than 1,200 people were tortured and killed during this period. Atrocities included cutting out the hearts of detainees, using them for flag sacrifices, scalping men with modern hairstyles, cutting off women's breasts, and forcing victims to consume human flesh.

"I can send some of these books and notes, not because they're connected to your ancestry, but because they might be interesting to you as a national who grew up in a foreign country," *Avid* wrote. He also sent internet links containing more information on the historic topic.

11

It was December 21, 1994, when my father and I drove the black car down Oxford Street between Cherryhill Mall and Mount Pleasant Cemetery, embracing my beloved mother's ashes. This day is the beginning of winter in the northern hemisphere, the shortest day and the longest night of the year.

We had received her cremated remains, as my beloved mother had requested, and on my way back with my father, I swore that I would never forget the Mongolian language. Because the only person who spoke Mongolian to me was no longer with us, I thought that if I kept my letters in Mongolian, which comforted me all my life since I was 12 years old, I would be able to grasp my mother tongue for the rest of my life. That day, when I spent the night in Mother's room, I tried to write my letters in Mongolian for the first time, but I could not write a single word.

The next morning, I got up early to make coffee, and my father, with eyes so red from crying all night, came in and sat next to me.

"My son. Unfortunately, we can't alter the hardships of life. You are young, and you have a long and beautiful life ahead of you. But for me, it is just an empty house, full of memories of your dear mother. I am going to miss her and reminisce about the times with her to the point of death.

"I don't know how to endure this long winter alone. But there is no other way in life than to follow the hard way. I want to tell you something. I'm going to transfer the assets I have to your account immediately. But on one condition. You go to Mongolia. There is a lot of work to be done there. You need to use this money to invest in your country and start a business. I have no doubt that your mother's spirit went there. I don't want to tie her here anyway. You work for a very prestigious organization and have gained a lot of experience. Now you need real-life experience. After all, democracy won in Mongolia two years ago, and this year the country has a new constitution.

"Also, I have contacts who are interested in working in Mongolia. I'm not forcing you to leave tomorrow. You work for the European Union in Brussels. But soon you have to get involved in a big project and use your stepfather's money to do big things in your home country. You have enough money to start a good business. I don't need to worry about anything now. I have no one to pass my property to but you. I'm keeping a small amount to live the rest of my life."

I went to Brussels that day, and when I boarded the plane, I began to reflect on everything—how I had followed my mother from an early age and later set out to explore what I considered my homeland, even though I wasn't born there. I hadn't returned since becoming an adult. Even though my mother was gone, I felt as if she had returned to the land she came from, where the wind blew so wildly and freely. On the plane, I felt her traveling beside me on the white clouds. In that moment, I realized the word "motherland" held a meaning so profound for me; it was overwhelming. I used to call Mongolia my "fatherland" because my late father lived there, but now, I think it's only right to call it my "motherland."

I arrived in Brussels and was writing this at home, staring at a photo of my mother and me hanging on the wall. She is smiling at me, an eight-year-old wearing a white t-shirt with a black bow tie and a kilt. This photograph was taken by a London photographer. My mother did her hair in the fashion of the day, an elegant bun, her head slightly tilted, and her white teeth gleaming behind her beautiful smile. I remember being embarrassed to be wearing a Scottish skirt.

I still wonder why the bald-headed, fat Jewish photographer had chosen the skirt for me. I thought I was in a woman's outfit. That old Jewish photographer recognized me and gave me candies even after I started school. Later, in middle school, I learned that he was a German Jew named Klaus, who had escaped during the 1942 Holocaust of Jews in Nazi Germany. I made fun of him, calling him Santa Claus.

Looking at my mother's photo, I knew my decision to see my grandmother *Khanddolgor*, as Mom told me to, was the right idea all along.

It's been many years since Granny Mariusya's death, and I didn't know how to find *Khanddolgor*. So, I decided to contact the Mongolian Embassy in Brussels first.

12

The reason why *Avid*'s wife suddenly decided to divorce him was not clear to him. There seemed to be no reason for it. Reading about the girl *Avid* wrote about in his "sad diary" must have become an excuse for his wife to attack him in every argument they had since. It is said that it is difficult to understand a woman, but he never imagined she would make such a strange decision to read his diary.

…On a quiet, drizzly evening, *Avid* was on his way home and saw two people fighting next to a dumpster. It was almost funny to call what they were doing a fight because they were too drunk to even lay their hands on each other.

"Who are you, huh?" one of them shouted as he slipped in the mud and fell to the ground. The other clung to him without giving up, so he too landed in the mud.

"Who's talking? You're kidding me, aren't you? You're some kind of big shot, huh?" asked the other drunk. He headbutted the other's face, and the skinny man's nose began to bleed. He roared in pain and tried to grab the other guy.

Avid watched them for a moment, deciding whether or not to get between them.

It was getting dark, and it was difficult to walk down the street, so *Avid* carefully walked around the puddles to keep his expensive shoes from getting ruined.

Recently, the dumpster was relocated to this area near their home, and the homeless from the trenches began to gather around it and squat in the unfinished building nearby.

Poor things, he thought. *They're so drunk, so poor; all the same, they want to overcome each other.*

He walked around them and tried to enter the house with the key from his pocket, but the key did not turn because the door had a key inside. He pounded on the door, but no one answered. Surprised, he took out his phone and called his wife.

Soon he was lying under his warm blanket next to his wife, staring at the television.

It was still raining.

The next day, they had to go to the German embassy to apply for a travel visa.

"What time do we have to be there tomorrow, honey?"

"Ten-thirty. All documents are ready. I also got a bank statement. It's all on the table. Let's go on vacation at least this once, not for work," *Oyunaa* said.

"Yes, it is difficult to be a citizen of a poor country. What if an American citizen is asked to show all his or her bank statements to obtain a visa? But here, I'd show them the copies of the bank statements that I don't even show to you, my wife."

His wife asked him what she should wear to the visa appointment.

"Just wear whatever you like. We're just going on a vacation, not a business trip!" he said over a cup of coffee.

"Oh, I've heard that the people responsible for reviewing the documents are Mongolian ladies. They must be pretty picky. We should look as trustworthy as we can."

"Oh, is that so?"

They put the plates into the sink after breakfast, dressed neatly, and left the house.

The air was damp and fresh; the morning was calm and pleasant, just the right day to take a walk. After a while, the couple entered through the glass-fronted door of the light green embassy.

A very polite woman checked their names and let them in. But behind the glass window sat a rather proud-looking and stern middle-aged woman.

Avid put the papers in the drawer and pushed it, staring at her face.

She took the documents and without lifting her eyes to take a look at him asked coldly, "You have no invitation letter. What kind of business are you traveling for?"

"Traveling."

"What does that mean?"

"It means relaxing!"

"Why do you have to relax, especially in Germany? Who will you visit?"

"Madam, I want to go on vacation with my wife. I just want to relax. I have visited Germany many times before."

The word "madam" must have offended her, and for the first time, she looked at him.

"We do everything according to the rules. We can't issue a visa to an applicant who has no invitation or hotel reservation."

"Why? Can't you see we have enough money to travel?"

"It has nothing to do with the money. I'm asking according to the rules. Please come back in the afternoon for a consultation. Now, please, take back your documents." She put the documents in the drawer and pushed it to him.

"Hey, excuse me! What do I do now? I have even booked the plane tickets and have an official letter."

"Don't raise your voice. This is the territory of Germany!"

Avid lowered his voice and said, "I'm not raising my voice or being an asshole. I'm just asking what to do next."

"Don't use vulgar words. I'm reminding you again you're in another country's territory."

"Hey, Mrs. German, what should I do now?"

"You have no right to insult people. I never said I was German. Security, let the next applicant in, please."

The next applicant, who appeared intimidated by the previous conversation, looked at the consular woman with puppy-dog eyes. "Hello? Good morning?" he asked softly from his seat.

Avid looked at his wife, who was being interviewed at another window. She seemed to be getting approval.

He went outside and lit a cigarette. Oyuna came out shortly, smiling.

"They canceled my application," he said. "What about you? Will you be issued a visa?"

"Yes, I'm being issued a visa. And I observed you being such an arrogant ass with that woman, as usual."

"How come I was the arrogant one?"

"I just wanted to go on vacation together once. You deliberately quarreled with her and did not get a visa. Well, well. I guess I'll be going alone with some tour group. I suppose you'll be happy spending all your free time with the younger women anyway."

"Are you done talking? I haven't been seeing other women. Have I?"

"Stop it. You've become so entitled to treating people horribly. I wish you could hear that tone of your voice. You need to grow up! I'm leaving you. You call yourself a writer, and what do you write? You can't even be the writer of your own life. What do you write about anyway? Do you write about all your adultery? It's been a long time since you've figured that everyone else was stupid. You adulterer, you liar."

Avid could not stop his wife from walking away. Red-faced, he leaped through the door of the first roadside pub he found.

He wondered if the tone of his voice was really that harsh. So, *Avid* asked in a very sweet voice:

"A hundred grams, please, madam!"

The bartender reluctantly placed a glass of vodka in front of him and turned around, seemingly offended by the word "madam."

He chugged the vodka and asked for another hundred grams. The barmaid painted her nails behind the bar, glared at the annoying man who kept calling her madam, and handed him another glass of vodka.

On the counter were all the documents rejected by the embassy, as well as his passport.

Avid looked up at the dark ceiling of the bar. *Why create so many enemies? Maybe the barmaid will quit her job in a year's time. What has my wife said now? She must have found my notes and read them*, he thought.

13

January 13, 1996

My home was in an old house in the very center of Brussels, five minutes from the Grand Place, where the famous Manneken Pis statue stands, just down the Stoofstraat, along the sidewalk in Rue du Chêne.

There are various stories about this statue. Some say that in the 17th century, a tourist lost his son in the crowd and later found him urinating in that spot and that same tourist erected the statue.

I graduated with honors from the London School of Economics and Political Science, usually just called the LSE, a well-known university in the United Kingdom, and came to Brussels to work in a branch of the European Union.

Priya and I are still in touch, but after graduating from the university, she moved to her hometown of Manchester, where she got a job at a company, so we didn't see each other that often. In Europe, the tradition of getting married in the thirties or even the forties is still there. It's normal to fall in love, date, and live in the same house, but it's a different matter when it comes to marriage. There are many obstacles to it, such as family consent and religious differences.

Last September, Priya came to Brussels, and I took her on a tour of not only this city but also the most beautiful cities in Belgium, such as Antwerp, Bruges, and Liège. After a week together, she returned to Manchester. Belgium is so small that there is no time-consuming travel; I like this country very much, and I even plan to settle here. Belgium is a multi-ethnic, multilingual country, and many of my favorite writers and artists were born here.

Art was my favorite subject at school. I liked the romantic, expressionist, and surrealist artists of the late 19th and early 20th centuries, such as James Ensor, Constant, Permeke, and Paul Delvaux. René Magritte is from this country. There are many exhibitions and museums of artists such as Panamarenko, a sculptor representing the avant-garde movement since the 1950s.

Eddie Florence, my high school literature teacher, recommended that I read a number of famous Belgian writers, including Emily Verhaeren, Robert Goffin, Hendricks, Georges Simenon, Susanna Lee, Hugo Claus, and Amélie Nothomb.

The first time I met Belgian writers was when I read *The Negro* written by Commissioner Maigret's author, Georges Simenon. From that book, I learned that human life is unpredictable. The book tells the sad story of how the protagonist in a high position, with a beautiful wife and a child, suddenly became trapped in a foreign country, eventually fell in love with a black woman, and died in that country. I was wrong to think that Georges Simenon was a French writer who wrote only books about crime. I was surprised he wrote such beautiful novels about ordinary, yet intriguing, stories.

The country has two sections: the Flemish, who speak Dutch, and the Walloons, who speak French, so both languages are required, and all addresses are written in Flemish and French. I spoke French well in high school, and I'm still learning Flemish step by step. Another thing I like is that Belgium is located in the middle of England, France, Germany, and the Netherlands, so it has a lot in common with Mongolia, I reckon.

The British are very proud and sometimes appear to be a bit arrogant, just like my stepfather, while the Belgians are more friendly and very accepting of other cultures, partly because there are international organizations like the European Union and NATO. But with the arrival of the EU in the 1990s, the cost of living has become more expensive. When I first arrived, a pint of beer in a bar was worth thirty-five Belgian francs, or just one dollar, but now it's three euros. This is because even the cleaning ladies in the European Union are paid five thousand euros a month, and other professionals, tens of thousands of dollars. I am also a high-paid specialist.

Since I was a child, my stepfather taught me to live independently and economically, and even though I live in this city with a high salary, I don't want to spend a lot of money. I wear a few suits and shirts to work, and for other occasions, I wear the jeans and T-shirts I used to wear at school. I don't cook at home, so the only things in my fridge are beer and ice, and I hardly go to the grocery store. When I do shop for food, I go for the cheaper items. Belgium has somewhat socialistic ideals and differs from Britain in that all canned and packaged products have the same white label on the outside but cost twice as much in all stores. When I do need something, I'm used to buying canned food like those. Belgian beer is very popular and has almost 300 varieties, so sometimes, on the way home from work, I buy the kind of beer I've never tasted before, and now my fridge is full of beer.

When my mother's funeral was concluded and by the time I got home, the Christmas holidays had already begun, and I am writing my diary in great detail. This holiday season, a co-worker and I have agreed to travel to Antwerp to meet a few people. Antwerp is the largest diamond center in Europe and has a huge network of the Russian mob dealing diamonds. The people I'm going to meet are probably American businessmen who are interested in implementing projects in Mongolia, and my purpose is to network with them and find out what projects they're trying to do.

I also received a phone call from the Mongolian embassy yesterday and had a very friendly conversation. I didn't say I was Mongolian at first, and when I spoke in English under the official name of Jim Edmund as a British citizen, they noted that the embassy was open to anyone interested in investing in Mongolia.

14

Six hours later at sunset, *Avid* arrived at *Uyangaa's* workshop, but she was not there. No one could be seen on the long, dark top floor of a large, old building called The Workshop of the Craftsmen's Committee, and the door to *Uyangaa's* room was unlocked.

There was a picture on the wall, a mess of books and magazines on the floor, and a Russian magazine called *The Artist* lying on a pedestal table that sat on an old rug in front of the sofa. On the wall, two shelves made of thin black metal, known as the *five-ruble shelf*, were nailed to the wall and covered with brushes, paints, books, magazines, and multicolored candles.

Uyangaa's apartment was so colorful, so untidy, and so lighthearted it perfectly captured the painter's nature. Her workshop felt even closer to home when *Avid* thought about how many times before they had made love on this bad old couch. *Avid* lit a cigarette, got up from the couch, and pulled out the paintings one by one, leaning against the wall. There were many, some of which had been completed, some left unfinished and forgotten probably; most of them were bright-colored flowers and leaves. She used to do abstracts, but lately, she had turned to realistic flowers. Her paintings were warm in color; from time to time, a more than usually sharp-colored painting appeared, and he liked how it screamed from the warm soft colors.

Right in front of the sofa, on an easel painted pure white, a canvas seemed to have recently been pressed against a mixing plate called a palette. The sharp smell of the diluent, known as solvent in Russian by artists, wafted through the air.

Soon, he heard footsteps coming down the empty hallway. The door opened silently, as if sighing, and there was *Uyangaa* with a plastic bag full of wine and other treats. She put the groceries on the table and brought out the wine. *Avid* pressed his lips against her chubby pink lips, and he sighed, leaned over, sucked on her lips, kissed her, and stroked her pinky pale neck. *Avid* opened his eyes abruptly, intoxicated by her scent, but *Uyangaa* closed her eyes and pulled him closer and closer, kissing and biting his lips with such passion. *Avid* slowly moved away from her and sat back on the couch, panting a little.

"Shall we celebrate? I found a nice wine. What happened all of a sudden? Will we really go to Amsterdam together? I can't believe it. You're not kidding, are you?"

"Stop it. I won't kid about something like this."

"And when are we going?"

"Tomorrow I will take your passport to human resources. The meeting is six days later."

"That soon?"

"Yes, and the response will come out next week. You and I haven't been together for two days in a row, have we?"

"Nope."

She took a wine opener from the *five-ruble shelf,* handed it to *Avid* with a glass of wine, emptied the plastic bag, put a few grapes on a plate, took out two pieces of cheesecake, and placed them on a paper plate on the table in front of the sofa.

"I never thought I would go to Amsterdam. It felt like another world that seemed unreachable. But now I can't believe I'm going to go with you. Today has been a wonderful day—I sold a painting!"

"Oh, congratulations! You don't have any issues regarding the visa, right?"

"There is no problem."

"Very good. I'll take care of it now. Well, everything you own is in this workshop, huh?"

She chuckled like a child, handed *Avid* her passport, and said that she had been to China a few times.

"I was going to Beijing two years ago to buy some paint and almost left it here. I don't always go abroad like you, so I almost forgot. It will expire next year. What else do you need?"

"I don't need anything else. I just need you."

"It seems unbelievable. The first thought that came to my mind was to buy paint and a set of brushes in Amsterdam."

Avid's cell phone rang as he said that Dutch paint and brushes were the trend now. Janna was calling, so he picked up the phone and walked away from the couch.

"Hey, do you know what you did wrong?" Janna's drunken voice sounded through the phone.

"What's wrong? Are you drunk?"

"A bit. With your money! You are crazy rich. I asked you to lend me 900,000 *tugrugs*, and you transferred nine million."

"What? How did that happen?"

"Well, you're a rich guy, huh? Be glad it was me. If it were some other greedy girl, you would not see your money again."

Uyangaa filled two glasses with wine and looked at him, smiling.

Nearly faint with shock, *Avid* managed to say, "All right. Let me check."

Yes. In fact, he had really transferred nine million. He called Janna back, realizing he had inadvertently transferred nine million when he replaced the number one with nine and forgot to erase one zero.

Janna was not picking up the phone. *Avid*'s face turned pale. He hung up and called again.

No answer. Panicked, he grabbed his glass of wine and drank it at once.

"What are you doing?" asked *Uyangaa*. "Why are you making such a serious face? Is everything okay?"

He looked at her and decided not to answer. He continued calling Janna, who wouldn't pick up. He became increasingly frightened, poured, and drank another glass of wine in a gulp.

"I'm sorry, *Uyangaa*. There's a money problem. I have to leave now."

Surprised, *Uyangaa* followed him along the hallway with her mouth open, holding her glass of wine. Just as *Avid* went out the door, he received a text message. He hurriedly looked and saw that eight million *MNT* had been transferred to his account. He let out a sigh in the empty hallway, slumping against the wall. He managed to call Janna. She now picked up the phone.

"Ha! Were you scared? I was surprised and wondered if it was a gift or not. But I felt sorry for you. Anyway, I bought a bottle of wine with it. I'm different from other people, you know." She was quiet for a moment, and *Avid* couldn't speak. Thoughtfully, she said, "But you're a very rich man, aren't you?"

Uyangaa had followed him out of the workshop and watched him slide to the floor with his phone to his ear.

"What's going on? What happened to our celebration? Is it that serious?"

He suddenly came to his senses and said, "Everything's alright. I've figured it out."

When *Avid* returned to the workshop, he poured another glass of wine to calm down, locked the door, hugged *Uyangaa*, kissed her mindlessly, and began to undress her as if he were angry. She grabbed *Avid*'s pants and put her hand inside them.

Avid's cell phone kept ringing on the table, the screen lit up with "Janna" on it.

The curtains fluttered, and a faint blue light shone through the window. In the dim light of the studio, the white bodies of the couple shone brightly. *Avid* and *Uyangaa* panted in lust. As *Avid* let out a loud cry, *Uyangaa* moved her sweaty body beneath him.

Avid was confused by the fire of lust on top of the fright of his life. He felt as if someone was watching them from above, and *Avid* was incapable of stopping until he came and collapsed on the woman like dead weight.

15

In addition to his work as an author, *Avid* corresponded with Mr. *Aajim*, and while translating the diaries from English into Mongolian, he realized he hadn't received any new notes from him in two months.

Avid grew concerned.

Aajim's diary was interesting, readable, concise, and did not require much editing. However, at times, it seemed as though the diaries were written by two different people taking turns. It was even stranger that, in a recent note, a dream about the past began to emerge from the dark tunnel of the subconscious. *Why have I waited to investigate the reason he hasn't written to me in so long?*

For the first time, *Avid* had doubts. Could it be that this person has been sending me a completely false story? *Why have I never checked if the address under the email was real or fake? Why has it never occurred to me to investigate if Jim Edmund even exists?*

I have friends in Belgium, he thought.

Nothing came of it for another month, however, due to *Avid*'s habit of letting things go. He later regretted ever trusting a stranger, but his curiosity got the better of him, and he decided to meet the old woman named *Khanddolgor*; she was described in the notes and might ignite the last strand of faith he had in the man *Aajim*—if such a bloke even existed.

While refreshing his inbox each day, he researched the old woman and asked around to see who might know her. When he found out that she was 100 years old and lived in the Chingeltei district, *Avid* grabbed his recorder and set off on the bus.

On the way to the woman's neighborhood, he was lost in thought. *A hundred years is a long time to be alive. Will she remember anything at all? The strange man who's been sending me his notes must have met this old woman when he came to Mongolia. What kind of name is Aajim, anyway?*

He realized the reason he had believed in him. *As soon as the money was transferred, he believed everything he told him, he thought.*

The background check was easy to complete because the only thing he had to do was call the Ministry of Foreign Affairs and inquire about the man named Purevjal Punsal.

The address in his hand read: 12 Chingeltei District, 4th Khoroo, 12 J. Sambuu Street. The address system in the slums was so bad that he had to ask for directions from kids playing in the neighborhood. Eventually, he found the right house.

"Who are you looking for?" asked a young boy from behind the fence.

"Does an old woman named *Khanddolgor* live here?"

"Grandma does live here. But now she is at Uncle Ojig's in the city because she hasn't been feeling well."

"Oh, really? Where does your uncle live?"

"Be right back," said the boy and sprinted to the house. He returned with an address and a phone number written on a piece of paper.

Avid backtracked and found the address, entered through the open entrance door, and went up the stairs to number 32. He rang the bell, but no one answered, so he sat on the steps, waited, took out his cell phone, and checked his e-mail.

But *Avid* did not need to dread disappointment; he heard someone walking up the stairs and got up to greet a man in his late fifties who stared at him with a strange look.

"I'm inquiring about an older woman named *Khanddolgor* at the behest of a man named *Aajim*," *Avid* said hurriedly.

The man, grocery bag in one hand and a five-pound bucket in the other, looked at the writer intently again. "Are you talking about the man who lives in England?"

"Yes, yes. I am a writer and journalist. I met him a few months ago. I mean Jim Edmund."

The older man unlocked the door and let him in. "She's been a bit unwell lately, but she's fine now. Her ears are no good. Probably won't hear you."

Avid now realized how tactless he was. He could have brought a carton of milk for the elderly woman. *Oh, well, I'll just give the man some cash to buy milk.* He calmed himself.

In a small room on a single metal bed sat an old woman eating a bowl of beans from a cup on a chair in front of her.

As soon as *Avid* came in, the first thought that came to him was that she really resembled *Ayurzana*, one of the generals of the Tariat uprising.

He pulled up a chair next to the bed and sat down in front of her. "Hello? How do you do? Your grandson *Aajim* sent me," *Avid* almost shouted.

"Oh, my goodness! May God bless you. You must be an angel carrying news from my poor grandson," she exclaimed. "It has been a long time since we last saw each other. He came to see me in the nineties. My poor daughter-in-law, how has she been doing? There's no news of her. But my grandson, he has grown up to become a handsome, tall boy just like his father. Will he come here again? Why didn't *Tsogzolmaa* come? Is she still in England? Is the Embassy still located on American Hill?"

Oh, so Aajim's mother's name is Tsogzolmaa, Avid thought.

Khanddolgor continued, eager to talk. "My poor daughter-in-law; she left in the 1960s and never came back. My poor son suddenly fell ill and died. Probably not a good place, that England! My son went there and passed away, and my daughter-in-law went there and disappeared. But my poor grandson, all alone, came and met me. Once. You want to know how I am doing? Alive and kicking, thanks to my adopted son Ochirbat." She waved over at Uncle Ojig, who sat reading, paying no attention. "I have lost my father, mother, sister, and even my poor son. I think it's all about my karma coming back to haunt everyone I've loved and cared for."

"Well, yes, I've heard about your family, and it intrigues me, ma'am. I am kind of a journalist myself, and I heard that you've submitted a request to have your father exonerated officially. How is that going?"

"My father was literate, very wealthy, and deeply devoted to God. He joined the Yellow Army and was later executed. Before I die, I want to be granted a state apology for my father and have him exonerated. You said you were a journalist; did I hear right? Could you please go after it and rehabilitate my father's reputation? He was recently even mentioned in a book."

Avid wanted to extract more information from the old woman, but she kept repeating the things she had said about the deaths of her parents and sister, which *Avid* already knew from *Aajim*'s notes. And he realized that the book the old woman was talking about was Britannica.

He took out two bills of twenty-thousand tögrög from his pocket while the granny kept talking about how good a person her father was and how her mother and sister were poisoned. *Avid* tried asking Ochirbat, hoping that he would know something more, but apparently, he wasn't aware of anything regarding the family history.

Avid left the bills on the bed, stood up, said he would come back, and left.

As he walked down the stairs, he was embarrassed that he had chased an old woman out of curiosity. Everything *Aajim* was writing to him turned out to be true. Now he didn't even have to check on his father. That, too, was true. *But it's a little strange why Aajim suddenly went silent. Khanddolgor's adopted son Ochirbat seemed not to know much about them or care. He simply took care of Khanddolgor. Aajim's mother, Tsogzolmaa—they don't even know she is dead.*

Avid decided not to write to *Aajim* about the day's meeting of the old woman. Better to just wait.

At the time, *Avid* was editing a book translated by a man called Ts. Tseren, and he had received a series of emails from him. He was scrolling down to see if maybe there was an email from him when he found that not only had *Aajim* replied to his letter, but he had also attached the continuation of his notes in email attachments. *Oh, Avid! It's obvious why I didn't check the attachments—Aajim used to send them simply in the form of an open letter.*

He felt like a fool for not thinking to check for attachments for two whole months.

He replied to *Aajim* immediately in a letter: "Over the last few days, I've spent a lot of time editing my Mongolian notes and rearranging them to make them even more distinctive. I just realized that I had sent you a very vague message about what I had done before and what exactly I did for the European Union. It took me a long time to figure everything out again. I also did not mention my first visit to Mongolia. In addition, I have sent you a copy of the contract. We're getting along so well; I'll send you more money soon. If you agree to the statements in the contract, you can sign it, scan the signed copy, and send it over. Then the contract can be effective.

"The contract is made in English because I am a British citizen, so it did not need to be translated into Mongolian. My personal lawyer prepared this contract, so it can be considered legal. Good luck to you, Jim Edmund."

PART 3

Running out of words to describe the shortness of the night

Lusting for the satisfaction that was not just right

Realizing what a sucker I'd been for this empty pleasure

Addicted to the blind fantasy beyond measure

- Galsaa Axt

: "The Himalayas, a backdrop of serene strength against Avid's reflections."

1

In the middle of the steppe, there is a group of mourners in a procession, followed by a wind ensemble playing a mournful melody. The procession is led by a mounted man, Batbold, the flag-bearer. He sits on his horse with his head almost hanging from his neck; from time to time, he chugs vodka from a strange bottle labeled with a skull. The pinto horse walks slowly and surely, as if she knows the solemnity of her role. Following the flagman is a person being carried on a rolling hospital bed, pushed by four doctors in protective clothes and face masks.

After the doctors, two young men, one Mongolian and one foreigner, who resemble common missionaries, carry a large wooden cross.

Following them is a crowd of people wearing glittery, shiny clothes.

The person being pushed on the rolling bed is a woman whose eyes are wrapped in a piece of cloth dripping blood, seeping and leaving stains on the sand—a red trail.

The woman shouts blindly, "Where are we going? What's happening? Doctor, please, what's happening? What is wrong with me?" She struggles, but to no avail, as she is tied tightly to the bed.

"The operation was unsuccessful," said one of the doctors.

"What operation? What happened? I can't see!"

A doctor looks down at her. "You gouged out your own eyes," he replies coldly.

"What do you mean?" she begins to screech.

Some of the mourners cry, all of them with their heads down. The procession stops at the brink of a steep canyon. Batbold holds up his hand. "The time has come!" he announces.

A man runs to the woman and tapes her mouth shut. The music stops, and everything goes silent.

Oyunchimeg, the woman, does not give up; she struggles.

No one cares.

Soon Batbold dismounts, shakes the bottle, sips what is left, throws it over his shoulder, tosses the flag to the man next to him, raises his hands to the sky, and stands in prayer.

At that moment, the foreigner carrying the cross, dressed in a suit and tie, approaches the woman. Without a moment's notice, he throws her to the bottom of the deep, dark ravine.

"Mother!" *Oyunchimeg* screams as she wakes from the nightmare.

What a vicious dream. She sighs heavily. *Oyunchimeg* does not rush to get up, lying there, buried in fear of the horrible dream.

A while later, her mother peeks through the drapes separating her bed from the other parts of the ger: "*Oyunaa*, are you awake? It's Sunday. Is Batbold picking you up?" she asks with one eye still closed.

The mother gets up slowly and starts to make a fire to boil tea.

"I had a nightmare, Mother," *Oyunaa* says from behind the drape. "Batbold has been running around with some troubled men." She wants to converse with her mother, but her mother is occupied with the fire and watching TV and does not hear her daughter talking.

The TV narrator is saying, "Nationalism is not an ideology of hatred but of love. The citizens of a small nation should treat each other with love in nationalism. Racism is hatred toward other nations."

There are two *gers* in this yard on *Tsagaan Davaa*. Because they are located high on a hill, the *ger* dwellers think the city would fit in the palm of one's hand. As *Oyunaa* comes out from behind her hanging drape, a stray dog comes running to her, wagging its tail.

She pours a small bucket of water from a big bucket of 40 liters and pours that into a bucket hanging on a small pole. Soon, a boy of about ten comes out of the door and begins to wash his hands and face.

"Did you let that stray dog in the yard?" asks his sister.

"No, she came with you."

"Hey, go away, you! *Baatar*, chase this dog out. Get away! Last night, this dog was following me around, so I gave her food, and now she's making herself at home."

The yellow dog hesitantly looks back at the woman and walks out the front door that the boy has opened for her.

It is early in the morning, and there are no people or animals except the yellow dog, who proceeds to run down the street. As the girl walks down the dirt road to the corner, a yellow bus passes by. She remembers yesterday following a woman who had just gotten off that yellow bus. For some reason, she felt so close to her that she couldn't stop following her for a while.

Sharik the dog tries hard to understand why people hate stray dogs so much, but she doesn't get it. Sharik has a strange ability to distinguish between the scents of a person who is about to suffer and that of angry or good people. She knows that many people reek of evil, especially when they spot an innocent stray dog running around looking for food. She misses her country home. In the countryside, dogs are men's best friends. Every family has a dog, and they are like a member of the family, but that's not the case in the city.

City dwellers have dogs in their yards tied to the fence, and it is common for city dogs to hate other dogs and despise their homes as well as their owners. They don't have any livestock to take care of and direct, so they bark at everyone who comes near them. Although some people living in apartments own dogs, those dogs, like their masters, hate strays, too. They even smell like human beings, those apartment dogs.

Everyone has a different mindset, and the people of the city are different from the people of the countryside, even though most of them came from the country. They are always angry, fierce, and full of evil thoughts.

But like angels of the day, women do not despise the strays.

The daughter saw a dog shining in the rain the night before as she came down from the yellow bus, and the dog followed her into the yard. The woman was sorrowful to find the dog following her, so she came out in the evening after the rain and threw food at it.

After eating what the woman had given her, Sharik went inside their yard and lay down. When the woman came out in the morning to wash her face and hands, Sharik wagged her tail and approached her, but the woman had a child chase her away, and so Sharik ran into the street, not knowing where she was going.

During this time, a car entered a dirt road and came down a curved street. Batbold was in the car with two of his friends, with whom he had been drinking the previous night. Sharik knew that he was drunk and coming for *Oyunaa*.

When the car stopped outside the fence, Batbold staggered to the side of the road and pulled the gate open. Sharik attempted to follow him inside, but the door had shut right at her wet snout. She managed to get inside through a small opening.

Soon there was a scream in the yard, and when *Oyunaa* came out of the fence crying, the young man followed her with a knife in his hand. Unaware of what was happening, *Oyunaa* saw her husband being bitten by an angry dog. After a moment, *Oyunaa* realized it was the dog that had followed her here the night before. Sharik bit the man's hand. Batbold fell down, got up, and threw a stone from the ground. Sharik dodged the stone and bit his leg.

At that moment, two young men came out of the parked car and threw stones at Sharik. As she fled, she looked back and saw that the light of the radiant girl was fading.

2

"You shameless liar!" cried *Oyunaa* as she slammed the door and left. In a fit of rage, she forgot her school bag. She went back upstairs, took her bag from under the closet in the hallway, ran to the bedroom to pick up her notebooks, and turned to the door. A shirtless man looked at her sternly. She pushed him out of her way and attempted to leave again.

"Where are you going to go this early in the morning? I just said what I thought. Our life is not working out. It's true that I didn't spend last night at home. I'm sorry, but it didn't turn out the way you thought. We drank and met a man who wanted to trade red mercury. Do you know what red mercury costs?"

"Tell that story to the girl you were with last night. You still reek of vodka and a woman's perfume. You should become a fiction author! How dare you insult me like that when I'm with your child in my belly? I'm leaving you. Do whatever you want!" She slammed the door and left.

Oyunaa had become intimate with Batbold two years ago when she was a graduate student in the French department of the Institute of Foreign Languages. When she first met him, he seemed like an interesting and passionate person. But two years after moving in together, he was completely different. He would always say things that were incomprehensible, like, "I'll be rich soon." The young people he hung out with were a gang of traders, gamblers, and troublemakers, not friends—never visiting Batbold and *Oyunaa* at home.

When they first met, Batbold used to say that he trained dogs at the canine training center in front of *Gandan* Monastery. *Oyunaa* was from the countryside, and she loved dogs and assumed men who loved and cared for dogs must be kind. That was one of the reasons she believed in him. Batbold later brought in a lot of money. She was happy now that she had money to buy furniture and other things for their apartment, but Batbold told her to save it.

One night, Batbold came running in and told her to give him half of the money. "My friends are having a hard time. A friend in need is a friend indeed, right?" he said. "Be patient, I'll see you soon. Money will come around, but friends won't. They say it's better to have a hundred friends than to have a hundred *tugrugs*, right?"

Later that night, Batbold came home hammered. *Oyunaa* quarreled at first. But as time went by, she stopped saying a word. She went to school thinking that their relationship had failed completely. He was a handsome young man, but that fact no longer attracted *Oyunaa*. By the time she decided she was no longer in love with the man she had been living with, *Oyunaa* found out she was pregnant.

Oyunaa graduated from high school in Bayankhongor. She and her mother set up a dairy factory but did not succeed. They spent four or five years working in the *Aimag* center. The year a French family moved into town, *Oyunaa* regularly visited the family, and after one year, she could speak French fluently. She moved to the city after passing the entrance exam to the foreign language institute.

Her mother sold the animals and followed her daughter to the city.

On one Women's Day, *March 8*, she had a fierce argument with her partner and decided to break it off. She went to her mother's to spend the night. As she walked along the edge of a ravine, her lower belly ached, and she sat down.

Oyunaa didn't like to bother her mother, but she had nowhere else to go on Women's Day. She came in moaning and lay down on the bed in the back of the ger. Her mother was worried and called an ambulance.

Half an hour later, an ambulance arrived, and the doctor listened to the girl.

"You don't have to worry. You seem to be distressed." He smiled. "Don't be too concerned."

When she lay down for a while and began to cry, her mother worried and asked her if she was okay. She sighed and sat up on the bed.

"I am leaving Batbold. He's a little over the top. He went out every night since I told him I got pregnant. You do remember him chasing after me with a knife, don't you?"

Her mother tried to comfort her. "No, you go back to your husband. You cannot break up now that you two are going to have a baby. There are always such quarrels in life. You are also a strong-willed person. He will gladly welcome you back. Come on, it's *March 8th*!"

Shortly after that day, *Avid* met *Oyunchimeg*, a young man who had studied with him in Russia and later hired him at the time when the Institute for Strategic Studies became independent from the Institute of Military History.

They both got jobs and enjoyed each other's company. Not only did *Avid* love his wife, but he was also proud of his wife's French-speaking skills and bragged to his friends. He'd even hire her for written translations required from the Institute from time to time.

They got along very well both physically and mentally. They would make love every couple of days. *Oyunaa* had never had an orgasm before in her previous relationships. In the month after the miscarriage, *Oyunaa* and *Avid* first had sex, and she had a climax for the first time in her life. As amazed as she was with the immense pleasure she had experienced the night before, *Oyunaa* even made the first move on Avid, which she had never done until that point. That night, *Avid*, even though he was not as fierce as a stallion, managed to make her orgasm three times. *Avid* was the kind of man who rejoiced as much as the women he was giving pleasure to. He also asked *Oyunaa* to speak French during sex, and he would be even more turned on. They had sex all night and conversed happily in between. *Avid* also excelled in Russian jokes, so they both laughed and clung to each other. Such happiness lasted for three years; she got pregnant four times in those three years, but lost them all. During the last pregnancy, she had not left the house for three months. One night she experienced contractions, called the ambulance, and had another miscarriage. *Oyunaa* decided to follow doctors' recommendations to apply permanent birth control. Since then, they hadn't discussed having children.

Fifteen years have passed since the eclipse.

Avid took the coffee he had left on the table and tasted it. Because it had gone cold, he decided to make one more cup. He turned to his wife. "Are we going to sleep like this forever? Three months apart? Is that okay for you?"

"But it's what you wanted for a long time now. Isn't it? You are the one who decided to distance yourself from me. You were the one who even rented an apartment to get away from me! You are living your life just as you wanted it. Promiscuous and writing about it."

"So, you're not to blame? How sweet and sexy you were when we first met. Now you are completely frozen, dry, and in a constant bad mood."

"Don't you put the blame on me. You made me like that. You killed that beautiful *Oyunaa* that I once was. You will never find a loyal woman like me again. I am a saint. I am disgusted to lie in the same bed as you, let alone be near you. You should be thankful to have me around you, you filthy animal!"

"Well, well. Not again, please. It's impossible to have a conversation with you. I have a lot of work to do. You are living in your head, filled with anger and frustration from the past. I don't know what to do with you anymore."

Avid got dressed and went out the door while the coffee was boiling.

"A journey into the past unfolds as figures converge under the weight of memory."

3

December 19, 1999

In the winter of 1999, I contracted jaundice.

I turned 33 this year. I read that Jesus Christ was crucified at this age. But it seems very reasonable for Mongolians to consider every twelve years as a cycle. Because everything seemed to change from cycle to cycle, I believed that physical illness and emotional instability were common symptoms of those changes. At the age of twenty-five, I committed a major failure.

According to Oriental scriptures, the thirty-seventh year of a human life coincides with the year the planet Earth is positioned on the opposite side of one's birth. In the sixty-first year of human life, one sixty-year span is replaced by another. I remember reading those ages thirty-seven and sixty-one can be the toughest years in anyone's life. A person of the same generation, a friend of the same generation, means a person who falls within these twelve years, and a person outside that twelve-year cycle is deemed to be of another generation.

Jaundice was the "reward" for my three-month visit to Ecuador, where I worked on a project. My mother told me that I had jaundice when I was three, but I don't remember. My mother used to pay a lot of attention to my diet because jaundice is more likely to recur.

When I was in Ecuador, I ate a lot of spicy food, mostly fried food, and I drank unsafe water and lived in a dirty environment.

A colleague of mine, Fernando Silva, used to drink a sixty-percent alcoholic beverage called Aguardiente, which is widely consumed in Mexico, Chile, and Portugal, almost every day. That might've been a part of the problem.

A few days before I returned from Ecuador, I felt exhausted. When I got to work two days after my arrival, my co-worker, Odo Halflans, greeted me and was so surprised to see me in such a condition that he pulled my lower eyelids down to inspect them.

"You go to the hospital right away and get tested. Didn't you notice that your eyes are all yellow?" he asked.

My Belgian friend Halflans' parents were doctors. It wasn't a surprise that he was the first to notice.

I became a patient at Cliniques Universitaires Saint-Luc, a hospital near the northern train station of Zaventem. Jaundice is a serious liver disease, and because it is contagious, it is forbidden for me to see anyone. I'm not even allowed to read books or watch TV. It was going to be hard to pass time there for two whole weeks with such restrictions. Luckily, because I was hospitalized straight from work, I had a small laptop with me. Although I was not allowed to work on a computer, I thought it was still a good opportunity to compile and edit my notes behind the doctors' backs.

For the first few days, I was constantly on medication, so I was alone in my room, staring out the window. Also, because jaundice is a liver disease, I could not take sleeping pills; I would wake up in the middle of the night unable to fall back to sleep.

My father in London, although he's old now, does not sit idle and occasionally works as a consultant for a company other than the one he worked for. He told me his job was somewhat connected to economic intelligence, and I've been receiving reports from him about Eastern European countries, such as Mongolia, of economic hitmen known as financial fraud-based investors.

Ecuador, where I stayed for three months, has had its worst economic crisis this year. The mining-based economy seemed to manifest the potential risks that Mongolia might face in the future.

In 1996, Abdala Bucaram, the leader of the Ecuadorian Roldosist Party, won the presidential election after campaigning for socio-economic reforms.

Following the elections, Ecuador's economy declined sharply from 1997 to 1999 and faced a deep financial crisis. That's why I went there with six people to do research, and we found that the crisis was caused by external factors, such as U.S.-invested companies, the country's tax laws, and the involvement of populists in its politics.

I was to write a review on "Transparency and Restrictions on Foreign Investment in Ecuador and Other Factors," so I summarized the research I had done while I was in the hospital. I woke in the middle of sleep from night sweats and thirst, and I occasionally vomited because of the bitter taste in my mouth from the medications I had been taking all day.

Another strange thing about this hospital was that the windows of the brothels on the long street next to the North Station, which was not far from my window at night, were directly visible. The half-naked prostitutes sitting behind the window looked like mannequins.

At night, when drunken men passed by the street next to our hospital, they laid their eyes on the prostitutes as if they were making their choices while shopping for clothes.

Why do people live like this? The young men who had done their business came out with a satisfied look on their faces. But it was sad to see a woman sitting there with her bare thighs, smoking as if nothing had happened.

We've all come out of this thing called sex. However, the sacred act is despised everywhere, especially in religion; everyone having sex is persecuted as immoral. According to the Crusades, mankind was created from a man named Adam and a woman named Eve. Adam and Eve ate of the fruit, and their desires were aroused, and everyone became a sinner. It is even more ridiculous to preach that if they had not eaten the fruit, there would have been no sin of sexual intercourse. But intercourse is an easy thing to finish off in under one song. Some people are selling their sexuality for money, some are falling in love and getting married.

The wars of this world are almost entirely caused by lust, which is beautifully called love. Doesn't a wife sell herself to her husband at a high price for the rest of her life? Trading is in every aspect of life. In Ecuador, the richest people in the world sell their oil to foreigners; in Europe, mostly Eastern European women sell their bodies to foreigners. What does the woman do with her earnings? She buys an expensive car or an expensive house. When you think about it, it all starts to look like madness driven by lust. Is momentary pleasure the essence of every being? Most books and movies don't talk about it; they just show it.

I recently read a book called *You'll Never Make Love In This Town Again*, which was published in 1996 and gained a high readership. That's how I got to know a little bit about the lives of those in this business. The book describes three prostitutes having affairs with Hollywood celebrities, and because it is based on true events, it has become very popular.

In fact, many books in this field have been published in Europe for a long time. One such book, *Prostitution, Considered in Its Moral, Social, and Sanitary Aspects, in London and Other Large Cities and Garrison Towns, with Proposals for the Mitigation and Prevention of Its Attendant Evils*—a book with its ridiculously long title—was written in 1857 by William Acton. I read it in high school as recommended by my favorite teacher, Eddie Florens.

I, alone in a hospital ward, with prostitutes lined up to sell their time and lust outside my window, younger and older men going and coming one after another... This world never ceases to amaze.

4

Although I was ill and could not sleep at night, I managed to have a strange dream one day. I will try to relive it.

I don't dream much; dreams seem to come to me only when I, the dreamer, am unwell. I thought I was dreaming because of discomfort. I dreamt about drinking from a river whenever I was thirsty.

That day I heard George Harrison's *My Sweet Lord* playing somewhere through the hospital window. I fell asleep listening to the song, but my mind was empty, my heart was pounding, and soon I felt I was in a strange, deaf silence.

I felt like I was dying, and I felt like I was hanging in empty space. All my bodily fluids were gone. If I think about it carefully, I can remember that I died four or five days ago.

I know I've been asleep for five days. But right now, I hear an unfamiliar sound, and I open my eyelids a little; I'm forced to remember what I thought five days ago: Am I in heaven? I heard the sound again, and when the footsteps grew louder, I had a hard time with it, being afraid, and I forced myself to listen for the man with the cane in his hand. The sound of the cane became louder and louder.

Five days ago, I was walking alone through a brothel near Brussels' Northern Station when I heard the George Harrison song ring out. I loved the song, and I hadn't heard it in years. I stopped and listened to the faint sound that would lead me to the window where a girl sat. It seemed as though the girl behind that window was Irina. As I walked up the stairs to the entrance and found the flat where the melody was coming from, I heard a voice behind the brown, wooden door and the smell of grilled meat. I knocked, but no one answered. I felt uneasy pounding on the stranger's door, and I kept listening for an answer. I hoped it would be Irina's.

The downstairs front door slammed open, and I heard the sound of a cane's regular tap, tap, tap. I knocked on the door again, wondering, *Why won't Irina open the door tonight?* As I walked downstairs, the sound of the tapping cane and footsteps approached.

The footsteps and cane grew fearfully louder and closer, and the sound echoed in my ears like an alarm clock. I was amazed at what was happening, especially when the sound of a cane echoed through the hollow entrance. It seemed like the old man was Russian. All of a sudden, I experienced severe pain in the back of my head, probably due to being axed, I remember thinking. The man holding the ax appeared to be Chinese, and he looked evil. All of these thoughts were incoherent, and I wondered if I'd been reliving a dream I'd had before. I really wondered why I was still in the hospital alive if someone had killed me with an ax.

Is this real, or is it a dream? I couldn't wrap my head around it. Even when I died, I could still hear my favorite song playing in the background and the sound of the old man's footsteps. The thought of why… At that moment, I could see from above that I'm lying unconscious in the middle of the narrow street where the brothel was. But in the street, where many girls were lined up, a few people were standing in a crowd, a screen with a white sheet hung in the middle, and a few Mongolians on horseback were watching a movie. The movie was Jerry Maguire, starring Tom Cruise.

"From space, I see a blue marble. We hear the calm voice of Jerry Maguire talking to us. The light in the air is the earth, where five billion people live. When I was a child, there were only three of us.

Someone said, "I remember."

The great continent revolves around the misty sky. (Satellites and other celestial bodies are floating here.) The audience whistles and shouts, "Dui, dui!" The film mechanic rewinds the film.

Next to me appeared a taxi that was traveling in a dark alley in the *ger* district of Ulaanbaatar, where I had walked through a few years ago. It stopped by me, the car window rolled down, and an old man with glasses said, "Is this J. Sambuu's 23rd street? Isn't that the warehouse I see there? And this twenty-three?"

I nodded, and he said, "Thank you," through the window, and the car drove off into the dark alley.

I hung back in the air, watched the movie, and stood in front of a crowd of insects. It was strange to see prostitutes sitting behind a glass window, waiting for a movie on the street, ignoring their customers and smoking.

As soon as I woke up, I recorded this strange, chaotic dream so I wouldn't forget it.

Today is December 3, 1999.

5

We think that what's real is what we see, Avid thought. *We seldom realize that truth and love are invisible.* Continuing in my journal: *Do people see mental and physical pain? Happiness and misery are all invisible. I can't see my thoughts, but still, I suffer from them. You can neither touch love nor disease. It's not about looking for love; it's about bringing it out. I think my wife Oyunaa loved me very dearly at first, but now she's buried it deep inside; at least, what's left of it. Unfortunately, she's reluctant to dig it up; she's even forcibly suppressing every attempt at it.*

I had returned home for a while, but *Oyunaa* did not hold a human conversation with me, let alone sleep with me. After months of separate bedrooms in the same house, I returned to the apartment.

I, Avid, gave myself credit for at least trying to make things work—I and *Uyangaa* were going to go to the Netherlands together. But suddenly the Institute decided to send someone else in my stead because I'd already gone on an international trip to India.

I was very bored. All I did was translate a few files sent from the Institute and email them back.

I had a few empty bottles of beer on the table in front of me and was chugging another early in the morning. *How do I change the heart of someone who can't see me and doesn't love me? It doesn't make sense to ask for something that is not there anymore. Why don't I call Uyangaa or Janna right now and spend this time of mine happily for at least a whole day? Uyangaa says I haven't spent a whole day with her; it's true for all of them. Does Oyunaa fathom how much pain I'm in right now? I asked myself, but to no avail. She would probably laugh at me and even be happy knowing she hurt me.*

My landlord is an elderly woman living alone after being widowed recently. She told me that the apartment was furnished and redecorated to be rented to foreigners. Located in the north of the food market called *Dalai Eej* (Mother Ocean), the place is perfect for renting to tourists and ex-pats who search for convenient locations in the center of the city where everything they need is within walking distance. Everything in this apartment is brand new and seems a bit soulless. In front of a white table and a black leather sofa is an expensive Persian-style carpet. There are two new cabinets with glass doors on the opposite wall. The bedroom has a spacious wardrobe, coupled with a king-sized bed from Ikea. The kitchen is small but fits with the custom-made furniture and a few new pots, pans, bowls, and buckets that have never been used for cooking so far.

Thanks to the three months I spent in this apartment, the place has, at least, a shallow resemblance to someone's home.

Through the window, I could hear a faint sound of rain falling, and somewhere a dog was barking. I scrolled through Facebook on my cell phone and realized it was Father's Day. When I saw people posting pictures of their fathers, I remembered my father, who passed away five years earlier.

When I was in high school, my father worked as a bus conductor, and I was embarrassed to tell my classmates what my father did. Later, when I grew up, I was very happy to learn that my father was an employee of the Ministry of Home Affairs but wondered why he worked as a conductor. One evening, before he was sent to the intelligence school by the Ministry, he told me a story.

"Son, you will be a secret agent like me. So, let me tell you something. You know, I was a conductor at the bus depot for a long time. But you probably didn't notice that I used to suddenly disappear at night. Your mother knew, however. I would be sent on a secret mission—a state secret. There are things the government should run covertly. You will get a grasp once you start school. There are secrets that cannot be shared."

It was now clear that my father worked as a bus conductor to cover up his real job. "I want to give you a few instructions. You just keep it to yourself. The first thing you should focus on is becoming a very good sniper. Your school will teach you anyway. I don't have any other children, so I raised you at your will. But now that you're going to a very important special school in the great Soviet Union, it's going to be different. You must be patient, disciplined, and sophisticated. Russian is the most important and richest language. Life will be easier for you if you learn good Russian and good shooting. The country is in transition. But it doesn't matter. The quality of life depends solely on your discipline and independence, regardless of the environment and the social changes," my father told me.

To this day, I never found out what kind of secret missions he was on. I remember thinking just once that maybe my father was an executioner.

6

October 17, 1997

In the fall of 1997, during the world premiere of James Cameron's *Titanic*, several of our staff received invitations to the official opening and reception of the film in Brussels.

The Titanic was built at the Harland and Wolff shipyards in Belfast. My invitation allowed for a plus one. I had to decide whom to bring.

Priya, of course, couldn't come from Manchester to attend the opening with me, and she and I had been drifting apart in the last couple of years. It seems to me that love needs a lot of nurturing. At first, we missed each other a lot when we were apart, but then the feeling slipped away. Our conversations grew lifeless. When it came to sex, I had no one to compare Priya with. How passionate and sultry she is in bed can't be forgotten, a sharp contrast to how she, an ordinary geeky girl, is in other situations. We don't talk much. When we actually see each other, we feel the instant physical chemistry that leads us quickly to the bedroom as if intercourse were the most important part of our encounter. As the days went by, a gray space like a fog appeared between us.

As soon as I received the invitation, Irina Polishuk, whom I had met recently, immediately came to mind. She is a gorgeous Ukrainian girl who works for Adamas Diamond Tools NV, a diamond testing company in Antwerp. We never run out of conversation as she shares my interests in literature and movies.

"Good evening, Irina. Titanic is premiering in Brussels tomorrow. Can you come to the premiere with me?"

"Wow! Of course! I didn't know what to do with the three-day bonus vacation, which is starting tomorrow, anyway. I was just about to call you. I'll be there by tomorrow."

"If you don't mind, you can stay at my place. I believe I've told you I live in a multi-room apartment right in the center of the city. It's much better than staying at a hotel."

"Of course I don't mind. Honestly, I have a lot of interesting things to tell you. You talked about investing in Mongolia. I have two prospects interested, one is Russian, the other is Chinese. The Russian is even a pretty big deal. I heard he has some influence in the Russian Duma. He's one of those people who buys diamonds from Antwerp. Anyway, I'll give you a call tomorrow when I get on the train."

The next day, Irina came and stayed with me. We watched the premiere together and went to the Kafka Café on 21 Rue des Poissonniers, where I used to grab a beer. Later that night, we opened a bottle of champagne and slept together. She was a wonderful woman, beautiful in every way—physically and intellectually; she read a lot of books and watched a lot of movies and, at this time in my life, felt like an angel sent from heaven just for me.

At that time, I had become one of the senior executives in my institution, and as a Latin American specialist, I traveled to Ecuador, Chile, and Brazil to support project implementations; I was responsible for consulting on economic issues in developing countries.

Irina obtained her degree in London, specializing in banking and finance. She says she first came here with a headstrong young man from a wealthy Ukrainian family. Eight years had passed since she split from her rich boyfriend and started working for the diamond firm. She once told me the young big shot was the nephew of Alexei Kuzmichev, one of the partners of a German-born Ukrainian oligarch who runs the Alfa Group and the Luxembourg-based Letter One. German Khan has a net worth of $10.6 billion, according to the latest issue of *Forbes*.

She left Kyiv sixteen years ago and had no intention of returning to her hometown. Another thing we shared was that her father served in the military in Mongolia. According to Irina, her father was a retired colonel who spent three years at a military unit in Choir. When she was little, her father was freshly discharged from his mission in Mongolia and returned to Ukraine to marry her mother.

Irina was interested in Buddhism, as her father was friends with Buddhists and people from Buddhist countries, including the editors of Garuda Magazine.

Irina was also an only child, like me. However, she did not like the strictness of the military man, but under his influence, she grew up to love literature. It sounded very appealing to me when she told me about how they had an entire wall of their apartment as a library.

"How did you like *Titanic*?"

"I was impressed with how everyone, at the time of the sinking, tried to rescue their valuables."

"Really? I found it strange how the band members kept playing their music and sank with the ship. I wonder if it is more important to die doing what you love than to die trying to survive."

"Everyone has different values. Some on the Titanic put their selfishness aside and helped women and children board the lifeboats. For some others, the highest values were their own lives, and they were leaving women and children behind to save themselves. Both acted logically. It's just that their logical starting point is different... Death comes to everyone at the right moment."

I liked the part where Irina claimed that everyone's values differed. I asked her about her job at the diamond firm for the first time since I met her.

"Diamonds are amazing stones," she said, eyes glowing. "They are the hardest stones known to humankind."

"Is it true that a diamond is completely translucent? How do you know their quality?"

"There are no other gemstones that can match the transparency level of diamonds. Imagine, for example, if there's a diamond wall between you and me; we wouldn't even know there's a wall. So transparent, invisible, amazing! As for the hardness, diamonds can only be cut with diamonds. Nothing else can make a scratch on diamonds.

"What is the structure and why is it so hard?"

"Actually, the chemical formula is just carbon. Same as the graphite used to make pencils, but very different in texture. I'll give you an interesting book about diamonds later. There's so much more to talk about diamonds; we could be talking all night. That book says almost everything about diamonds. It's not just a gem." She smiled at me. "Tell me about your work now. What is your role? What are your goals?"

"To be honest, I haven't figured out my goals yet. I was my mother's child. My mother died. Thanks to my stepfather, I graduated from a good school, and now I have a high-paying job. I like my work, but I can't say it's my passion. I inherited my father's entire estate, but I haven't decided what to do with it and where to invest it. I'm just one lucky person. I don't value money very much, but I think I should do some business and increase my wealth with my participation, and I should like what I do, and I should be proud of the fact that I did the right thing with that money. I feel that if I start a business in Mongolia and do something for my country, I could repay my debts to my mother."

Irina had a broad knowledge of Buddhism, which embarrassed me as a person of Buddhist background because of my mother. I knew almost nothing.

"What do you think about Buddhism?" she asked.

"I don't understand the idea of voidness. Do these real things around you seem void to you?" I answered the question foolishly by asking another question. "In my opinion, emptiness or voidness means that what is happening to others and what is visible to you is empty. There are a lot of people sitting next to you and me, but for us, they are empty. You and I don't even know their names; we don't know what kind of people they are, and we don't need to know.

"Yet my mother was not empty to me. She was the only support system I had as a young child. Since my mother's passing, the world seems to be empty."

"Yes, there is usually no one closer to anyone than a mother. The loss of yours is what creates this profound sense of emptiness. She is, however, still in your heart. Even if someone has become an enemy to you or no longer means anything to you, that person also has a mother and a family. To them, the mother is irreplaceable. You have to watch and observe everything around you just as it is, like a camera. Just as the camera doesn't get angry or fall in love with all its recordings, it simply observes the scene. We suffer and we rejoice because of the changes that take place in our hearts. All of these feelings are happening in your mind, and they don't depend on anyone else. But all these feelings are just temporary emotions. I'm a Ukrainian girl, but the Ukrainians are no different from the Belgians. If I'm here, and people are suffering, why is it that I, too, must suffer with them instead of just observing them and keeping my peace?

"Sounds a lot like selfishness, doesn't it?"

"It's called egocentrism, where a person is self-involved and self-important. But their self-importance also depends on the reactions of others."

"The selfishness in Buddhism is different. It's living in harmony with the world around you, not hurting yourself, not hurting others; in other words, accepting the things both good and bad with a positive attitude. There was a man named Vladimir Montlevich, a Buddhist and a Tibetan scholar, one of my father's classmates. He was the editor-in-chief of *Garuda* magazine. His words influenced me.

"You've said before that you didn't like your stepfather, but he turned out to be your pillar in life. So, it's just that the perception in your mind has changed, isn't it? Today, you are thinking about how to invest the money your stepfather bequeathed to you and to do something valuable for Mongolia. So, even though you are far from Mongolia, it means that you are still Mongolian."

"Back in my home country, we have a concept called '*Russkaya Dusha*,' which means the Russian heart, but that concept seems to me masochistic. It basically describes a person who likes to be involved in other people's affairs and suffer for it."

We spent three days together watching movies every night, and we sat together in the Kafka Café, talking about things such as the premiere night's excitement and discovering many new things about each other. I became accustomed to her in such a short time, and my life without her seemed dull and boring. She looked like a diamond herself. And like a diamond, she was tough and precious. She also had a bright, optimistic outlook. I thought women, especially Russian women, were full of complexities, but Irina wasn't. She was optimistic and kind-hearted. When we completed such a wonderful three-day vacation together, we decided to take our next date to the Karlovy Vary Film Festival in the Czech Republic the following year.

The reason for choosing that place is that in the early 19th century, the spas of Karlovy Vary became so popular throughout Europe that many writers visited and wrote their prominent books there, as Eddie Florence used to say.

The famous German poet Johann Wolfgang Goethe went to the spas in 1820 to write, and Wagner composed his operas there. Of course, *Franz Kafka* of the Czech Republic and Mark Twain, the legendary American author of *The Adventures of Tom Sawyer and The Adventures of Huckleberry Finn*, which I read over and over as a child, also wrote there.

7

June 29, 1998

Irina and I arrived in Karlovy Vary in the afternoon. The hotels were full because of the international festival, but as soon as we got to the Hotel Promenada, which we had booked and confirmed almost a year before, we heard the first amazing news as we checked in.

The legendary American rock star Lou Reed had landed at the hotel where we stayed. A documentary about his band *The Velvet Underground* was opening at the festival, so the film crew was also staying at the same hotel.

Built in the 16th century next to the *Tržní kolonáda*, this hotel had the best restaurant in Karlovy Vary and one of the top ten in the Czech Republic. Other celebrities, including Richard Gere, Antonio Banderas, Jude Law, and Robert De Niro, have stayed at this hotel.

The Karlovy Vary Film Festival has been a prestigious festival since its founding in 1948, and the spa town is home to some of the world's most famous hotels and rented accommodations where celebrities stay.

As soon as we dropped off our luggage in our room, we went back downstairs to the lobby to get to know our surroundings. One of several people sitting around on the couches was a man in an expensive gray suit who stood up and approached us, smiling at a familiar face.

Irina recognized and greeted him warmly.

"*Irichka, Irichka! Kakimi sudibami!* (What a fate!)" The older man embraced Irina, and they both exclaimed and had a loud conversation in Russian and did not object to my being ignored. But Irina suddenly felt embarrassed and turned to me, speaking in English. "I'm sorry, Avid. This is Boris Petrovich. Boris, this is my boyfriend, Jim Edmund."

"How are you? Jim, you're a very lucky guy to be considered by our Irina. Are you Japanese?" asked the well-dressed gray-haired man.

"Indeed. I'm so lucky. I'm British. In fact, a Mongolian national."

"Oh, our Mongolian brother! My name is Boris Petrovich Arbatov. But everyone calls me just Arbatov. Let's eat together."

He turned to Irina and continued talking in Russian.

As the three of us walked together, Irina in the middle, she translated a few words about him in English, saying he was one of Russia's richest men who had just come here to relax. "I met this man in Antwerp a few years ago and helped him get the diamonds," she said of her old friend.

The man turned out to be an oligarch, one of the men the Russians called "the new Russian."

The restaurant, with its light yellow walls and arched roof, was full of white-clad tables in a modestly decorated hall. We ordered dinner. Arbatov remained talkative. He spoke to Irina in Russian nonstop but did not forget to occasionally exchange a few words with me in very harsh English. He seemed to be a quick-witted and businesslike man, especially when he took out his cell phone while eating and called someone. Within minutes, a young man my age brought in his handbag. Arbatov took out papers and started a direct business conversation with Irina. I escaped their business meeting by excusing myself and going outside for a smoke.

At sunset, the narrow cobblestone-fronted hotel with its gleaming view of a temple to the west was reminiscent of London, the old English city.

Nearby, in a bright tent with a Pilsner logo, many people were drinking the world-famous Czech beer. The window where we sat in the restaurant looked directly at the street, so I could see Irina and Boris getting up from the table and coming toward me.

The three of us roamed the streets of Karlovy Vary that evening. Boris Petrovich Arbatov appeared to be a frequent visitor, as he knew everything about the town. We walked a long way and talked, and finally, we came to the open beer house outside the Grand hotel Ambassador Národní Dům, where we drank beer and continued our conversation late into the night.

He and Irina spoke mostly Russian, but I learned that this person was the Russian with whom Irina had promised to connect me about doing business in Mongolia.

He said that since the adoption of the Minerals Law under the auspices of the World Bank in 1997, Mongolia had been making significant progress in exploration, but no real investment had been made in mining for a country so rich in mineral resources, such as the huge coking coal deposit of Tavan Tolgoi in the South Gobi.

Arbatov's friends were associated with Mongolian mining, such as in Erdenet, and he had a close friend who owned a bank in Mongolia called Chinggis Khaan.

He also said that Chinese companies had started lobbying to turn Tavan Tolgoi into a raw material base, as it was now the closest source to the Bugat steel plant in the Inner Mongolian region of China, as it had been in the past for the former Soviet Union.

He was also close to a Chinese businessman named Chen Yi. This man, he said, had penetrated the real estate and mining markets in Central Asia, including in Kazakhstan and Uzbekistan. Arbatov promised to provide me with information through him. We ended our evening walk and came back to our hotel with an invitation from him to take us to a beer bath later that day.

Not only was Irina tired from the long night, but she was also exhausted from Arbatov's constant conversations. She went straight to bed and fell fast asleep.

As for me, I sat behind the desk writing the day's activities on my laptop. Irina had a valuable set of skills, one of which was her fascinating ability to keep up a conversation to a broad extent, from personal to business. Her network of contacts was as wide as her kindness.

8

"Have you ever considered adopting a child?" *Oyunchimeg*'s lawyer, a handsome woman in her thirties, picked a book from the top shelf of her office cabinet.

As her blouse lifted, revealing her torso, *Avid* managed to notice her feminine figure: *What a nice body*.

"I don't think it's solely a matter of having a child. Now that the three of us are together to talk about this complicated personal relationship, it's probably best to talk openly. I don't believe that someone else's child can rekindle our relationship that is already so broken."

I looked at my wife, wondering where she came from.

The pretty, chubby-faced lawyer with fancy glasses blew the dust off the book, pursing her lips, clad with bright red lipstick. She sat back at her desk and took turns looking at us.

"Divorce is not a good solution. After all, *Oyunaa* and you are not young people anymore. You're in your forties and fifties. Moreover, in the event of a divorce, any court will first grant three to six months of reconciliation. People come to me every day with the same problem, so I know what I'm dealing with. And the fact that you two haven't had a child for so many years seems to have had a big impact. Let's be honest with each other, since it's a big decision."

The previous night, *Oyunchimeg* had called me and told me to come with her for a meeting with a lawyer, and that she wanted to put things in order once and for all. Although I had an important meeting, I explained to my boss what my wife and I were going through.

"*Badamsuren*, please," *Oyunaa* was saying. "I tell you everything. This man has not cheated only once in fifteen years. He has gone behind my back many times. I don't even know who this man is anymore. I have no choice but to divorce. And when he's drunk, he's even more unrecognizable and unbearable. I'm scared for my life. When I smell alcohol from him, my heart starts pounding. Because of this man, I might have a mental illness. No matter how hard I try to make things right, my eyes are sore just looking at him. There's no place in my heart to let him in."

"But you haven't slept with your husband in three months." The lawyer opened the book and turned the pages. "Here is an example like yours:

"Question: I love my husband, but I hate sex. It creates conflict for us.

"Psychologist: How can you love your husband and hate his sex?

"You want to hold a man's hand because you love him, and when you love a man, you want to hug him, don't you? When you love a man, you don't just want to hear his voice; you are more satisfied when you see him because the voice alone is not enough. Do you feel more warmth when you touch him? You are happier if you taste him, aren't you?"

Oyunaa stares at the table, embarrassed.

"There was a time like that. Now I can't even look at him, let alone hug him or have sex with him."

The lawyer looks up at *Oyunchimeg* and reads on:

"What is sex? It is a meeting of two deep energies. Not only shaking hands, but also hugging each other and meeting at the highest level of intimacy. Only through sex can we penetrate each other's energy. If you love a man, you want to share everything with him."

The lawyer looks up from her reading and asks *Oyunchimeg*, "Do you hate the entire idea of sex? Or do you just despise having sex with your husband? You are neglecting to 'feed' him physically and mentally. He can't stay without 'food' for a long time, so he will definitely look for a 'meal' in other places."

The lawyer takes off her glasses, cleans them while staring at *Oyunchimeg*. "Do you have a job now?"

"I am currently unemployed. I do occasional translations at home, but it's rare to find translation work from French."

"You want a man to take care of you financially. You take a house, a car, and a mink coat. Just so many things you want from him, but how can you not feed him? Isn't that a basic responsibility for you? You always want to use the other person? You call it love? You'd think it's his responsibility to give you all these just because he loves you. But you don't want to share anything with him? It's not just love you want."

Oyunchimeg gives the lawyer a look of distaste.

"What are you talking about? What's this nonsense about looking for a meal elsewhere? You can maybe get away with cheating once and be forgiven, but this person has written in his diary that he has been philandering with multiple women for four or five years. It's his words, not someone else's or a vague rumor. What can I share with him now that the love has gone?"

"Sex is not all about love. The truth is love is more important than sex. But from what you said yesterday, I understand that you started giving up sex a long time ago. Sex is but the foundation of love! Sex is the ultimate goal. Yet, sex eventually disappears from the relationship. It's true. But hating sex is not the way to go about it. When you stop sleeping with your husband, you stop giving him food, and the exchange of love and energy is lost."

The pretty lawyer is serious. *Oyunaa* suddenly jumps up and walks out the door without a word.

I shrug, rewarding the lawyer with a grateful look.

"In general, this is what is happening," she says. "People don't like the truth. But the truth is that one day it will have to be accepted." Her eyes widen. "There are two sides to everything. It's true that you've been committing adultery. She also told me about how you act when you get drunk and what disgusting words you throw at her. Your wife has endured your actions for many years and has looked the other way. Many years of wounds do not heal overnight. So, you'd better sit quietly in that rented apartment for a while. Don't talk to your wife. Experience has shown that the farther away you are, the longer it takes to reconcile, but for now, give her time to think. Besides, if you get divorced, your wife will be left homeless. If you divide your assets equally, everyone will be left without a place to live. A man like you can stand back up from that condition even when you're short of money, but your wife will have a hard time. It is useless to talk about it now. A woman follows her heart first."

"That's right. But I still love my wife. I just want a little warmth; I don't want much. I think I'll be looking for another meal like the one in the book if I had not had sex for so long."

"Don't justify yourself first. In fact, you won't die from not having sex. In your time, the army was for three years without sex. People who have been in prison for decades don't die from not having sex."

Badamsuren returns the book to the top shelf of the cabinet where it was in the first place.

9

Oyunchimeg runs down the stairs and out of the courthouse, forgetting to hand over a note that she has met with a lawyer on duty, and hurries angrily to her car, which is parked very far away.

This Badamsuren is full of shit, she thinks angrily. Comparing sex to food? So ridiculous, this Badamsuren. Can she be conspiring with Avid? It's probable, judging from the fact that she's been siding with him in there. I saw Avid looking at her back like an animal in its mating season. He could eat her with his eyes. Such a pervert! Oyunaa harumphs in disgust.

Why does the whole world turn against me? Heaven knows I'm a loyal woman. I divorce Batbold and marry Avid. I was so young. And now the guilty one is me? He's been wearing me down to my core. Is he really that stupid, thinking I'm not aware that he has been meddling with the work of the National Security Council and taking bribes? Well, even if that's considered okay, he hides the money from me. Who knows how much he made in the last eight years? Those sluts are only attracted to his dirty money.

Aloud she repeats the lawyer's question: "You're unemployed at the moment?" What a ridiculous question! This *Badamsuren* is definitely in it for him.

She realizes she has passed the spot where she'd parked her car. She turns around and almost runs into a man.

"Excuse me, miss, do you have a lighter?" asks a handsome young man in jeans, a yellow hoodie, and sunglasses. He looks to be in his late twenties. *Oyunchimeg* looks at him carefully from his white Adidas sneakers to his head, staring at the cigarette in his mouth. She reaches inside her purse and hands him the lighter.

"Thank you." He lights his cigarette. "You're just like a ripe fruit," he adds, returning the lighter.

"So overripe that I'm dry," she says acidly.

He hurries on to a white Toyota SUV, and she unlocks her car. Her hands are shaking, so she digs into her purse and pulls out a thin Esse cigarette, lights it, and blows the smoke out in a fury.

"*Ferme ta gueule! Ferme ta gueule!* (Shut up! Shut up!)," she shouts to the lawyer, to her husband, to the young man needing a light. She begins to cry. She throws out the cigarette and pulls into traffic without looking.

She eventually slows down, takes out her phone, and dials.

"Hello, Chimgee! We need to talk. Haven't seen you in a while. Let's go to that Chinese restaurant at Shangri-La—it's close to you. Okay. Deal. See you soon!" She has a desperate need to win someone over, hoping that her friend will take her side.

It is a beautiful, sunny day, and many people are on the street. Amy Winehouse's *Love Is A Losing Game* is playing on the radio when she hangs up the phone. She turns up the volume to the max.

Oyunchimeg enters the space between the two glass towers of the Shangri La Hotel Ulaanbaatar. She gets out of her car and rushes around the corner to plunge into the crowd at the mall. From the corner of her eye, she sees the Wedding Palace, where she married *Avid* fourteen years ago.

At the time, the palace looked magnificent and beautiful, like a palace of true happiness, but now she is surprised that it looks so small and shabby, like a cat's house. Their love, too, seems so small, so fragile, so old that she feels sorry for the old Wedding Palace. In fact, it is her love for *Avid* that fills her with sorrow. She walks slumped into a closed area surrounded by hotels, restaurants, and shops. *Oyunaa* remembers coming to this place for the first time, when it seemed like a foreign country—interesting, exciting; everything was exciting. This time, there is no feeling at all.

She hurries to meet her friend and talk shit about *Avid*'s dog-like behavior; she is overwhelmed by the urge to be defended by someone.

Oyunaa manages to think about how much their life changed from when she first met Avid. *After all, the Wedding Palace seemed to be the same as before, but in fact, the problems in her life grew bigger and bigger, and they overshadowed her happy memories. Where did that hot love go? How did we do that? I never cheated on Avid, but why did he have to cheat on me and go somewhere else in search of happiness? Is what Badamsuren read earlier true? I started to drift away from Avid after I had my first miscarriage. I was afraid of conceiving again and having another miscarriage. The second and third miscarriages made me even more disgusted with sex, didn't they?*

When did I first feel cold and reluctant to let my husband in? Not everything goes unnoticed; some things rot like a vegetable. You only realize it's gone bad when you dive in with your nose. By the time I found out, Avid was already rotten. It's true that Avid has a toxic habit when he drinks alcohol. He would come home drunk and have sex with me until I was dry, and he wouldn't finish. When I found and read that secret note, I was even more repelled—I could smell another woman on him. That's when I stopped sleeping with him. When he came back after staying away for three months, I felt even more depressed and alienated.

She walked quickly on the marble floor of the mall, up the stairs and into the Chinese restaurant, calling Hutong on her cell.

When the restaurant first opened a few years ago, *Avid* brought her here and told her the story of how the name Hutong dates back to the Great Yuan Dynasty of Mongolia, during which the Chinese language borrowed the Mongolian word "hudag" (meaning "a well" in Mongolian). Oh, poor me, there is nothing in my life that doesn't have a connection with this Avid.

10

May 2, 2011

Al-Qaeda leader Osama bin Laden was recently assassinated by U.S. special forces in a compound in Abbottabad, Pakistan.

There are many buildings in the center of the city whose purposes are unclear. We are outside a massive mansion, waiting to meet someone. There's a stone-paved courtyard, a fence surrounded by a beautiful green garden, and a black BMW and a black Benz parked inside the wrought-iron fence. The mansion's brown porcelain roof is decorated with various antennas. It was once a palace inhabited by princes and queens during the fifteenth and sixteenth centuries.

As soon as we arrive at the gate, Irina pulls out her phone and lets our host know we're here. The heavy oak door opens silently.

"How are you, Jim?" Boris Petrovich Arbatov greets me with a hug. "The first time I saw you, I knew you were from Central Asia, but now you look a lot like young Bat Khan." He stroked his mustache, picked up a cigar from the table, lit it, and immediately walked to the window to speak to us as we stood by.

"Belgium is a country of fairy tales," he declared. The old man kicked the window several times, almost like performing karate, before veering off-topic to show off. "It's made of very strong glass that won't break under any circumstances—it's bulletproof," he bragged.

"But let's get down to business. I'm not particularly interested in Mongolia, but I told you earlier I have a Chinese friend who is—and increasingly so. Many of Mongolia's mineral deposits were explored during the socialist era. The biggest potential is the Tavan Tolgoi coking coal deposit, which I mentioned in Karlovy Vary. In 2006, the mine was taken over by a few Russian oligarchs, but a movement rose against it, and eventually, only one company retained a share while the rest went to the state. If I understand correctly, you've worked in mineral-rich countries like Ecuador, so this should be easy for you to grasp. Plus, you're a Mongolian. Tavan Tolgoi has 7.4 billion tons of coal reserves, of which 5.4 billion tons is coking coal. That's basically food for steel plants. I'm going to connect you with my Chinese friend now. China produces sixty percent of the world's steel. This Chen Yi is a key player in that field. I'm a diamond trader, like Irina. It's a very risky business. You don't seem like the kind of person suited for the kind of business we're in." He glanced down at the papers on the meeting table.

He and Irina then have a long conversation in Russian about the diamond trade. I catch bits and pieces I can understand, including a mention of the Russian film *Kandahar*, directed by Andrey Kavun. The hijacked plane in the film is supposedly connected to Victor Bout. I've heard of him before.

They continue speaking in Russian, and I don't catch much beyond Bout's name. But I get a bad feeling, so I step outside to smoke. Soon after, Irina calls me back in. We say our goodbyes to Arbatov with a hug and leave.

"What were you talking about in Russian?" I ask her. I mention my eerie feeling that Arbatov might be connected to Bout's mafia.

Irina smiles. "Maybe there was some kind of connection, but this man isn't particularly close to him. We were just talking about a movie that was released yesterday. The film is about Victor Bout's hijacked plane. In 1995, Bout was negotiating the release of a Russian crew of Il-76 hostages in Afghanistan.

"According to Interpol, in the 2000s, Bout owned around sixty Soviet-made Antonov planes and had set up an airline in Miami, USA. In 2002, they tried to arrest him in Antwerp, where I live now.

"You've probably seen *Lord of War*—it's based on his life. According to Arbatov, Victor Bout was mentioned by President George W. Bush as the leader of a large arms trafficking group. I'm sorry we kept speaking in Russian. As you can see, Arbatov's English isn't great." Irina smiles at me reassuringly before continuing.

"He said he'll provide more information about the Chinese man. He speaks Russian, English, and even a bit of Mongolian. Arbatov is a good man—an honest Russian. I was telling you the other day about *Russkaya Dusha*—the Russian soul. He has that. If he believes in you, he won't hesitate to give his life for you."

11

"Oh, Gagarin. Why have you taken off again?" sighed Janna.

"There is no gravity in that house. No matter how hard I try to land, there's no gravity to pull me to the ground."

"But you always say that one should seek the easiest solution to any problem. You are directing your problems to the most difficult situation."

"What is there to seek when the love is gone? And yes, this was the situation in the first place that made our encounter possible. It's as if I met you to fill that void in my heart. But the situation has not improved. Nothing has changed since then. It's getting worse, actually. I'm not going back now. Maybe time can change it. But the question remains whether it will change. You know I still love her."

"I don't know. It's as if a writer is destined to live alone. But if I go out of your life, you'll be lonely."

Avid got up, took one of the Marlboro cigarettes from the drawer next to the bed, lit it with a match, and went back to bed. He stared at the picture of Angelina Jolie on the bedroom wall for a moment, thinking. *The poor landlords thought it was the kind of picture that foreigners might like.* *Avid* stroked Janna from her thigh and up to her waist. Her skin was as soft as a baby's, slightly damp with sweat. *Avid* caressed both of her breasts and wound her dark hair, which flowed down her chest, around his fingers.

"Why don't you get married? You're such a beautiful woman."

"There is no one to match. And I've gotten used to being on my own."

"It doesn't seem fair for a lot of guys who'd be happy to have you."

"I don't like those guys."

"Why not? You like being around an old man who's fifteen years senior to you?"

"Well, I'd have to feed those guys. Maybe even have to support his parents. I'm barely getting by myself. And it's nice to be with you. Occasionally we meet like this. I don't like to cling to you. We meet once in a while if we have a chance. We call each other whenever we please."

She turned to the other side of the bed to sleep.

For Janna, there are a lot of things that don't add up. She lives with her mother, who is in her seventies, but in all these years, *Avid* has never visited her home. She says her mother is a very peaceful person who doesn't even dream at night. She never talks about her father, and it's unclear whether she has one. When *Avid* first visited her place, it was a single, empty room with almost no furniture. She didn't seem to be getting along well, but for some reason, her life improved significantly after she met Avid. Janna started working for a foreign mining company, earning a good salary, bought a two-bedroom apartment with her mother, and began driving an expensive Jeep.

Ganbold, who was originally *Avid*'s contract translator, recommended Janna as a replacement when he decided to study abroad. At first, *Avid* wasn't very interested in her, but he sent her a multi-page contract in English with difficult legal wording and asked her to translate it into Mongolian as a test. Two days later, while *Avid* was sitting alone at work, Janna called. The previous day, he had another quarrel with his wife, and he was reluctant to go home. At nine o'clock in the evening, Janna said she had finished the translation.

"If you don't mind, could you bring it to the office?" *Avid* asked.

Shortly after the call, Janna came in.

Avid read the translation, which was very good. That summer evening, Janna wore a satin dress that highlighted her slender figure. With her hair in a swinging ponytail, she didn't look like she'd just come from the office. She was clearly on her way to a party. When he asked her, she told him she was waiting for friends and had some free time before they showed up. Then she received a call saying her friends had to cancel the get-together. Janna asked *Avid* if he wanted to have a late dinner at a newly opened restaurant nearby. They shared a glass of wine and headed out to eat. Hours later, they were checking out the last movie of the day, which happened to be The Duke of Burgundy, an erotic film directed by Peter Strickland.

After the movie, they went back to the restaurant and drank more beer. Having had a lot to drink, *Avid* just couldn't let go of Janna and decided to drop her off at her apartment, which she said was in the tenth Microdistrict. They caught a cab. *Avid* paid the cab driver and went upstairs with her. As soon as they entered the apartment, he undressed in the corridor and maneuvered her to the floor. *Let's just taste her once tonight, he thought. It can't hurt, and it cannot continue. What am I doing, cheating on my wife? I can't go on under any circumstance. I shouldn't be allowed to have an affair with a woman who works for me.*

"Wait, I'll go to the bathroom. Be right back," she said, leaving him in the middle of the room, naked. He felt chilled, so he grabbed the comforter off the bed, wrapped it around his hips, and went to the bathroom door. *Avid* looked around. Next to a mattress on the floor was a large table with all sorts of pictures and papers. This single-room apartment had no other furniture except an additional chair. However, he would later find out that the apartment was not hers but her brother's, which was a relief to him that she wasn't lying. She and *Avid* would come here often because her brother was away on business a lot.

As soon as Janna came out of the bathroom, *Avid* embraced her, and they made love for over two hours. Janna slept soundly afterward. *Avid* woke up early, as usual, so he got up and took a shower. On his way out, he paused for a moment to take a good look at the beautiful young woman sleeping on the floor in the middle of the room. He hoped never to meet her again like this. He picked up his underwear that he'd dropped by the door and left the apartment. At the time, he couldn't imagine they would meet over and over for the next six years without any complicated fights or misunderstandings.

Janna met him in every way, and there was no talk of moving in together or spending a few days somewhere, let alone marrying.

She had never asked him for money until a few days ago when she requested a loan of 900,000 *MNT*.

When *Avid* saw her sleeping naked, he was aroused, but he merely kissed her softly on the forehead, put on his t-shirt, and went out the door barefoot.

When he first rented his apartment for three months and lived alone, he was upset and lonely, but since he came back last time, he had learned to enjoy it. No one was disturbed, no one got offended, and it was only right to live one's life as one wants. What's the point of torturing oneself in hell, tiptoeing around someone else, hoping for love when the other person is already cold and isolated?

I have a great novel that I've started on. I have two beautiful women to choose from. I could even marry one of them if I wanted to.

He couldn't imagine it. The easiest way to solve a problem is important, but there seemed to be no easy way out in his mind.

Neither of these two women had bothered him. Until Janna, neither had asked him for money like his wife. But why did he always tell them that he had problems dealing with his wife and bother them with his issues? He lit a cigarette, opened the laptop on his desk, and sat down to add a few words to his gloomy diary. He burst out laughing like a madman, remembering what Janna had said today: "Oh, Gagarin!"

12

As I was walking down a street on the outskirts of Brussels, I saw a few vodka bottles on the side of the pavement. It was raining, and the glasses looked very shiny, as if they had been washed and deliberately lined up for an exhibit.

As I walked past the bottles, a conversation about vodka bottles I once heard in Mongolia popped up.

Chen Yi and I, introduced by the Russian oligarch Arbatov, whom I've written about, met a lot of people, and the work went well. One day when we went to Tsogttsetsii soum of Umnugovi *Aimag* to visit the mine, I wanted to return by car, not by plane. I told my partner I had seen the *Gobi* when I was very little, riding on a motorcycle with my father many years ago. I didn't remember most of it and wanted to see it again. I rented a Land Rover to take me back to the city. Chen Yi joined me for the car ride.

The driver, *Khurelchuluun*, was a short, good-looking man with a happy visage. As I sat next to him, I noticed that his neck was scarred, as if he had been strangled. It was a very hot day, so we went bare-chested, and it was impossible to ignore his scarred neck.

At first, *Khurelchuluun* thought I was some kind of big boss, and he was reluctant to converse. But after we had a few small conversations, he became closer and more talkative. He was not a man of few words.

"You're looking at the scar on my neck, aren't you?" he asked. "I call it a 'bottle-scar.' This one taught me an important lesson."

"Did you cut your neck with a piece of glass?"

"Oh, no. It's just called that because it has a connection to glass bottles. You probably don't know, but in the 1990s, every morning people would shout in front of your house, calling for dead vodka bottles. I would turn in bottles and receive cash in return."

"I wouldn't know because I didn't grow up here. Why buy used bottles?"

"At that time the glass factory was closed, and bottles of alcohol were scarce. People collected vodka and beer bottles and sold them to the factories."

"Oh, yes, it was the transition period."

"Yes. It was 1996. Then one day I thought, 'If I go to Russia and collect bottles and sell them here, I'll make a lot of profit.'

"So, I went to Russia with 300,000 *MNT*. Beyond *Kyakhta*, we went into a mountainous area called Titovskaya Sopka and started to collect bottles. In no time, we had a full car." He smiled broadly as he drove. "We had collected 12,000 bottles."

"For the 300,000? How much would the bottles cost here?"

"Well, it was important to go to the *ataman* of the village first. Then give them presents. Then he'd order people to collect the bottles. That means we didn't actually buy the bottles for money. When I came to the city, I sold them in bulk to the Noyod vodka factory of Buyandorj, in Selenge, owned by the husband of one of our famous singers, Ariunaa. I sold the first bulk supply of bottles for about one million *MNT*.

"You got it? You sold them at a price three times higher?"

"That's why I went again. I drove the trailer and returned with twenty-five thousand bottles. More than two million *MNT*. The bottles with screw caps would pay even more. There were a lot of vodka factories in the city. The business was good, so I went again. In three months and several trips, I brought a total of 100 thousand bottles, sold them, and made more than ten million *MNT*. After doing this for two years, I'd earned about eighty million *MNT*."

"Eighty million at that time was a lot of money, wasn't it?"

"Of course. Enough to buy several apartments." He grimaced good-heartedly for his own benefit. "That's not how it turned out, however. I started wasting a lot of money. Vodkas were piled up on top of each other because sometimes the factories would pay for the bottles with boxes of vodka. I thought I was living the luxurious life. I gained a lot of new friends and thought of myself as a small-time oligarch. I wasn't married, and I'd lost count of girlfriends at the time. Eventually, I stopped going to Russia by myself. I'd sign contracts with a number of drivers. I'd lend and borrow rubles from middlemen, so they got very close with me."

"You established a company?"

"It's hard to call it that. Occasionally, I would go myself for major buy-and-sell deals. I had established good contacts in Russia who would collect the bottles ready for us to take away. It had gotten easier. Then one day I decided to make a big move, and I rented three good trucks with most of my money and took all my rubles. On the way home from Russia, with all the bottles loaded on the trucks, one of the trucks broke down at night. Because the hazard lights would not come on, we piled stones and made a barricade on the road. But in the dark, a fancy SUV crashed into the stone barricade. A Russian came out angrily and shouted at us. One of my drivers got angry and came out swinging a socket wrench, threatening to kill him."

"In the morning, I sent two of the drivers to *Kyakhta* in one of the trucks to get spare parts. Only one driver was left with me and the trucks on the side of the road. The next day was so hot and sunny; it was getting late, and I was thirsty. The two drivers had not returned. Later, I learned that they had met some Russian girls and stayed with them to party. They had bought the spare parts for only 200 rubles— in Russia, if you have money, everything is possible— and decided they had time to spare.

It was late; they did not return. We were about to go to sleep when a car came along. We were stranded in an empty part of the country. *Ingoda* is a densely forested area along the river. Before I knew it, two gunmen came out shooting."

"Did the Russian from the previous night send them?"

"Yes, we later learned he was a governor of some local administration unit, as well as an oligarch. We not only broke his car but threatened to kill him. He must have been pissed.

"We ran for our lives. Imagine how fast a human being can run when he is being fired at from behind. Later, I was surprised to see that I had jumped across a wide ravine that I could not cross in my right mind. My heart was pounding like a clock. I didn't want to be killed. Just when I looked back and thought I'd lost them, I watched one of my trucks with a trailer full of glass pull out. Then the other one. Apparently, they knew how to fix trucks.

They took the brand new ZIL 130.

"Did you tell the police? Did you find the truck?"

"I told the police, who searched the area and did not find a single bullet hole or a shell. They had cleaned up and left without any trace. The man sent professionals. But when I found out later, it turned out that our ruble middlemen were the ones who gave us up.

"I waited for a few days in *Kyakhta*, where I found my two trucks with their almost empty trailers. One of the two drivers didn't believe me and got angry because he lost his truck. I gave what was left of the bottles to the drivers, and I was left in debt for a brand-new truck. All I had left were boxes full of vodka back home. What could I do but indulge my unfortunate self in alcohol?

"After drinking day and night, my mother found me strangling myself in the outhouse. She rescued me just before I was about to die from asphyxiation. That's how I got the scar. The teaching scar, I call it."

"After a year in the police force, I ran out of money, and a year later I got this job, and once again I am making a living.

"Our people are very ugly. How do you know this if you live abroad? If we don't treat people very carefully, our people will be shocked. Bad friends are like shadows. I will not leave the sun, but it will disappear at night," he reminded me.

At that time, I was preparing to go to Mongolia again.

There is a company called Mercury in Mongolia. Chen Yi said that his boss was a very influential person there, so he arranged for the undercover boss to meet in person with another subordinate and hold an investment meeting in Mongolia.

What worries me the most is the consumer society in my country. This was also the case in the South American country where I worked. After the war to defeat the Soviet Union, they were vanquished, and a strange system was established in the former socialist countries.

Those who originally planned to destroy the Soviet Union deliberately distributed American films with great care and precision. It wasn't hard for many people to understand, but in a way, it was an introduction to consumer society. Heroes like Arnold Schwarzenegger, along with a flood of simple films about sex, murder, entertainment, and violence, quietly changed the collective subconscious. Everyone who has never been to a socialist country dreams of becoming like James Bond. Superman seemed like a man who drank the most expensive tea and dated the most beautiful women.

And because socialism was collapsing, people wanted something new. In the Soviet Union, one government had been ruled by one head of state for half a century, so he deceived the people like children with beautiful words like "freedom" and "democracy" and showed them where to light the match. It's a match, and now people are free to choose who will lead them. The government that has weighed you down for so long will not last; it will be a temporary government for four years. If you like, you can extend it, but if not, elect someone else. The people loved the idea and immediately accepted it, and now we have a temporary government in a never-ending unstable game.

Because the government is temporary, the person who gets elected thinks only of themselves. There's no time to think about anything else, and foreign investors, attracted by the country's good reputation, have come in and devoured it. Elections have become a game. The Nobel Prize isn't an election. Democracy was embraced without people realizing it was a tactic to destroy the state they had built. Information is received differently by various segments of the population. Little children are given cartoons that not only entertain but also subtly program their behavior. Young girls read glossy magazines, unaware they're being taught how to live. Perhaps even you have unknowingly embraced consumerism in your writing—you might not know how you got there, but you buy into it and either use it or get used by it.

When I was working in South America, I immediately felt sorry for my own country once I saw how the nation I was working in was being looted. It was pure exploitation.

If you instinctively share a consumerist mindset, your artwork will reflect it. The artist doesn't always realize this; it's like the fruit of "free thinking." You have to understand that many young people in Mongolia are deeply dedicated to this kind of consumerism. That's why I want to implement my project in Mongolia and stay away from Chen Yi. I hadn't had any real desires for a long time, but now I do.

I'll write to you later—first about the money, then about what I plan to do. The so-called democracy in Mongolia since the 1990s is like magic! Today, everything is commercial. They say fair elections are taking place in Mongolia, but in reality, many people never choose the right person. And the person who is elected stays in government just long enough to think only about getting rich. I'll write more about this later.

13

When *Oyunchimeg* came home, it was two-thirty in the morning. She was so drunk she struggled to find the keyhole to her apartment in the dark hallway. Suddenly, she heard the whimpering of a dog. Shocked, she reached into her purse, pulled out her phone, and turned on the flashlight. There was a husky pup drenched in rain hiding in the corner of the hallway. Finally, with the help of her phone's flashlight, she found the keyhole and entered the apartment. She picked up the small dog and let her into her home.

She saw from her collar that the dog was called Daisy; a phone number was on it. "You got lost in the rain, didn't you, girl? What a cute animal you are. It was pouring outside, so you came in and took refuge in my building. You're scared, you poor little thing." *Oyunaa* cooed to the dog as she toweled her dry.

In the center of the room was a large blue sofa, a small table with a gold pattern, and on one wall a seventy-inch television. *Oyunaa* hugged the puppy, took the milk out of the refrigerator, put it on a small white plate, placed the puppy on the floor, and put the plate of milk in front of her. The puppy licked the milk as if she were dehydrated, and *Oyunaa* sat down and watched her as if she'd never seen anything so precious.

"How cute are you, Daisy? Well, you will stay with me today, and tomorrow I will call your master with the phone on your collar and return you to your home. Is that okay?" She pulled the puppy into her lap. "I had a drink with my girlfriend today. You probably don't know what being drunk means, do you? My husband used to kill beautiful animals like you. Then he was cursed by the murdered dogs, and he's flown from home. He must be a very bad man, right? Killing such cute animals like you? What are you looking at? Do you know me?" she blabbered. Daisy closed her eyes as if she were saying "yes."

Oyunaa took a sip of the vodka she'd found in the fridge, sat for a while, picked up the phone, dialed a number, and waited, smoking.

"I'm fine, Chimgee. I came home. The driver parked the car outside. Are you okay? Well, it was a fun night. My husband is a cheating, philandering piece of trash. Hey, by the way, I found a cute dog in front of my house. He's lost. His name is Daisy. The name is on the collar. Well, thank you, my friend. Good night!"

She threw the phone on the table and drank more.

"Daisy, let's listen to music," she announced.

I am sitting in the morning

At the diner on the corner

I am waiting at the counter

For the man to pour the coffee...

Daisy lay down to listen to the song. She stared at *Oyunaa* inquisitively, as if wanting to speak to her.

Oyunchimeg woke up the next morning and called Daisy's owner's number but was told the number was inactive.

PART 4

Nothing will come of nothing.

- William Shakespeare

1

In a small fenced-in parking lot at the intersection of 11th Street and 1st Avenue in New York City's East Village, people gathered on Saturdays and Sundays to sell extra clothing, books, records, and belongings of all kinds.

As the wet snow begins to fall, I stop at a street market stall to look at a Zippo lighter with a picture of Marilyn Monroe on it.

A black man sits with a few leather jackets, a hippie-era cotton shirt, and a woolen scarf hung from a metal mesh fence. On a small red rug in front of him lay a tray of candles, porcelain cups, bottle openers, cigarette packs, and ashtrays. He is talking to an old man in a black leather hat in a shed next to him. The older man talks, takes a puff, and looks up with one eye closed, dazzled by the sun.

"Very old one. But maybe this one is better," he says and stretches out his hand to me with a pink lighter, the image of a jazz musician on it.

"I like this one. How much?"

"Five bucks. Take both for fifteen. The purple one is really good—ah…." He continues his conversation with his neighbor.

The two Black men are talking in African American Vernacular English, their words blending together with shortened phrases. I leave the lighter he had given me in the middle of things, hand him five dollars, check to light the lighter with Marilyn Monroe on it, and put it in the pocket of my gray coat.

I look up at the sky, brush the snow off my shoulders and sleeves, and walk along the busy, wet, snowy street, passing by the old low houses of the East Village, the red-painted fire stairs, and in the distance, the massive skyscrapers black in relief.

I walk a long way east, take out my phone, and hold it to my ear while going into Barmacy Bar on 14th Street. Chen Yi called and agreed to meet at this bar, so I find this strange place with the amusing name, but it is not so strange when I enter: the interior is just like a pharmacy.

Because it is Sunday afternoon, only one person sits in the dimness. I remove my coat, take the lighter out of my pocket along with a pack of American Spirit cigarettes with a picture of an Indian on the front. I hang the wet wool near me and sit down for a drink.

"What Bo Xilai? I don't know. You'd better come and explain it now. It's a very strange pub," I say to Chen Yi while looking at the medicine bottle on the table with candles in it. I light a cigarette and nod at the bartender for a drink. In the corner, right next to the window, a beautiful woman leans her cheek on her palm, staring sadly outside. She's wearing a light-colored sweater, her blonde hair catching the weak sunlight from the window, making her shine like a fairy. She gazes out the window, lost in thought. On the brown wooden table in front of her, a cup of coffee steams. The heavyset man with a bald head and a snub nose, standing behind the bar wiping glasses, finally comes over to me.

"What would you like to drink?" he asks.

"Ketel One double shot and a Brooklyn pale ale beer in a large cup glass."

I take off the shiny black shoes I wore to work, now wet inside, and leave them below me, wiggling my toes on the bar stool's footrest.

Then I go to my phone, wondering what Chen Yi has to say. The bald bartender places a beer and a glass in front of me. I've already had one cigarette as I politely ask,

"Is it still legal to smoke in this bar?"

He just looks at me, so I light up another.

Yesterday, I watched a movie about a killer who axed an old man to death and stepped over the corpse covered in blood to dig out a safe at the back of a room. Watching this, I get anxious, like the killer in the movie, taking the killer's side, thinking, The door isn't locked... someone could come in! I remember getting the feeling of killing a man and burgling a house in real life. Yes, I was on the side of that man—the killer—until I finished the movie. I almost cried out of pity when he was executed at the end. Is this who I have become?

I drink the Ketel One Dutch vodka and have an unpleasant thought about Irina. I had taken notes, so I pull my notebook from my black bag.

March 19, 2010

It's three o'clock in the morning right now. Irina was in Brussels today, so we went out together to the Kafka Bar and had a lot of drinks, but she was tired, and because she is on her period, we came home.

She said, "I will sleep on your workplace sofa," and went to my office.

I go to bed alone, but I can't sleep, so I wander into my large room, watch TV, drink a few glasses of Belgian beer, and finally fall asleep. Suddenly, I wake up with a full bladder, and as my drowsy self walks toward the toilet, I think I hear someone talking in my office. I am a little surprised, but as I walk back from the bathroom, I hear Irina's voice, clear as day, only with a tone of anger I've never heard from her before.

What is going on in the middle of the night?

I look through the crack of the office door and see Irina standing by my desk, talking on the phone in a bossy tone that makes her seem like a stranger.

"I searched thoroughly, but I can't find it. There is nothing on this desk or on the wall shelf. There are a few research papers here, but that's not what you're talking about. I'm tired of you. Although I am promised a lot of money, you don't pay. I got as close to this Mongolian as I could and have seen no cash. This is not the person you are talking about…" She shouted a foul word in English and continued in Russian.

At first, I wonder if I am dreaming. I stop short as I was going to enter the room and hide behind the door to listen to what else she has to say. She speaks in Russian and then hangs up.

Although I do not speak Russian, I hear the names Chen Yi and Arbatov. So, it is clear that the person Irina is talking to is neither of them. Stunned for a moment, I feel cold creeping up my back. I step quietly away from the door and lie down in my bedroom. I am completely awake, my mind racing.

So, does this mean Irina intends to steal some project from me? It is unlikely that this kind of behavior began two years ago when we met. Or is it? And why are Arbatov and Chen Yi mentioned? Is this Victor Booth connected? I think for a moment and turn on my phone, searching the internet for information about Victor Booth.

Victor Anatolievich Booth, a businessman, agreed to give an interview to "Echo of Moscow" radio in November 2006 and said that the lawsuit against him was motivated by the desire of the United States to justify its failed attempts to influence the situation in Central Africa.

Two years later, on March 6, 2008, Victor Booth was arrested in Bangkok. Booth was detained by U.S. anti-drug police on suspicion of selling guns.

In May of that year, U.S. authorities sent a request to extradite Victor Booth to Thailand, but a Bangkok court rejected the request.

In August 2010, a Thai court ruled that Victor should be extradited to the United States, and at the end of the year, Booth was transferred from a Bangkok prison to a U.S. prison.

The idea that such a person would be spying on me seemed ridiculous. *But this is strange. Is Irina such a person? I had never thought of her suspiciously before. I've not even noticed the slightest negative feeling since I met her. I used to think she was an angel. Well, I'm going to sleep anyway. I'll just have to get up in the morning and ask. How do I proceed with such suspicions?*

I mark my journal at this and fall asleep.

I sip my beer, put my notebook back in my pocket, and when I look around, the empty bar seems too joyless for me. The girl at the table in front of the window does not seem as mysterious as before. She looks at her phone with a frowning face, or reads something sad online, writes a comment, or writes something very threatening. Her face is as white as a witch's, and her hair and ponytail are pale yellow.

I continue to watch her in amazement. The girl who had looked like a fairy just moments ago now seemed completely different, distant—like the black metal padlock on my family's backdoor in Mongolia, one that I could never seem to open no matter how hard I tried. I remembered, as a child, licking that cold padlock and thinking I was stuck forever. The strange sensation that frightened me then is the same I feel now, looking at this angel.

I figure I'll ask Irina in the daylight if I really heard the conversation the night before, but by morning, I feel very different. When I enter the kitchen, Irina greets me with a cup of coffee, salted pork, fried eggs, and a smile on her face. So, I don't have the motivation to tell the angel of breakfast that I overheard her angry phone conversation last night.

I wonder if she was talking about something completely unrelated to me.

We spend a pleasant day, and Irina leaves that evening, saying she has to go home for work the next day in Antwerp.

I forget about the incident, the phone call—was there one? I'm in denial, perhaps. But at the pharmacy bar, while waiting for my Chinaman, I see the mysterious woman, both captivating and intimidating, going through her cell phone, and another thought comes to mind. *Irina, why does it seem like you don't want to live with someone?*

Days later, when Irina is back in town, and after watching Lars von Trier's new film *Breaking the Waves,* I ask her to meet me for a beer at the Kafka Bar, where she looks at me fondly with those innocent blue eyes. I ask her, "Why does it seem like you don't want to live with someone?"

"You and I watch a movie," Irina says to me. "The movie is about a woman who lives with one person, and then because she doesn't marry him, she becomes trash to the town and dies for it. The idea that such a woman is a victim is not new. I also decided to live with a rich guy. It feels like a nightmare now. He wanted what the guy wanted in the movie."

"Why is that? It's a movie. In real life, everyone gets married and has children."

"And who is happy? Are you saying that your stepparents were a happy family?" she asks me. "Maybe your stepfather is living a happier life now. My parents were unhappy. Probably still are. Dad used to drink and torture my mother. When he got older, he stopped drinking. Then my mother started drinking and would get angry with my father while she herself was now under the influence—obviously something she'd always wanted to do when he was the drunk. She took revenge on the life she had spent in hell, but it didn't work well because he made her suffer every time she drank."

"Hmm. It's weird. In fact, it seems so. If you marry me, you won't quarrel, will you?" I ask her.

"Yes, we will quarrel. Women are quarrelsome by nature. So, what's wrong with you and me quarreling?"

"There's nothing wrong with that…"

But there is, so I go on.

"It's natural for people to live together," I say. "We could be happy that way. Couldn't we?" I hate the thought of suffering alone for the rest of my life.

"If you think you're happy, you're happy to be alone. You're a nice guy. You have an intimate relationship with several women." She looks at me. "Don't you? Isn't it enough to meet one by one on the schedule? Ha ha. And how sad is it to die with one person?"

I'd never thought of that before. I ask her quickly,

"Do you intend to do the same? Calling many young guys in turn?"

"A woman is different. One man is enough for us. But don't live together. If we feel someone is boring, that's it. With whichever woman it happens, you will have a child. You need to copy yourself; it is the human need. But if you need to have company as you get older, it is a child for the woman. So much fun and so much love. I will definitely like my copy."

"A kid needs to have a father."

"What for? Children only need their mother."

That night Irina is completely different from the Irina I know, more forthright. But she is correct. I never thought such a conversation would come from a woman. Irina soon told me,

"You always go to this boring bar Kafka. Will you come with me to a different nightclub? A secret Russian nightclub with live music." I agree, and we leave the apartment and hail a taxi.

Irina is drunk, so she sings Russian songs on the way.

We leave central Brussels and enter the outer city where we stop and get out of the taxi behind a building that is on the verge of collapsing. I am afraid she gave the wrong address in her inebriated state; we are surely at the wrong place.

"Is there a nightclub in a dump like this?" I ask seriously, and she unbuttons her black leather jacket, pulls down the neck of her red t-shirt, and reveals a small cactus tattoo above her breast.

"There is. It's called Cactus. Have you not noticed this little cactus tattoo before?"

How could I have not? But I had not.

"Follow me," she says, and when we walk around the corner of the old house, I see expensive cars parked at the entrance, and I realize that something really is going on here.

We approach a red carpet strewn haphazardly before the front door of a red brick house, the walls of which are wild with spray paint. At the entrance stands a pair of large male gatekeepers in black tailcoats and hats.

That's when I realize that Irina wasn't just showing off her breasts to me to be titillating; she goes over to the tuxedoed men, says a few words in Russian, pulls down her red t-shirt and shows them the top of her breasts. They hold a flashlight on them and check out the small cactus tattoo, smiles on their cold-eyed faces. They invite us inside.

I am greeted by a lively club that feels no different from a nightclub in downtown Brussels—a band plays, and people are dancing.

"Wow!" she yells. "Zveri is playing." She turns to me. "It's a very popular Russian band." Then she heads to the dance floor and starts wiggling with the crowd.

I'm pulled to dance, but I don't want to, so I pull my hand away and sit down at the bar, shouting to the bartender for two bottles of Duvel. He opens two bottles of dark beer in brown glass bottles—not Duvel like I ordered. I take a sip and calmly watch my girl dancing like a Tasmanian devil. The band has the Russians ecstatic; they're singing along, and I keep my eyes on Irina, dancing with joy, never taking *her* eyes off the lead singer.

The song seems to be about love; what else? Among the dancers are beautiful Russian women; the men dress in elegant attire as do the few middle-aged and older people.

Behind a long table extending from the bar is a daunting group of athletic guys scanning the crowd. The Russian bouncers—some in training uniforms, most in black leather jackets—all wear gold chains around their thick necks and large gold rings with diamonds on their fingers. A tall man sits at a large table close by the toughs—possibly the leader of the gang? Next to him stands a stunning girl, completely ignoring him.

The band announces a break, and a soft song from the sound system calms the wildness of the dancers as they drift back to their seats, glistening with sweat and the thrill of having danced. Irina can barely contain her happiness as she sits down beside me, quickly gulping the Devil beer. She gives me a quick peck on the cheek and starts looking around, as if searching for people she knows.

"Is this a popular band?" I ask, just to start a conversation she might want to engage in.

"Well, yeah," she says a bit derisively. "Look where you are; not a place for nobody bands, is it?" She perks up. "Looks like it's someone's birthday."

"It certainly is. The tall guy there." I point at the good-looking fellow I think is the boss man.

"Wow! That one is a legendary oligarch."

"What's his name?"

"Did you hear about the scandalous arrest at the French *Courchevel* ski resort a few years ago?"

I'd never heard of the place. "No."

"That is Mikhail Prokhorov. He is one of the richest people in Russia, according to *Forbes* magazine. He invested in a ski resort in France. He was arrested in the year of 2007 when many Russians were there."

"Why did he get arrested?"

"The *Courchevel* scandal erupted in early January that year when the French police, with more than 50 officers, arrested him for allegedly owning a luxury prostitution network."

"So, he sells luxury prostitutes? Big deal."

"Mikhail Prokhorov is a legend. Prostitution is just for fun. This man, with big business ventures, plans to run against Putin in the presidential election in two years." She watches the birthday cake ritual. "It must be his birthday since the girl is paying no attention. That's why

Zveri came here. The girl sitting next to him is also a star named Nyusha—Anna Shurochkina—a Russian singer, composer, and actress."

"What is this club about? And that tattoo?"

She looks at me speculatively and decides to tell me. "I didn't know anything about life when I first came here. I suffered a lot after breaking up with an oligarch's son. I'll talk to you later about that. In short, there are many such Cactus nightclubs in Europe. The center is in Berlin. All the female members have these small tattoos.

"I work for a company that sells diamonds, so you have to be able to enter places like this and do business. It's a very expensive tattoo; my company paid for it." Then she grabs my hand, gets up, says she sees a Russian she knows, and takes me to meet him.

We stay at the club until dawn. Irina is very drunk for a while, but suddenly she recovers and goes around meeting many people and starting conversations. She gives everyone a business card, doing her job.

It is mostly Russian spoken here, but oddly, when they get drunk, the Russians try to talk in English, so the drunker they get, the more I understand about the murder of a great oligarch named Globus, about the murderer of a big criminal named Alexandr Thessaloniki and his escape to Europe, and about Matrosky Tishina prison. There were countless rumors throughout the night about Solonik escaping from a terrible prison, about the fact that many gangs were moving to kill him, and about taking a large number of diamonds from Irina's diamond company.

Early in the morning, an expensive black car drives us home, and we sleep like the dead all day, Irina returning to Antwerp in the evening. To my surprise, all night long, Irina had told everyone I am not Mongolian but that I am British and of Japanese descent.

Since that night, I am wary of Irina. Although she is a lovely woman, she has a secret life, a world completely different from the one I know.

2

It isn't long before Chen Yi enters Barmacy. He has a very gloomy face, and he carries a newspaper in his hand and throws it in front of me.

"Read that," he spits.

I read the *New York Post* headline: Wang Lijun's head valued at 6 million yuan by local criminal gangs.

I continued to read: "At 2:31 p.m. on Feb. 6, 2012, Wang Lijun, head of the Chongqing City Department of Public Security, fled to the U.S. Consulate in Chengdu, Sichuan Province, and apparently sought political asylum in the United States. Wang Lijun was scheduled to meet with the British consul in Chongqing in early February but did not arrive."

I wonder why Chen Yi wants me to read this article. I glance at him as he wipes his glasses and stares at the floor, gloomy, unaware that I'm watching him. I pick up my recently purchased Zippo lighter and try to light a cigarette, but as I gaze at Marilyn Monroe with her plush pink lips against the black background, her eyes seem to magically stare at me in a seductively sexy way, and I give up on trying to light the cigarette.

I keep staring at the picture on the lighter; I can't take my eyes off her. I look at her, then look away, feeling a strange sensation similar to what I felt when I saw the woman sitting by the window. But when I glance over, she's gone. Blue smoke spirals out of a medicine glass used as an ashtray—the smoke is from the cigarette she was smoking but didn't put out. The lipstick stain on it is as clear and red as fresh blood.

I shake my head and continue reading the article: "On the morning of Feb. 6, he canceled all official events and drove to Chengdu in a car prepared by Wang Pengfei, head of the Social Security Department of Telin Xian, Liaoning Province.

Wang Lijun's Mongolian name is Unenbaatar. Born in 1959 in the city of Rashaan, Inner Mongolia, his father is Mongolian, and his mother is Chinese. In 1984, he became a traffic police officer in Telin, Liaoning Province. From 2008 to 2012, he was director of the Chongqing City Department of Public Security. When he contacted U.S. Ambassador to China, Gerry Locke, Locke immediately contacted the State Department."

The article finished by saying the American side contacted China and agreed to provide security for Wang Lijun to deliver him to Beijing, and not to hand him over to Chongqing. It was the headline of the newspaper that day.

"What does this mean?" I ask my still morose friend.

"Bo Xilai is not only related to us, Avid," he says, "but also to the business you and I are going to do in Mongolia. The reason I came here was to meet this man's relative, but he was caught by the other side."

"Then?"

"It will be a long conversation to explain the details," he says, wiping his glasses for the tenth time.

"It can be understood that Bo Xilai's group is about to be suppressed by the current leader, Xi Jinping. Their supporters know that I came here. I didn't tell you in detail, but if I had met this man who was about to be arrested, I would have deposited $160 million in Chase Manhattan's bank account. But all of a sudden, things changed."

Chen Li is two minutes into his explanation, and I don't understand anything. "Does that mean it's dangerous for you, too?"

"It is dangerous. In 2009, Bo Xilai launched a campaign against the mayor and mafia of Chongqing. The person who did it was Wang Lijun, or Unenbaatar, mentioned in the article. He betrayed Bo Xilai. During this time, he arrested 6,000 people on Bo Xilai's orders, including wealthy businessmen, mobsters, and their associated senior police officers. In a word, they began to take revenge.

"I just don't understand enough. What do Bo Xilai and Unenbaatar have to do with us?"

"It means that Wang Lijun betrayed the other side. The main thing is that I came here to meet a person close to Zhou Yongkang, who is on his side, on our side, and I took him everywhere.

"Then they knew I had come to see him. Zhou Yongkang's power and influence are almost equal to Hu Jintao's, and you understand that all the people we associate with are on their side... a great earthquake is beginning. What do I do now? Can you help me?" asked Chen Yi, pulling a towel from his pocket to wipe the sweat from his face.

"How can I help?"

"I want to go somewhere together. Brighton Beach. If I don't get help from the Russians there, I will be ruined. They are looking for me. I know the banking method, so they let me try to get the money I was supposed to receive. They are very powerful here. No one knows you, so there won't be any suspicion. I can't meet him myself, so if you just talk to one person, it will help."

"Shouldn't I have gone to Mongolia with you?"

"There's no point in going there when such a big earthquake is happening. The problem is here, in New York. If you can't get the money, nothing else can happen. He has already said he will take it from my account. And I'm the only one who knows this method. But I can't access the money without a solid connection to the bank. The person arrested recently was a banker. Well, there is a way to make a connection because the person in the middle is a Russian in Kazakhstan, so the only option left is to unite with the Russians."

"That's how it is now? Our work was going very well. And when will we leave for Brighton Beach?"

"Right now."

Chen Yi and I leave the pharmacy-like Barmacy, board a subway, and go together to the airport, to Brighton Beach in the States, where the Russians live. Chen Li stares thoughtfully at nothing. I've never seen him so sad. When Boris Arbatov and Irina first introduced us in Antwerp, he greeted us with a big smile and greeted us in Mongolian. And not badly.

He was a happy man, and he laughed a lot. I glance over at him, taking off his gold-rimmed glasses and wiping them with a handkerchief for the umpteenth time. I look away, thinking of how we became very close from the first meeting.

He invited me to visit Beijing.

And a month later, I went to Beijing for a week. I was greeted like the emperor in a long black limousine at the airport, took a trip to a luxury hotel, where he met me and showed me his city. We had dinner in a five-star restaurant every night, he introduced me to influential people, and he and I talked about our work. Since I returned to Belgium, we've talked on the phone, met one another here and there, always talking about our work together. The following year, we visited Mongolia for six days, and he showed that we knew many important people who were very influential.

But it was the first time I had seen him not happy, and I sincerely wanted to help my friend.

When my mother saw me sad, she would say, "Like a Chinese in debt..." and I looked at my indebted Chinese friend and wondered; he exemplified the meaning of the cliché of a Chinaman in debt. I didn't quite understand what he was talking about. I'm not very interested in China, and I'm very bad at remembering Chinese names. I have Mongolian blood, and I became a Brit. In addition to the fact that every dislike for China seems to be in the blood of these two nationalities, there is also the influence of my father being killed because he was issued a visa to China.

But I have a responsibility to help when my business partner is in trouble. From his speech and from an article in the *New York Post*, it is clear that a major political and economic change was taking place, a major "earthquake," as Chen Yi called it.

"Explain exactly who I need to meet and what I need to do now," I say to Chen. I think: *Have some will. Don't be so dull-witted.*

He stares blankly at the people on the subway, suddenly looking at me and forcing a friendly smile on his face and barely managing to hold it. He wipes his spectacles.

"Money," he says.

"I understand, but you said $160 million before, or $160,000?"

"Million. $160 million."

"Why so much money? And where do you get it?"

"If we can contact one person, that part of the Russians we were going to visit, we would succeed. Well, it's a long story. In the 1970s, there was a bandit named Gennady Karkov, nicknamed 'Mongol.'

"He was also known as the 'grandfather of racketeering.' There are Ukrainians among them. But now we don't have robberies like in the old days. The bank only conducts financial activities."

"And now we are going to meet with the Ukrainian mafia?"

"It's not the mafia. It has to do with the country of origin, but it's just a banker. You are an economist; you will understand. So, I put $160 million into my account with the help of a banker, and I had to put half of it back in another account, and I had to take 40 percent of the remaining $80 million and transfer the rest to other people's accounts. In the morning, I was called from Kazakhstan, and suddenly everything happened."

"Like what? What's going on? What should I do now?"

"Well, we'll both stay at the same hotel first. Then I will talk on the phone and look for that person. If you meet him, you'd better go back to Belgium. I'll just finish. In fact, it is very easy to complete a transaction in one day.

"Let's go to the hotel, and I'll tell you more. If this money doesn't come through, our work will stop. We need to connect with Beijing, but now even the phones are being listened to. We'll just have to take the long route. Our situation in China is terrifying. The announcement in the *New York Post* means that everything is moving very quickly in Beijing and is now almost one-sided. China's population is tough. Since it has been announced to the world, it means that our side is losing. Here, too, people have begun to move. It's a heedless commotion now…"

"A vivid snapshot of chaos and revelry where secrets intertwine."

3

February 23, 2012

When we arrive at Brighton Beach and get off the subway, we see a line of Chinese celebrities with paper dragons, dressed in ruffles.

"Chen, what's going on? Why are the Chinese celebrating here? I thought there were only Russians in Brighton Beach."

"Today is the Chinese New Year. Lunar New Year."

"Really? Do Mongolians celebrate it, too?"

"It's the same lunar celebration; Mongolians must have celebrated yesterday," he shouted as we moved in front of the happy crowd.

The area known as Brighton Beach is sometimes called "Little Odessa," home to more than 20,000 immigrants from Ukraine and Russia who migrated in the mid-1970s. The whole area is full of Russian addresses, so it's almost as if you're in Russia rather than the United States.

In 1995, I saw the film *Little Odessa*, directed by the American James Gray. Tim Roth plays the main role.

We have come to the hotel BPM Brooklyn, 11 kilometers from the beach. The hotel is painted a gloomy dark gray, although the front is bright pink. At Chen Yi's request, we enter a room in my name; it has two beds.

"What is the reason for staying at this hotel?"

"No reason other than it's better to stay in an unnoticed hotel; is it okay to share a room together?"

"Of course. But I can't hide the fact that it all feels like a crime."

"You are a financial person. There is no crime here. There is no crime without victims. Do you know which bank is the best?"

"As a rule, a simple well-known and guaranteed bank is called a good bank."

"No, it isn't. The best bank is a bank without money. This means that all the money should be in circulation, not in the bank. You know, money is just a number."

"That's what I was taught. But you said you were going to get $160 million. It's definitely someone's money, isn't it?"

"The main reason is that it's no one's money. The money isn't visible in the clearing of the bank. It's about taking money out of thin air. A hacker in Kazakhstan can change that number. So, no one will be harmed. It's not a crime because there are no victims."

"Are you laundering money?"

"Not laundering. It's just a way to get money out of nothing. This can only be done by Deutsche Bank, although Chase Manhattan can do it, too. It's a little hard to explain. But trust me. There's a lot of money floating in the banking space. It's about pulling it down. But it's quite complicated. It won't work without a banker. Or, on behalf of a person with a financial history, a request could be sent to a Botswana bank by MT 103. Then comes IT 104. This means that the money went between the two banks in the middle of the road. It's all about code. So, a hacker in Russia will go in and pull the money from here to there. But in the bank, it won't look like it's been extracted.

"I'm not going to get you involved, don't worry. I came here because we agreed that it would go smoothly. But the commotion in our country made it a disaster, and it started to smell like a crime. Now that my partner has been arrested, I'm in danger. He probably didn't tell them about me at all. But there's nothing wrong with being cautious. As our people say, 'A cautious man is a man who got caught.'"

Chen is lying on one of the beds, talking to the ceiling.

We spend three days searching in several places to meet a Russian man named Yuri Nikolayevich. We can't find him. He's not only a banker at Chase Manhattan Bank but also the owner of a large club. He often travels to Russia to invite the "DTT" band to play at the Brighton Beach bars, so I call Irina and tell her everything that's happened.

She says, "I don't like it. I'll call Arbatov anyway."

The next day, she calls me back.

"There was a big mafia boss named Marat Balagula. He was recently released from prison after being charged with selling $750,000 in credit cards while trading in gasoline. He also lives here in Antwerp. There's another big boss named Boris Naifeld, nicknamed Biba, who was Balagula's bodyguard. But these two are big guys you can't just find. Arbatov says to go to the *Tatiana nightclub* and ask to see someone named *Pavel Korchagin*. Of course, it's a nickname or pseudonym—Korchagin is the name of the main character in Nikolai Ostrovsky's novel How the Steel Was Tempered. It's said that you can meet someone reliable in banking and finance through him. Korchagin is the accountant for that restaurant. But it's better to let Chen handle the meeting. Big changes are beginning in China."

4

We come to the end of a series of notes from Jim Edmund. After the last note was sent, he disappeared again. He was supposed to be in Mongolia soon with Chen Yi to meet with some government officials to discuss investment. However, this was written and sent before *Avid* had been in contact with him during his time in Mongolia.

Life continues, driven by the money that is worshiped around it. This cruel form of capitalism does not love anyone, and the struggle for survival will consume the human heart to the point of nothingness. People with kind souls will become fewer and fewer, leaving only those who have benefited. The word "love" will lose its full meaning, and the struggle for survival will begin with the sale of love, beliefs, values, and even the body, regardless of where it happens.

In such a poor society, ready to sell anything for food, only the rich can be happy and buy whatever they want. They buy dozens of the most beautiful young women in Mongolia, taking turns calling and using them for money.

Avid was in no hurry to have another woman. He remained inactive, wondering if someone would come along who could truly understand him—someone who understood what he was writing (or even speaking from his heart) and could share his support. But he had neither such a woman nor even a close male friend. He had reached this point in his inner world, and unfortunately, he had not found anyone.

However, *Aajim*, who had only been in contact through notes over the past year, gave him great hope and faith. When *Aajim* suddenly disappeared, *Avid* felt as if he were living in an airless space of loneliness. The nourishment that fed his soul was cut off. There were several notes left that were not included in the two sections compiled above. In particular, *Aajim* noted what he saw when he first came to Mongolia, which reflected not a public but a personal opinion. These notes were not included in the previous two sections because they seemed irrelevant to someone unfamiliar with Mongolian life.

However, on the way from Umnugovi to Ulaanbaatar, the note about his conversation with the driver was chosen because it was more interesting than the others. He wrote extensively about his life between the ages of 18 and 25. Since he had an affair with a Ukrainian girl named Irina, he kept a detailed record, and in the second part, he chose that name and compiled a note about her. However, at the end of the last note about his meeting with Chen Yi in New York, the situation became even more obscure.

Tired of waiting for an email from Irina, *Avid* searched Facebook to learn more about the kind of woman Irina Polishuk was and found her page. He didn't know if she and *Aajim* had been in contact, and it wasn't clear if *Aajim* had told her about Avid, so he didn't rush to message her.

Anyway, *Avid* thought he should work on his notes first. When he opened Irina Polishuk's Facebook profile, he found that she didn't write much or post many pictures. But on October 10 of the previous year, a black-and-white photo of a woman in a military uniform holding a rifle was posted with the caption:

"She is a hero of the Soviet Union and my father's sister. She died on this day, October 10, 1974. Lyudmila Pavlichenko, nicknamed 'Lady Death.' She was born on July 12, 1916."

Adolf Hitler called my sister Luda "a Russian bitch from hell." Sister Lyudmila Pavlichenko was the most famous female sniper in history, having killed 309 German soldiers during World War II. U.S. President Franklin D. Roosevelt invited Pavlichenko to the White House in the United States, and she traveled to 43 cities. In Chicago, she publicly said,

"I'm 25 years old. I killed 309 Nazis during the war. They couldn't hide from me, gentlemen."

After the war, she graduated from Kyiv University with a degree in history and worked as a research assistant to the Soviet Navy. My heroic sister from the Soviet Union died on this day.

After digging through Irina's Facebook, he found another interesting photograph, this one of her father serving in Mongolia with a group of friends. In the black-and-white photo was a group of Russian friends holding champagne in front of a prefabricated building. It appeared to be a celebration of the Russian New Year in military barracks in Choir. In the center of the picture was a man with a bare head and a smile. That was her father.

5

It's been two months without a reply, and *Avid* has emailed Irina several times about why he's worried, but there has been no response.

However, *Avid* spent all day sitting in the archives to find what he needed for another book he was writing. That night, he decided to ask Irina why *Aajim* was so quiet, and he turned on his computer and checked his email as usual. He made a cup of hot coffee and sat down to text Irina. But where to start to address *Aajim*? He wrote, "First I will introduce myself, and then, because I compiled your notes into a book, I will explain how I know you well."

Then he lit a cigarette when he opened Irina's Facebook profile, hoping to sit back and relax with her and the cig.

However, there was nothing special about her Facebook, except that it appeared a picture she took with a woman was posted eighteen days ago. He wrote the following message in English, as if she were smiling at him to indicate that nothing bad had happened: "Hello, Miss Irina Polishuk. My name is Avid. I am a Mongolian writer. A year ago, I contacted Jim Edmund by email and compiled a book of his notes, but I received a recent email from New York that stopped contact, and I'm worried about him. Can you tell me about him?" I pushed "Send."

Another month has passed since that day. Irina doesn't answer either. There is nothing added to her cover; but does she not see his message? Since we are not friends on Facebook, she maybe didn't even see my message; she hasn't been active on Facebook for about a month.

As a writer, I have an increased workload, and from time to time, I look at my email, write a letter once or twice, and stop waiting for a letter from *Aajim*. After more than a year of emailing him and receiving his interesting notes, *Aajim*, who had become accustomed to reading them in a hurry when the next one arrived, suddenly disappeared.

But one day, Irina Polishuk sends a Facebook direct message with notes from a Russian newspaper.

Cops: One killed, four injured in Brighton Beach Posted: Oct. 10, 2012, at 11:00 p.m. UST

Police say two men with guns shot a man to death and wounded four others at around 2 a.m. outside the Tatiana restaurant in Brooklyn's Brighton Beach. One of the two gunmen was identified as a Russian, and the other was identified as Jim Edmund from Britain. Police say the man killed in the shooting was a Chinese man, Chen Yi. And it is not clear whether the victim was shot on purpose or accidentally killed. Chen Yi died on the spot, and the other victims were taken to Lutheran Hospital and Coney Island Hospital, one man in critical condition. No arrests were made by police. The suspect is a tall, British man of Asian descent. Anyone with information about the crime is asked to call 1-800-577-TIPS, as there are reports that the person who went with him was a Russian citizen with a Georgian face.

Irina had sent this bad news and then blocked his profile after he read it.

PART 5

No master can be kept in the presence of a woman who has no respect for her man.

No virtue can find the door to the house with no master.

- Turu Khan

"In the surreal dreamscape, the dog embarks on a journey between reality and imagination."

1

Avid hurried home after buying groceries from the Mother Ocean market. It's been half a year since he left his home one night, slamming the door shut behind him. Since then, the ordinary humdrum days have been passing along one after another. He still visits *Uyangaa* from time to time, but he rarely sees Janna. She did not repay the one million *MNT* he had borrowed, but he waited calmly. It was obvious that Janna wasn't in a hurry to pay off the loan, and she'd been drinking a lot lately, and *Avid* didn't like the way she called him on the phone while she was drunk.

"These women get worse as their lives get better. Their intentions are pure only when they are suffering in life. For *Oyunaa*, the case is the same. When we first met, she had nothing but me. When she started to have everything, her heart had changed…" *Avid* unknowingly stepped in a puddle.

He came home with one of his shoes wet, hurriedly took off his socks, put the groceries in the kitchen, and sat down at his desk. He is now accustomed to this apartment, and once, in the absence of his wife, he went home and let himself in to bring with him the record player and speakers along with a number of his favorite records.

In addition to his work, he was taking part in a project to publish a collection of the best Mongolian short stories in Russian. He had been translating several short stories into Russian from scratch. He was moved by one of them, which happened to be an actual note, written in 1948 by the famous Mongolian author Donrovyn Namdag.

He doesn't understand why this note touched his heart so, but guessed it was because he had killed dogs for a living. He could not fathom the fact, at that time, that the dying dog in this story was born in the United States as a girl named Daisy Maria who was shot dead and reincarnated as a dog named Sharik back in Mongolia. How could *Avid* have guessed that Sharik was the same dog he killed fifteen years ago?

TWO DEATHS OF ONE ANIMAL

By 1948, my personal life did not seem to meet the standards of what was considered normal at the time. In fact, this was largely due to the decline in my artistic work. I had no reason to believe I had lost my creative ability. It is true that my experiences over the last few years did not weaken my mind in the slightest but instead drew me deeper into the realm of life experience. In other words, one of the keys to understanding the art of writing is to experience what you are writing about firsthand and to know it in your heart—and that is certainly true.

For now, though, I'm not going to write about art theory. I'm going to write about a tragedy I witnessed with my own eyes. But I'll also be at a loss if I don't include part of my personal life. For example, when the cool of autumn came and winter's chill began to set in, I found myself without a roof over my head. However, I was fortunate. My only nephew, a close relative, worked for The Pioneer newspaper, and the paper was kind enough to lend him a ger to live in. We decided to live together. But the question remained: where would we set up and assemble it?

As the director of the library at the State Drama Theater, I ended up in the courtyard of the homes of the actors and staff. The location was north of the State Central Press Committee, where dozens of households lived in gers, and there was a mud house for three families with west-facing doors in the northeast corner. The spot I found to set up our ger, of course, was the worst. It was right next to a large gate that served as the entrance and exit for everyone. Not only was there a toilet on the east side of my house, but the people in the yard constantly dumped their wastewater nearby, turning the area into a dirty iceberg. Still, I didn't see the place as bad; I thought it was actually quite good. The most important thing was that people walked through the front gate day and night, so things like firewood and spilled coal wouldn't go missing. On the other hand, because it was such a poor spot, it was rare for animals or people to be running around. I didn't want to interact with others so often anyway—I had plenty on my plate. In addition to handling all the household chores, I cooked for the two of us. Luckily, I had built the stove myself, and it turned out to provide more warmth than expected, so we were able to save on firewood.

Most of the time, I didn't leave the house. I stayed in, reading and writing by candlelight, so life didn't seem too shabby back then. On the contrary, it was a valuable lesson to experience the difference between real life and what is taught about life.

Now, let me get to the real point of what I'm writing about. One sunny day, I went out to gather groceries. As I approached the front gate, I saw a little boy, probably younger than 10, standing near my house with a wooden stick in his hands. A man in a brown coat, holding a long stick, was waiting nearby for the same thing the boy seemed to be anticipating.

"Get out!"

"Hey!"

"Hit him!"

People were shouting and chasing some animal. A yellow-furred bitch, a shepherd dog, was running toward the gate, followed by a well-fed black Mongolian dog. I realized they were trying to kill the black dog. As the yellow dog darted through the gate with the black dog close behind, the man with the truncheon struck the black dog, knocking him to the ground. They kept hitting him until it was all over.

Watching the entire scene unfold, I not only felt deep sorrow for the poor animal, but I also found myself sinking into darker thoughts. Incidents like this have been recorded in ancient and modern myths and histories alike. The poor dog was left lying on the ice-covered ground. I thought about the little boy holding the willow branch, wondering what would become of him when he grew older. Will he be willing to kill more than just a dog then?

Nature gives life to any animal to keep it alive and to allow it to thrive, but also to those who would destroy those lives. In other words, as the city has been overpopulated with dogs, it must seem natural to keep their number as low as possible. The dog that had been beaten to death is one of the beautiful creatures of nature.

But what was even worse was that the poor creature wasn't dead yet. As I went to the outhouse before sunset, I could see that he was struggling to breathe through his bloody nose.

I was heartbroken and said, "Oh, you are not dead yet? You'd better die."

The next day I had just gotten up, and the dog was still breathing.

I sighed again: "You'd better die."

Then I saw a middle-aged woman, the mother of many children, who lived by the far north entrance of the yard, feeding a bowl of leftovers to the poor dog. It made me think, "Well, there's nothing purer than a mother's heart." But the dog did not have the strength to pay attention to her.

When I returned from work that evening, the dog was still lying down, but the bowl in front of him was empty.

For a few days, she gave the dog a little food every now and then, and I also couldn't help but nurture him. Then one day when I came home from work, he was gone. All that was left was the melted lair next to the ice mound. But the poor animal was lying in a circle on the left side of the door of the compassionate woman. I couldn't help but rejoice that he had joined the company of his beloved. Then, a few days later, I noticed that the dog had switched his lair and was lying on the right side of the door, keeping a close eye on everyone coming in and out. To find out exactly why, his left eye had been struck hard, and his sharp fangs had fallen out. Obviously, the animal had to use his good eye to guard the rescuer's home. I'm naturally amazed at his sanity now.

As the days went on, the dog got better and better. He would stretch well from time to time and noticeably observe everyone walking down the narrow alley between the houses. But as the animal recovered, his behavior began to change. First of all, it was difficult for strangers to enter, especially for a few sticks of firewood and powdered coal waste. But he would let me in. Maybe it was because I was treating him well when he was lying on the ground near death.

Then, as the cold of winter passed and the call of spring came, an awkward conversation arose among the people in the yard. They started saying ear to ear that the black dog was going to be mad because of rabies.

There is no one on my side who can say, "How did you come up with such a conclusion?" Obviously, I was having a conversation in my head saying, "No, rabies is a contagious disease that affects the mind of an animal only when contracted through saliva, not an injury."

The first woman to save his life was so shocked that she had to go to the ward and bring in a man to have him beaten to death. For me, the only way to save him now was to take him home without saying a word, but he didn't seem to think I was the real master. On the other hand, I could not make such a decision on my own because I was sharing a home with another. Also, if I went against the crowd, the only place I called home could be confiscated. I had no choice but to remain silent about him. But not long after, two men with wooden bats came in through the front gate.

"Where's that crazy dog?"

Now the alley was full of people who gave him up. When the two men came to the door, there was no sign that the dog had any idea that the man had come to kill him, but he began to fight, thinking that the man was about to break and enter his master's home. However, his fight was useless. The crowd shouted:

"Beat him!"

"Pound him!"

"Kill him!"

The poor dog came to an end, and finally, he was dragged past our house by a wire rope around his neck and disappeared...

Avid was upset when he read it again.

When he sneaked into his house to get his music, and when he came out of the living room into the kitchen, a dog saw him, whimpered in fear as if he had seen a demon, and ran away, crashing into a large cupboard in the middle of the kitchen.

He remembered that on the morning of the day he met *Oyunaa* in 1997, the same morning he visited the Inner Mongolian woman's house, the dog he had shot and killed had crashed into a fence, running mindlessly away from him. The reason he remembered the kill was that she was the last dog he shot.

Avid hasn't killed a dog since the day he met *Oyunaa*. A month later, he was offered a decent job by a friend who had studied in Volgograd. He wondered what this strange dog was doing in his house. However, having read the upsetting note by the famous writer, he put his phone back on the table, stopping himself from talking to his wife to ask where the dog had come from.

For the past six months, *Avid* had been living alone, accustomed to his lonesome life. This was the best way for him to live now. Unsatisfied, *Avid* took a glass of beer from the refrigerator and drank it. He lay down on the couch for a while, but he wanted more to drink. *Avid* opened the freezer and found vodka in an almost empty bottle. He poured the remaining liquid into the beer stein he was holding and chugged it in one swallow.

He lay on the couch, staring at the ceiling, waiting for his stomach to heat up.

2

Just as *Avid* lay alone, waiting for the cold vodka to warm his stomach, *Oyunchimeg* was waiting for a man she had met a month ago in her house. She stood in front of a large mirror dressed elegantly. She was surprised to see a beautiful woman in the mirror, who was getting a bit thicker but still had a nice figure. Her eyes sparkled with anger.

"I was a woman of few words, which were 'shy' and 'calm.' But as soon as I learned that my husband smelled of another woman, I turned into this sad, angry, and 'monstrous' woman as *Avid* described me in his diary."

It was the first time she'd welcomed another man into her home, and she felt like a sinner about to commit a crime. As she looked at her body, she saw in the mirror her dog Daisy behind her, staring at her master.

Oyunaa called the phone number that was on the dog's collar many times, but the machine would answer: "The number you have dialed cannot be reached at the moment. Please check your number and call again." When she went to Mobicom and asked who the number belonged to, she found that a foreigner had once owned it and had returned home. She took Daisy straight to the vet for a test and found that she was perfectly healthy. Daisy is a smart dog, and it's weird that she acts like she's reading *Oyunaa*'s mind. The husky pup spoke with her eyes, but for some reason, it seemed as if she had been around for many years. Living alone in a five-room apartment is not a life to wish for, so it was a great opportunity for her to suddenly have such a beautiful dog. Since Daisy's arrival, Oyuna's loneliness disappeared, and her hatred toward *Avid* diminished.

One day, however, her husband had come home and taken the music he used to listen to. Surprisingly, Daisy was left so frightened that she sat in the corner until *Oyunaa* came back, and as soon as she entered, Daisy came straight to her and lay down on her lap.

Now *Oyunchimeg* stared at her own body with unhappy eyes.

"This body did not please my husband. This body is not destined to produce eggs. Isn't it just a mechanism that digests food and excretes feces? Isn't it just a piece of meat I need to get rid of? But now I'm trying to give this abandoned body to someone else and try to deceive that person with a fancy outfit. Who needs a body with such an evil spirit?"

She wanted to break the mirror into a million pieces and was astonished when she felt relief at the thought of killing herself. She felt like she had the power to turn her "useless" body into a corpse and burn it in an incinerator.

"Should I really have to commit suicide and end this meaningless life? What's the point in living like a housekeeper in so many rooms, with no money I can spend in my old age? And the person whom I chased out is still paying for this apartment. Everything around me is the life he gave me, the life he built. From the car I drive to the clothes I wear; they are all his. Is there anything I have added to this house? Only the creams and perfumes I use on this ugly body were paid for by myself. It's okay to take out this useless body like a cabbage." She hated herself.

"*Avid* is never coming back. He's living happily ever after. Whereas I don't have a job or a community to fall back on. There were a few frenzied women whom I called friends, but at first, they seemed to feel sorry for me, but now they don't care. They even take pleasure in gossiping about my miseries. If only my mother were here. Who do I have now? How will I live in the future? Whom will I live for? Is it for this corpse that no one needs?"

The thought came to her mind that it would be better to drink poison and die.

Suddenly, the Husky barked, chasing away the gloomy thoughts.

"The only thing I have is you. Another abandoned soul. Well, at least I have to live until you die. Don't I?"

Daisy barked at her as if to say "yes." *Oyunchimeg* picked up the phone, feeling uneasy.

"Shall we cancel tonight, *Gerelsaikhan*? I have a headache."

"What do you mean? I'm almost outside your house. I brought a gift."

"Okay, then, I'll take some pills and will feel better."

As she was finally ready to welcome her guest, *Oyunaa* tried on a sultry evening dress but hesitated because it would look odd, as she was at her home. She put on a rather modest skirt paired with her black blouse.

At eight o'clock in the evening, someone knocked on the door. Daisy was lying on the floor with her head on her front legs, and suddenly she got up, barked at the door, and ran at full speed. As *Oyunchimeg* approached the door, she glanced at herself in the mirror and opened it. A well-dressed man in his late forties with a bouquet of roses was standing there smiling. He kneeled down to take a good look at the dog sniffing his feet.

"How are you? What a cute dog. Wow, two different colored eyes!"

Daisy wagged her tail and began to lick his face.

"Hmm, it's bad if you're good to everyone."

"She's not like that at all. She barks at everyone. I don't know why she's acting like this all of a sudden, as if she knows you."

"I don't know. It's as if I left in the morning and came back here. Dogs can tell if a person is good or bad."

He took off his white coat, hung it on the rack in the corridor, took off his shiny Lloyd's shoes, put on slippers, and came into the living room.

Oyunchimeg went to the kitchen with the bouquet of flowers, put them in water, and placed the glass jar on the table. *Gerelsaikhan* opened the bag in one hand and pulled out a box wrapped in gold paper that contained a gift.

Oyunchimeg took a bottle of cognac called Camus from a glass-faceted cupboard on the kitchen wall and placed it on the table.

When *Gerelsaikhan* took off his jacket and leaned back in the chair, it was strange that Daisy jumped on his lap and licked his face.

3

Oyunchimeg awoke from her shallow sleep at the sound of the dog whimpering at the door. She got up to go to the bathroom, remembering that she had been sleeping under the same blanket as a stranger. She lifted the blanket and slowly stood, deliberately avoiding looking back, afraid that if she did, last night's encounter would feel even more real—though it already was. Wrapping herself in a small blanket, she walked softly. As she opened the door, Daisy jumped right onto the bed next to the sleeping man. *Oyunaa* finally turned to look back.

The man, who was snoring with his chest exposed and looking up, smiled a little in his sleep, resembling her husband. The man sighed as she saw Daisy lying in a circle on the blanket, staring straight into his face. *Oyunchimeg* closed the door behind her.

She walked as fast as she could as if she were escaping from a bad person, and when she pulled open the bathroom door, she was greeted by a luxurious room decorated with vermeil walls and floors. Many years ago, when *Oyunaa* had a quarrel with her husband and went to her mother's for a few days, *Avid* had turned this bathroom into such luxury. Everywhere she looked, she was surrounded by *Avid*'s creations. At first, she had been amazed and respected what *Avid* was doing for their life, but then she stopped appreciating both the house and *Avid*. She wanted to lock the door and sit on the toilet until everything was over.

The only thing she proudly owned and left with was her loyalty, which she lost the night before. She wanted to cry, but her eyes could not produce tears. *Oyunchimeg* was with a man for the first time without any love, and after less than a month, she realized that she was even emptier.

Last night, I was quite drunk, and in the back of my mind, I had a secret desire to take revenge on *Avid* by having an affair with someone else.

But it felt strange. His embrace was firm and strong, and she found herself breathing heavily. It was unsettling, different from the way she felt with *Avid*. This wasn't about love or connection, but something more primal, something instinctual. Being with a stranger in this way made her feel conflicted—both empowered and disoriented, as if she was disconnected from herself. With *Avid*, there had been moments of overwhelming emotion, moments when she'd cried after reaching pleasure—tears of joy and release. But this was entirely different. As heat spread through her body, she thought about telling him to stop. Yet, even as the idea crossed her mind, another part of her wanted to keep going. The conflicting emotions—wanting control but also feeling desire—were confusing, but in the end, she decided to continue.

She hadn't been with anyone in nine months, and she thought she wouldn't be affected by this man, but there was a raw and unfamiliar desire stirring inside her.

What happens now? Oyunaa wondered. *Gerelsaikhan* hadn't hidden the fact that he had a wife, even speaking about his three children with affection. He didn't come across as someone driven by lust or recklessness. He seemed gentle, a good listener, and respectful of women. And yet, she couldn't shake the discomfort she felt, knowing he was still betraying his family, much like *Avid* had. He first came to the city from *Choir* in 1992 when he was twelve. He was now 44 years old. He went to Russia for peddling, later ran a tannery, and then he and his brother started a company together. He seemed like a very resilient man. *Oyunaa* had first attracted him with her French. He seemed to be a good father. *What kind of woman is his wife?* she wondered. *What have I done?*

She got up from the toilet and flushed. But the ache in her heart seemed to be swept away with the flushing water in the bowl. In fact, we clean our bodies every day. But for the first time, she felt as though she had reached this point in her life by digging up filth and throwing it at her husband instead of washing it away with the toilet water. It was the first time she had ever felt like that. *The number of good days in our lives is greater than the bad days*, she thought.

Oyunchimeg came out of the bathroom, went to the kitchen, lit one of the cigarettes from the table, and stood by the window.

The full moon of the fifteenth was shining down a blue ray from the sky. She was reluctant to go back to her bedroom and into the man's arms.

I hadn't opened my arms to my husband for half a year... Why? Why did I do it to this man? She was filled with sadness.

She took a shower, put on her clothes, and decided to sleep in another room.

4

Three months after that full moon in mid-Autumn, a modest divorce case was tried in a civil court. Amazingly, during the trial, *Avid* read his "sad diary" to the jury in full. The court ruled that the marriage of *Oyunchimeg* and *Avid* should be dissolved, and an expert was appointed to divide the property equally.

Oyunchimeg had nothing to say in court. She was even more shocked to learn that not one but two women were involved in *Avid*'s life.

Another remarkable thing was that *Avid*'s lawyer presented a strange piece of "evidence" during the trial. She said:

"Although these facts are not directly related to my client, I'm going to discuss monogamy and polygamy. There are three forms of polygamy. The first is polygyny, or the practice of a man having multiple wives. Then there is polyandry, where a woman has multiple husbands. Lastly, there is polygamy, which refers to any form of multiple spouses.

"In Islamic countries, a 1932 law allows for up to four wives, but in addition to providing a dowry, it is only allowed with the written consent of the first wife, or 'queen.' Polyandry is common in Tibet, where it is not unusual for brothers to share one wife.

"In countries like China, India, and some West African nations, especially where Islam is predominant, and in Polynesia, the practice of polygamy is not considered illegal. Historically, polygamy was common in ancient Greece. The Bible states that a man can have more than one wife, and the American Church itself recently acknowledged that the founder of Mormonism, Joseph Smith, had 40 wives, one of whom was only 14 years old.

"Joseph Smith (1805-1844), founder of the Church of Latter-day Saints, commonly known as Mormonism, is revered as

a missionary by his followers. According to the Mormon Church's website last month, Smith had 30 to 40 wives and fathered over 50 children.

"During the Roman Empire, Catholicism promoted monogamy, although polygamy was practiced throughout much of the world at the time.

"Mongolia has an ancient tradition of polygamy. Some historical texts state that Genghis Khan had multiple wives and many concubines during his reign. It is well-documented that Kublai Khan's great queen helped him find additional wives and treated them as sisters.

"Even as recently as eighty years ago, it was common to have first and second wives.

"If polygamy had been legalized, our population might be much larger now. We might not even have become a 'country of single mothers.' More importantly, children wouldn't have been orphaned, and men's value in society would have increased, along with the value of women aspiring to marry prestigious, healthy, and wealthy men.

"HBO's Big Love, an Emmy and Golden Globe-winning series, portrays the life of a man with twelve wives spread across Madagascar. The series shows that the man is a loving provider for his wives, who live in different parts of the country, demonstrating that he is capable of caring for all of them.

"If Mongolia, a country with many beautiful women, were to allow dual citizenship and recognize such polygamous arrangements, we could potentially attract wealthy foreign men to our country.

"According to The Secret History of the Mongols, Dair-Usun, the *leader of the Uvas Merged, presented his daughter Khulan to Genghis Khan, and the Khan was pleased to meet her. Khulan became one of the Khan's beloved queens and played a significant role in his life. Temujin's father, Yesukhei Baatar, had two wives, and Genghis Khan had four queens: Borte, Khulan, Yesugen, and Yesui (Article 241 of The Secret History of the Mongols). Among his many wives, the first wife held the senior position. Each wife had her own house, livestock, bodyguards, and servants."*

This was a strange defense, unlike anything ever heard in court. The court listened to it but ruled that it was irrelevant to the case and merely informative. The issue would be resolved in accordance with current laws, and the couple was not granted time for reconciliation.

While collecting materials for the magazine, *Avid* found and read Plato's Feast. According to legend, in ancient times, there were no males and females, and humans were called Androgynies.

Considering that the Androgynies were as powerful as the Titans, they could attack the gods, and Zeus divided the Androgynies into males and females, arguing that they needed to cause conflict. As a result, their power was halved, their divisiveness and misunderstandings multiplied, and the power of the ancient Androgyny diminished. Sexual love and marriage are not only a search for each other, but also a desire to have sex. So, for the first time, *Avid* wondered if most people mistakenly think that they have found the other half of themselves but married the other half of a different person.

But even though it was a made-up story, it seemed strange that Plato had written such a tale.

5

Avid was sitting on his hind legs. His brown, wiry fur blew in the wind as he breathed deeply through his white-tipped nose, puffing out his white chest. A blue bandana was tied around his neck as he sat next to a wooden bench with cement legs in front of a small white house. A road sign nearby depicted an adult and a child playing football, and an old suitcase lay on the ground next to the bench.

As if rain were coming, a flock of black clouds gathered in the sky, and the wind suddenly blew, sending all the hair on his body fluttering. The dog jumped off the bench and ran down the path. Then, just as suddenly, the wind stopped, and the sun broke through the clouds. He noticed a television set hanging from the sky by two strings. A man was talking on the TV, and the dog recognized him—it was *Avid*, his human self.

The dog barked at the television because the man's voice was barely audible. He stood up, trying to listen more closely, but *Avid*'s face remained expressionless, his eyes vacant. Suddenly, the screen filled with images of dog snouts. One snout's two nostrils zoomed in on the screen, and from one of the nostrils, a small man emerged, like a fly, and stretched. Each dog watching nodded in surprise and looked up at the screen, recognizing that the little man was also *Avid*.

Suddenly, the wind picked up again, and the dog jumped into the air.

Before long, the dog was flying through the sky, riding on the suitcase. Behind him, many identical suitcases followed in a line, with a few white gulls trailing behind. Sitting happily on his suitcase, the dog occasionally glanced down and barked. Below him, he saw cities and towns, their shadows moving across the ground like clouds, cast by the many suitcases flying above. Then, in the distance, he saw a wave of blood.

He watched as a number of dogs swam in the sea of blood, all wearing blue scarves around their necks, each sitting on a suitcase and looking up at the flying dog. Suddenly, the flying dog plummeted into the sea of blood.

Avid woke up and saw that he had fallen from the couch and was lying on the floor. He raised his head and thought, What a strange dream. *I'm going to die and be born a dog. As a man who killed so many dogs, I'm probably ending up in the sea of blood with those slaughtered dogs. Or maybe I'll go to hell. And what was that about flying on my father's brown suitcase? That suitcase is definitely my father's. It was one of the same suitcases stacked at the back of the house when I was little. It's a strange dream. I might have been riding my father's suitcase to hell.*

Since he began translating the story about two deaths of the same animal, he had been filled with a strange, mysterious fear and evil instinct.

When he came through the door, he was shocked to see a dog licking up a puddle in front of his building.

"What is this now? A dog in a dream, a dog in a thought, a dog in what I'm translating, a dog even when I'm out… I'm starting to go crazy, aren't I?"

There was a dog when I went to Oyunaa's to pick up my record player. Then the dog ran away from me as if it had seen a demon and crashed into the cupboard. What was a dog doing in the house, anyway? I had rushed to the people who were helping me move the albums and the record player. I saw that dog disappear around the corner after hitting the cupboard, dripping its urine on the floor. I never saw this dog again. Am I starting to hallucinate?

The strangest thing was that when I went to see Oyunaa back in the house, there was no Husky with two different eyes.

Well, that house I once called home is gone now. The bailiffs came and assessed the property and, in the end, I found someone to buy the apartment and sold it. I left enough money to Oyunaa for her to buy at least a comfortable, single-room apartment. I saw the life I had built for fifteen years disappear in one day.

I'm used to living alone. Getting married is not something that can be taken for granted. I can't even imagine getting married again, and the idea of living with another person seems strange to me.

The last time he met *Oyunaa* to give her the money, she was crying and saying:

"It was all my fault. I ruined the life we had built together for fifteen years. How would I have imagined neglecting you would lead to such tragedy? I still love you! Where and for whom will I live now?"

But *Avid* felt it was too late to go back to *Oyunaa*. He walked down the street to the store nearby, where he had bought groceries before. He knew they sold alcohol. Behind a small counter was a young man who was dozing off a bit. *Avid* greeted him and looked at the vodka on the shelf.

"How much is that *Finlandia*?"

"It is $82,000."

He took out his card and handed it to the young man. "A bottle of *Finlandia* and a spicy instant noodle," *Avid* said.

When *Avid* returned home, he took a sip of vodka, boiled water to soak the noodles, and opened the refrigerator to grab the sausage. He had found a hearty sausage called *Servalat*, but it was as dry as wood. He pulled a knife from the drawer, but it was dull. So, he took out a grinder and sharpened the knife.

When he tried to cut the dried sausage, it rolled away from the cutting board and onto the floor. The knife snapped, and in the blink of an eye, he saw the tip of his ring finger on his left hand lying on the counter, blood splattering all over. He let out a squeak.

He was looking for gauze to wrap his finger, but there was no such thing in this house. Panicked, he grabbed a tissue and wrapped his finger with the tip that had been cut off. His finger ached, the wrapped paper was quickly soaked with blood, and it began to drip onto the kitchen furniture. *Avid* hurriedly poured the vodka into a large glass and drank it.

The full moon of the fifteenth shone through the kitchen window, inspired by the red moon. He sat at his desk and typed the title "Rootless" awkwardly because of his now well-wrapped finger.

Two years later, *Oyunaa* had separated *Gerelsaikhan* from his wife and kids and married him. Afterward, the Husky died suddenly, and *Oyunaa* became pregnant. *Avid* was surprised to hear that she had named her daughter after her late dog, Daisy.

They say that it requires half of the time that you were together to get over the relationship. But it had been proven false this time.

6

That snowy night, writer *Avid* walked out of the house into the darkness, walked into a store, and bought a bottle of champagne and a box of cigarettes. He remembered he didn't have fancy wine glasses at home and bought four very expensive glasses.

He had finished writing a good story. *Avid* remembered watching a movie where one writer had finished a book and celebrated by drinking a glass of champagne and smoking a cigarette. He lit a cigarette, drank a glass of wine, and laughed alone like a madman.

When the champagne was gone, he poured wine into his glass and stood up. *The Emerson Lake & Palmer's Brain Salad Surgery* was playing on the record player when he suddenly fainted and fell onto his desk.

Like the ending of the last song on the second side of the record, 3rd Impression—when a piano still played strangely fast and suddenly stops—his mind ran as fast as if it was exhausting the last of his energy and stopped working right then and there.

Just as he was bored from the book he had started reading before finishing it, his life ended abruptly before he could turn 49.

Everyone's death is like the life he lived.

… A story was left on his computer.

7

"ROOTLESS"

All that could be heard was the oppressive darkness around him—the stinking water of the Selbe River, the grinding of stones under the ridges, and the lowing of cattle from the fence along the river.

He didn't understand why he was lying beneath the bridge over the Selbe River. Leaning on the frozen ground, trying to stand with his numb limbs, he muttered, "Morality. The hell with morality..."

Feeling his injured knee, likely from a fall, he grabbed the hem of his wet coat and crawled up the stone embankment. A truck passed overhead, rumbling loudly across the bridge.

Slowly, he swayed across the road and leaned against a wooden fence. His face was pale, as if fevered, and he looked every bit the drunkard, with mud smeared on his cheeks. Anyone who crossed paths with him on this dark night would probably avoid him.

He paused, leaning against the fence, before finally attempting to walk down the crooked street.

He was amazed by how calm he felt, as if he didn't care whether it was the darkness before dawn or still night.

Didn't I fly to heaven and die to be reborn in heaven? he thought.

Taking a deep breath, he felt at peace, as though he no longer needed to worry about anything. But he couldn't understand why he had woken up here. The question began to bother *Aajim*. Now, thinking about why his body ached like a living person's, it saddened him to realize that he had a body again.

No one was around. Only wooden fences, mud houses, and gers with their lights off behind the fences. Dogs barked occasionally in the distance.

As he walked, he reached the edge of an empty square, its boundaries unclear. It was as if there was no limit to the space he was in.

He continued through the darkness, heading northwest, which seemed to call to him from afar.

The thought came to him that he had fainted at sunset and had fallen off the plane. Finally, he closed his eyes and opened them again. It was a strange feeling, as if one thought was hanging over another thought. After walking for a while with his eyes closed, he opened them, hoping that the public square was coming to an end. But it wasn't.

He was just walking northwest. Suddenly, the ground seemed to collapse, and he stepped one foot into a hole.

It wasn't long before he woke up. He could hear a giant fan spinning, but that turned out to be flies running over his face.

Here and there the bells rang, the wind blew, and the stench of the jacket wafted through the air.

Then he heard a woman sigh beside his ear. Slowly he regained consciousness, in a clear but pale voice: "Who is this person?" he whispered.

"It's *Tsogzolmaa*, your mother."

He was shocked. "*Tsogzolmaa*? My mother died in London twenty years ago." The day flashed through his mind.

"Son, you had too much to drink, haven't you? I'm lucky to have been found by you."

His heart sank as the wind blew.

"You're very drunk. Go to sleep now, son."

His mother's words sounded strangely warm, as if she were resurrected or had never died.

The moon could be seen through the clouds. He forced himself up and looked around. The place he was now was full of stone pillars here and there; locusts and snakes scurried and slithered by.

He was startled when he learned that his leg was stuck up to his knees in a ruined tomb. Panicked, he pulled his leg out of the hole, and a few brown mice climbed up and out of the tomb.

Slowly, he knelt on the ground and stopped again to read the inscription on the stone statue, slightly tilted forward. Even in the shadow of the night, he could read what was written: "R. *Tsogzolmaa* 1937-1994."

He could hear the woman again: "Slowly, my son, come here."

For some reason, little by little, he was not afraid or surprised anymore. Gradually, he moved to his mother's side. She instructed her son to cut off the head of the corpse lying on the ground, which was himself.

"My poor boy, don't be afraid."

"I'm not afraid, Mom!"

"Then take that head and give it to me."

"But, Mom! It's me!"

Without saying a word, his mother put a spear in his hand. Without a moment's hesitation, *Aajim* put the iron spear on the corpse's throat.

"Don't be afraid, my son. There will be no bleeding. It won't hurt at all."

Slowly, *Aajim* plunged into his own esophagus. He cut around the neck and dipped the spear deep until he reached the bone. He snapped the neck bone, and the head came off. He looked up at his mother's face as he held his head, careful not to drop it to the ground.

"Now carve off the scalp," his mother ordered.

Slowly he cut the skin of his forehead to his ears and forcibly peeled off a piece of yellow felt underneath the scalp.

"Don't be surprised, my son. This is the last piece of upholstery from the throne of the last great king of Mongolia." She pulled a piece of orange silk out of her pocket to wrap the felt.

He wrapped a piece of cloth around his head and handed it to his mother. "Well, son, you can go now," his mother said.

Aajim tried to ask, "Where?" but his lips wouldn't move.

It was pitch black all around. He walked and walked until he reached the boundary of the cemetery.

He stopped when he saw a short man in a yellow cotton jacket and a Russian military uniform standing before him. The man's bald head gleamed faintly in the moonlight.

"Have you been here before?" *Aajim* nodded, though it felt pointless.

"Don't be afraid of me. I'm the guard here."

The old man smelled of alcohol. He was a stocky little man with a sarcastic expression on his face. He smoked a cigarette wrapped in a piece of newspaper, which he tossed on the ground as he walked toward his house.

"One cow is missing." His voice was hoarse but surprisingly calm.

As they walked, they approached a mud house with a lighted window. *Aajim* hesitated.

"Come on, come in. Why are you standing there?"

He stepped inside. Wood burned in the open-hearth stove, and the orange glow illuminated the back of the room. The familiar scent of an elderly person's home brought him a sense of comfort.

The old man took off his cotton coat, threw it aside, and pulled up a chair.

"Sit down," he said, setting a brass kettle on the fire. "Smoke?"

The old man pulled out a round box of tobacco and placed it on the cupboard. Then, reaching under the table, he retrieved a bottle of distilled vodka, popped off the cap, and poured *Aajim* a glass.

Aajim took the vodka and downed it quickly.

"Uncle, I'm cold," he said.

"Sit closer to the fire," the old man replied. "I'll go out and get some firewood." But even as he sat by the fire, *Aajim* felt even colder.

The tea in the brass kettle began to boil.

"Hey, son, you're burning up. There's steam coming off of you."

"Who's outside, brother?" *Aajim* asked.

"What do you mean? No one! Who's supposed to be out there? There's nothing but graves and cattle."

Aajim regained consciousness and touched his face. His skin was ice-cold. He gave the old man a startled look and hurried to the door. It was silent outside. A few of the old man's cows lay on the grass.

The cold still clung to him. He let out a long sigh of despair and walked back to the cemetery. As he moved, he dissolved like vapor into the darkness.

*** *** ***

When the morning sun shone on the peak of Sambalkhundev Mountain, the first line of funeral cars appeared.

The guard let go of the cows and hurried to the cemetery to greet the procession.

He remembered the madman from last night and went to the place where he was lying. A snake crawled out from the nearby tomb.

When the old man touched the snake with the tip of the whip he was holding, the black snake raised its head, hissed in a way that sounded more like a sigh, and slid back into the tomb.

Surprised that the snake gave him the same feeling as the madman had last night, the old man walked on. He laughed at the strange thought. *How could a man and a snake seem similar to each other? he wondered.*

PART 6

Maybe this world is another planet's hell.

-Aldous Huxley

"Under a tempest of wrath, escape becomes the only solace."

1

The first thing he felt were the 10,000 eyes of the nonmaterial world, free from consciousness.

They were the eyes of souls that had once been lost in the maze of suffering, grudges, joy, and hurt—souls that had passed into this world, waiting for rebirth. These souls had now dissolved into thin air, finding eternal peace and breaking free from the chains that once bound them to the material world. The souls of thousands of humans, dogs, monkeys, birds, and even insects had now transformed into these extraterrestrial eyes after their deaths. They only gazed down at life below.

The lower depends on the upper, and the upper depends on the lower.

It was unclear whether he had a body or not, as though he were suspended in emptiness. He thought calmly, *I think I'm dead.* In the first few days after death, things hadn't made sense, but now they seemed to come together, becoming one. Gradually, a light entered his awareness as he realized the peace of mind he had been searching for all his life would never leave him now.

Is death so easy and painless? he wondered. *Of course, my body is gone, taking all the suffering with it. But where am I?* As he thought this, his vision lit up the house he had rented, revealing a white desk and a white floor.

The computer he had left on flickered in front of him. He saw the headline "ROOTLESS" as if he had written it down a hundred years ago, and a calm sense of relief washed over him. I knew I was going to die, he thought.

Next to the computer, on the large white table, appeared two books: *Nothing is True and Everything is Possible* (2014) by Russian writer Peter Pomerantsev and *Franz Kafka's Diaries 1910-1923*.

I bought these two books at Kinokuniya Bookstore when I was in Singapore, he recalled. *I didn't read Kafka, but I took it off the bookshelf and put it on the table to read later. It might be useful for compiling Jim Edmund's notes. There is no such thing as death. Everything is immortal; it just means moving from one state to another. Things don't disappear—they become clearer and sharper.*

But am I dreaming? he wondered. *I think I've read all this before in Jim Edmund's diary. It feels like a continuation of a dream Jim had when he was in the hospital with jaundice.*

In the light, his voice began to speak. At first, it was vague, and he couldn't make out the words. Suddenly, his eyes became as white as the walls of his house, and the wind began to blow. Time became incomprehensible. Everything seemed to happen in an instant, but not in the order of time. He floated in the air like a man in a dream, and below him stretched a white field. There was no time in that strange place. The sky was white, and there was nothing but white snow. The snow had fallen silently into the stillness of the morning, and it too was silent. The white space seemed endless.

The fact that he didn't feel his body at all was surprisingly peaceful, and he realized that if he could control his thoughts, he could go anywhere.

But I can think! And think more clearly. I can smell, I can see, I can hear, but I can't seem to taste. Every word, every image, every sound—every thought—I used to feel or enjoy. But now, I'm neither happy nor upset about it. It's just strange to experience such peace. Every moment of my life, I was either happy or upset. How odd that my estranged wife is now lying in front of me, yet I don't seem to feel any desire or resentment. Everything is very simple, and I'm relieved to think that I was the only one who could make myself happy.

First of all, there is no day or night. Since there is no day or night, there is no time. It turns out there are only thoughts—thoughts without bodies. There is no sleep here. There is no hunger or pain. There is an eternal peace, completely different from the human world. I was listening to music at the time of my death, and perhaps that brought me to such a divine place. There is nothing to think about, yet everything is here. I can go anywhere I want, and there are no limits. Avid thought all of this as his soul floated on the clouds.

However, he couldn't see white wings or a body, like in some movies, but he could see everything outside. Over time, the idea of thinking about the past became uninteresting. The past felt so distant, so meaningless.

Why did I write when I was alive? What did I work so hard for? Wasn't it all just to avoid loneliness? But now, when a strong wave of that past or the underworld comes from somewhere, he can go to that moment if he wants. Everything aligns now. In other words, he will always exist in the present, and in a mind that has no past or future, everything is at peace.

How long will I be here? Since he could be anywhere, anytime, he wondered whom he might meet. But then, he felt a bright, warm wave approaching from afar, and he thought about moving toward it.

His current existence was a balance of energy—the kind of energy that is sometimes unnecessary in life. A wave of more energetic beings began to draw him in.

It was as if *Avid* were moving in the direction of a wave of joy.

2

From above, the bright light gradually shifted to a green hue, and it began to resemble a city with a few buildings that had mud-colored roofs and a narrow street winding through brick fences surrounding the structures.

A food market in the center of Yangon, Myanmar, was set to open early in the morning. At the bazaar, a European man walked toward a variety store at the end of the street, passing stalls piled with fish, snacks, and vegetables. He was heading to a meditation center.

"How much is the desk clock on the top shelf?"

"1,700 *kyat*. Are you choosing this clock to give as a gift to someone?" the middle-aged, brown-skinned woman asked politely.

"You guessed it. I didn't have time to buy a gift for my teacher from my homeland."

"This is not a gift for a teacher. At the entrance to the northern center, there's a kiosk that sells books related to meditation. If you have time, you can walk farther up the main road and then down a little. If you choose a gift from there, you'll find better-quality items. There are only a few such shops around the food market. For our stall, we only sell necessities, mostly Chinese goods."

The tall man, wearing a tan hooded sweater and wool trousers to match, thanked the woman and walked back through the green-painted metal door. As soon as he entered the next street, he found the kiosk with wooden shelves in the doorway, just as the woman had described. The tall man looked around the counter, where meditation and religious books lined the shelves. He decided not to buy a gift, but a book titled *The Beauty Begins Not With The Visible but With The Invisible* caught his eye, so he bought it, slipped it into his maroon backpack, and walked out of the kiosk toward a low white house visible in the distance, beyond a long wooden bridge. *Avid* descended from above, observing it all. The towering man in the crimson clothes lived in Brussels, but it was easy to tell he was Dutch, not Belgian. As *Avid* focused his attention on the man, he felt a strong surge of energy guiding him, radiating from the European.

When the man entered the teachers' quarters at the meditation center, only one woman was sitting at a low table, looking at a note. The foreigner took off his shoes at the entrance and stood quietly, looking around.

Black-and-white portraits of several teachers hung on the walls. The woman slowly approached him, astonished to see him looking at the portraits of *Lady Sayadov, Sayaaji U Ba Khin, Saya Tetji,* and *Satyanarayan Goenka*.

"How are you? I am a humble servant. How may I help you?" she asked softly.

"I'm well, thank you. I had an appointment to meet Lama *Tipitakadhara* Ugandahamala. He recently visited Mongolia and returned. I got in touch with him before I left Amsterdam."

"*Ugandahama Bandid* is meditating alone in his tent. I will inform him of your arrival," the Burmese woman said as she stepped out gracefully. The tall man pulled up a chair at a wooden table, unpacked his backpack, and took out the book he had just purchased.

Observing all this, *Avid* followed the humble servant.

The center was nestled among palm trees, a large facility with rows of wooden houses and stone pathways running between them. The meditation center appeared deserted, as a 10-day meditation retreat had begun two days earlier, so all the meditators were sitting in *Padmasana* in the meditation hall, practicing *Anapana*—a form of meditation focused on the breath.

The servant walked along the cobblestone path between the buildings, entering through the gates of a structure with a golden top resembling a stupa, where people were meditating.

When *Avid* followed her inside, a bright blue light radiated from the space, and a powerful energy emanated skyward. Everyone meditating in the tent was connected to the sky by waves of energy. *Avid* rejoiced in this wave of energy. But there was an even brighter light at the back of the tent—it was the great Ugandkhamala Bandid in a deep state of meditation.

Avid saw and felt a multicolored, rainbow-like light rise from the monk's chakra, and he was irresistibly drawn to it. The warm, vibrant light surrounded him, and he became absorbed in the tranquility of Bandid's mind, as if intoxicated by a peaceful euphoria.

3

Bandid is a monk who received the title of *Tipitakadhara* after studying and memorizing all the *Scriptures of the Kanjur and the Danjur*, which were said to be revealed by God. The Great Bandida *Tipitakadhara* of Ugandkhamala is one of the most famous monks in Burma today. Born on February 19, 1968, in Mandalay, Burma, he began studying at the Buddhist monastery in his hometown at the age of eight. He began to study with the help of Burma's greatest clergy.

In 1988, at the age of 20, he was ordained a postulant, became a perfect monk, and, with the support of virtuous devotees, passed a series of exams.

Avid wonders why he had come to Mongolia and thought of Mongolia—colorful rainbows and the events that took place there, one after another.

When he arrives in Mongolia, the monk presents the *Lagshin* idol of the Buddha and his twenty-one disciples to Mongolia, and Shirendev, a meditation teacher, exalted all the sacred *lagshin* ashes a few days ago. *Avid* sees all this in its actual form, and when he comes to the door, he begins to recite the thought of the man who is waiting for *Tipitakadhara* Ugandkhamala.

Adrian Calvin, the man waiting at the door, is an assistant teacher at Dhamma Pajjota, a meditation center in a forested and agricultural area bordering Belgium, the Netherlands, and Germany.

When Ugandkhamala finishes his meditation, he goes to the man who waits for him at the door. The man seems to have some kind of connection to *Aajim*; the tall man is meditating with his eyes closed.

Adrian, who is in charge of renovating and expanding the meditation center in Belgium, lives in Brussels in the same apartment building as Jim Edmund.

Soon the monk enters the room, and the two begin their conversation. At first, they greet each other, talk a little about the meditation centers in Belgium and the Netherlands, and then move on to discuss their main topic.

"Dear teacher, many texts in the *Kanjur* mention that *Tushita* is the heavenly realm. The Dharmapada commentary also refers to the six divas of Kamadhatu in the Buddhist tradition, with *Tushita* being the fourth of the celestial worlds. It is said that *Tushita* can be reached through meditation. It is also known as the heavenly realm where Buddha Siddhartha Gautama resided before coming to this earth. Does the *Kanjur* say that *Tushita* helps us here on earth?"

"Yes, it does. *Tushita* is the abode of bodhisattvas, the beings born to help others. The heavens are always trying to assist us on earth, but the reason we feel helpless is that we are unable to receive their waves due to being bound by our kleshas (mental afflictions). Those who meditate can benefit because they gradually attune themselves to the same wave as the heavens.

"Four hundred years on earth is equal to a day and a night in *Tushita* heaven. It is written in the *Kanjur* that one month in *Tushita* is equivalent to 12,000 years for us, and that the lifespan of beings in *Tushita*, in our terms, is 576 million years.

"*Tushita* is the heavenly abode of all bodhisattvas. After all, it is a place where perfect enlightenment is to be achieved."

As their conversation continues, *Avid* begins to realize that he is still in the middle world, not in heaven.

Although *Avid* doesn't understand the connection between *Aajim* and this man called Adrian, he starts to sense that, in Adrian's subconscious, Jim Edmund's whereabouts and the disturbing waves coming from him must somehow be linked.

The discussion about Buddhism gradually fades from his awareness, and a bright light fills *Avid*'s vision. He begins to feel himself moving away.

As he ascends higher and higher, it feels as if he is getting closer to the sun, as the mist over Yangon starts to dissolve, bringing him great relief.

A few hours earlier, an English-speaking Russian lawyer had come to see him: "Now we have no choice but to take your case to the U.S. police and court. Although you are currently being held on Russian premises, we can no longer cover up the incident that took place on U.S. soil. If we hand you over to the authorities, you will be sentenced to death under the Death Penalty law for the murder of two people."

"What does that mean? I didn't shoot anyone!"

This is not a nightmare. He feels the grip of a dark, terrible force tightening around him, and he begins to lose his mind. But it all feels like an unbelievable lie. He still hopes that someone is playing a very realistic, though far from funny, practical joke on him.

Behind a barred window in a dungeon-like room, the light flickers momentarily. *Aajim* kneels to pray, staring at the dark sky. The night is black, with a faint blue glow. As he begins to realize that what is happening to him is real, he feels himself becoming more and more lifeless.

Long after Chen Yi had left the hotel that night, at two o'clock in the morning, a Chinese man burst in with his eyes wide open.

"I managed to collect our money, but a group of Russians is coming to kill us," he said.

As they rushed toward the Tatiana restaurant, *Aajim* was struck in the head by a Georgian-looking man. A faint sound of gunfire echoed in his disoriented mind. When he woke up the next morning, he found himself lying in the same dungeon as the Georgian. A group of Russians entered, wrapped a black cloth around his head, and took him to an unknown location where they detained him alone.

In the morning, they gave him a glass of water and a slice of bread. Meanwhile, the Russians—who were served ready-made meals from a Chinese restaurant—did not speak to him or serve him for five days.

"I am a British citizen! You are illegally detaining me. I didn't do anything. Where is my friend, Chen Yi?"

No matter how much he shouted, no one cared. After a few days, he fell ill and lost consciousness. When he woke up, he was in a Russian hospital.

One day, an English-speaking Russian visited him for the first time and spoke to him with a semblance of humanity.

"You shot and killed a Chinese man named Chen Yi and a well-known businessman named Eugene Ustinov, also known as *Pavel Korchagin*, a U.S. citizen," the man said. "Avtandil Aliko, the Georgian who was with you, has already confessed. If you don't cooperate and confess, your life will be on the line."

Aajim screamed and resisted. He even tried to escape from the hospital, but several burly Russians caught him and forced him back into bed. They treated him for four days before taking him back to the basement, where they covered his head with a black cloth bag.

Aajim had never, in his right mind, imagined he would encounter such terrible luck. After more than a month in the dungeon, he became desperate, realizing, with deep sadness, that his life was slipping away.

At that moment, *Avid* was watching him from above. For the first time, *Avid* was seeing the face of the man he had corresponded with for almost a year, though they had never met in person. Indeed, *Aajim* had the features of an Azerbaijani and could easily be mistaken for an Arab rather than a Mongolian.

Although *Avid* had been reborn in an unusually calm and lifeless heaven, he still didn't understand why he had first traveled to Burma and met those people, or why he was now connected to *Aajim*'s situation from the perspective of a Dutchman. The prison cell was located in the basement of an old building, and directly above it was a Russian-run disco club.

That night, there was a lot of noise in the club because a Russian band was scheduled to perform. *Avid* listened to two Russians talking.

"Alesha, let's get rid of that Mongolian in the basement today. It's pointless to keep him locked up much longer. We've already taken the money from Chen Yi, and now he's the last witness. He's dying anyway."

"Well, then, let's dump his body tonight. DTT is playing, and there will be a big crowd. Everything is lining up perfectly for us."

When *Avid* heard this, he looked down and saw the man listening to his own thoughts.

One of the Russians went down to the basement, unlocked the door of the dungeon where Aajiy was being held, and set fire to the circuit panel next to it. *Avid* rushed downstairs to wake *Aajim*, but he lay unconscious on the floor, unable to receive any waves. As the smoke filled the room, *Aajim* coughed and stirred. Seeing the open door, he struggled to his feet and staggered out.

By then, people were already shouting, "Fire!"

Screams filled the air, and people were running back and forth.

Aajim pushed through the crowd and stumbled out into the snow-covered street. As he stepped away from the chaos, he saw a yellow taxi approaching. He raised his hand, and the taxi stopped.

The yellow cab sped off through the snowy streets of Brooklyn.

A red fire truck passed them, its horn blaring.

Watching all of this from above, *Avid*'s heart became clearer.

"Now it's time for me to move on. I may live for 576 million years in the land of *Tushita*, and perhaps I will see you again. Or I may be born in hell for killing hundreds of dogs in my youth. But many, many years from now, I will probably remember you when I am reborn. However, Mongolia will still be there even after 575 million years."

This is the story of those who encountered stray dogs and, by karma and fate, did not wish to be reborn as human beings.

"Contemplation under a wintry sky, a study of the self within the infinite."

EPILOGUE

At the entrance to the cemetery, a man stood silently, watching the soft snow fall from the cloudy skies of Brussels. The *Laeken Cemetery* housed the tombs of famous kings, nobles, politicians, and other dignitaries.

Beneath his slanted black beret, a gray beard hung down, and he wore a pair of spectacles with glossy rims. The man took off his glasses and wiped them with a cloth he pulled from the pocket of his yellow leather jacket, which was paired with a woolen scarf. He stared at the giant statue before him. He was a man in his sixties, with an Asian face that reminded one of an artist.

A bronze statue called *The Thinker* stood before him, a muscular, naked giant with his right hand resting beneath his chin, deep in thought. The statue seemed to sway slightly in the falling snow.

Originally a place of worship for the Virgin Mary, *Laeken Cemetery* was established in 1831 as a burial ground for the royal family. It had been home to some of Europe's most celebrated figures since the Queen's burial in 1850. By the early 20th century, it had come to be compared to *Père Lachaise* in Paris, and it remains the only underground burial gallery in Northern Europe.

Aajim, also known as Jim Edmund, stood by the entrance of Laeken Cemetery, gazing at one of the world's most famous statues—*The Thinker* by *Auguste Rodin*. Many years ago, he kept his mother's ashes at home, intending to return them to her homeland. But when his stepfather passed away, he buried her ashes next to her second husband in the oldest church-style cemetery in Brussels. Before his death, his stepfather, Thomas Edmund, had written in his will that he wished to be cremated and buried in Laeken Cemetery, where he had bought a burial plot years earlier. Following Catholic tradition, Thomas had planned to be buried alongside his wife. According to his wishes, Jim buried him in a small tomb next to his mother's ashes.

Jim Edmund lost his job at the European Union after rumors began to circulate that he had been involved in a crime in the United States. However, he later found great success establishing a consulting firm to advise private, mostly startup companies. He was also appointed by the British government as an honorary consul to represent Mongolia. His father, Purevjal, had served as a consul representing Mongolia in the United Kingdom, and his son now represented Mongolia as a consul in the same country. It was a coincidence that seemed destined to happen for two generations of father and son.

A Ukrainian girl named Irina suddenly disappeared from his life as quickly as she had entered it. A Chinese man named Chen Yi also vanished. All that remained were newspaper reports claiming Chen had been killed by gunfire, possibly assassinated. After Xi Jinping's rise to power in the political struggle that began in China in the 2000s, a group led by Bo Xilai was imprisoned. Thousands of people disappeared, were executed, or incarcerated, and now no one remembers that time. When his stepfather died, he bequeathed the family house in central London to Jim, the house where Jim and his mother had lived. Jim sold the property for a great price and bought an apartment in Brussels. Outside the building, he hung a Mongolian flag and a sign on the door that read, "Honorary Consul of Mongolia to the United Kingdom." He had *Avid*'s computer from Mongolia, compiled *Avid*'s diaries with his own writings, and published this book, on the back cover of which he wrote:

My name is Purevjal Aajim.

I live in Bruges, Belgium.

I have kept a diary since I was 18 years old, which I sent to the esteemed Mongolian writer Avid, who was unable to finish his book and passed away at the age of 49.

Though I never had the chance to meet him, I completed and published the book of the author.

Needless to say, everything in this book is based on true stories.

Dedicated to the memory of the Mongolian writer Avid.

Respectfully yours,

Aajim Purevjal

THE END

Glossary of Mongolian and Cultural Terms

1. Aajim (Аажим)
    - Meaning: A Mongolian name implying something done gently or with care, reflecting cultural or familial significance.
    - Context: In the story, Aajim is a central character, symbolizing his connection to Mongolian heritage. His dual identity as Jim Edmund reflects the complexities of his cultural background and the themes of identity and belonging.
2. Aimag (Аймаг):
    - Meaning: A province or region in Mongolia.
    - Context: Used to describe the administrative divisions of Mongolia.
3. Airag (Айраг):
    - Meaning: A traditional Mongolian alcoholic beverage made from fermented mare's milk.
    - Context: A popular drink in Mongolian culture, often consumed during celebrations.
4. Aldous Huxley:
    - Meaning: A famous English writer and philosopher, best known for his dystopian novel "Brave New World."
    - Context: The epilogue opens with a quote from Aldous Huxley: "Maybe this world is another planet's hell," setting a contemplative tone for the conclusion of the story.
5. Altai Mountains (Алтай):
    - Meaning: A mountain range in Central and East Asia, stretching across Mongolia, China, Russia, and Kazakhstan.
    - Context: Represents the rugged and diverse landscape of Mongolia.
6. Anapana (Анапана):
    - Meaning: A meditation technique that involves observing the breath to focus the mind.

- Context: The practice being performed by the meditators.
7. Anji (Анжи):
    - Meaning: A colloquial term for "father" or "paternal figure" in Mongolian.
    - Context: Refers to a father figure, used with affection or respect.
8. Arhat (Архат):
    - Meaning: In Buddhism, a person who has attained enlightenment and is free from the cycle of rebirth.
    - Context: Represents spiritual achievement and the pursuit of enlightenment.
9. Ataman (Атаман)
    - Meaning: "Ataman" is a historical term used in Russia and Ukraine to refer to a leader or chief, particularly of Cossack communities. The ataman was a military leader or the head of a village, regiment, or army group, responsible for leading the community in battle and making decisions on behalf of the group.
    - Context: In the story, the term "ataman" is used to evoke the historical and cultural significance of leadership within Cossack communities or to draw a parallel to a character who exhibits leadership qualities or authority.
10. Auguste Rodin (Огюст Роден):
    - Meaning: A French sculptor, widely regarded as the progenitor of modern sculpture, best known for works like "The Thinker" and "The Gates of Hell."
    - Context: The statue of "The Thinker" mentioned in the epilogue is one of Rodin's most famous works.
11. Avid (Авид)
    - Meaning: Avid is a Mongolian male name that derives from "Amitabha," meaning "Timeless Light" in Mongolian. Avid represents one of the Five Noble Gods in Mongolian culture. Associated with eliminating cravings and fostering actions that bring positive outcomes, God Avid vowed, "If someone in pain and at

a dead end remembers my name with reverence, they will be reborn in a holy place."
  - Context: In the story, Avid is the protagonist whose name reflects a deep spiritual connection. His life, marked by intellectual exploration and emotional complexity, mirrors the symbolic significance of the name, representing renewal, enlightenment, and the overcoming of life's challenges.
12. Ayurzana (Аюурзана)
    - Meaning: A Mongolian male name combining "Ayur," meaning "longevity," and "Zana," relating to "good fortune" or "protection." The name is associated with wishes for a long, prosperous life.
    - Context: In the story, Ayurzana is a historical figure who led the 1932 Tariat uprising. His legacy directly influences the storyline, particularly through his granddaughter Khanddolgor, adding historical significance to the narrative.
13. Baatar (Баатар):
    - Meaning: A title meaning "hero" or "warrior" in Mongolian.
    - Context: Symbolizes bravery and valor in Mongolian culture.
14. Baldantseren (Балданцэрэн):
    - Meaning: A Mongolian male name, belonging to a minor character in the story who is suggested as a contact in Bulgan.
    - Context: Reflects Mongolian naming conventions and cultural references.
15. Badamsuren (Бадамсүрэн)
    - Meaning: A Mongolian name combining "Badam" (Бадам), meaning "lotus," a symbol of purity and enlightenment, and "Suren" (Сүрэн), meaning "strength" or "power." The name can be interpreted as "Lotus Strength" or "Pure Power."

- Context: In the story, Badamsuren is a character whose name embodies qualities of purity, resilience, and spiritual growth. The use of this name highlights Mongolian cultural and spiritual values, often tied to Buddhist symbolism.

16. Bayarsaikhan (Баярсайхан)
    - Meaning: Bayarsaikhan is a Mongolian name composed of two elements: "Bayar" (Баяр) meaning "joy" or "happiness," and "Saikhan" (Сайхан) meaning "beautiful" or "good." The name can be interpreted as "Joyful Beauty" or "Happy and Beautiful."
    - Context: In the story, Bayarsaikhan is a character whose name reflects a positive or cheerful disposition.

17. Bogd Khan (Богд Хаан):
    - Meaning: The religious and political leader of Mongolia, considered a reincarnation of the Bodhisattva.
    - Context: Represents the fusion of religious and political authority in Mongolia.

18. Bogd Mountain (Богд Уул)
    - Meaning: Bogd Mountain, also known as Bogd Khan Mountain, is a prominent mountain located just south of Ulaanbaatar, Mongolia's capital. The name "Bogd" translates to "Holy" or "Sacred," and the mountain holds significant cultural and spiritual importance in Mongolian tradition.
    - Context: Bogd Mountain is one of the four sacred mountains surrounding Ulaanbaatar and has been revered for centuries as a place of spiritual significance. It is a popular site for pilgrimage, meditation, and nature worship, particularly among Buddhists.

19. Bogd Nasten Tumen Amgalant (Богд Настэн Түмэн Амгалант)
    - Meaning: The name "Bogd Nasten Tumen Amgalant" can be translated as "Holy, Peaceful, and Blessed Place." The term "Bogd" is often associated with something sacred or holy, while "Nasten Tumen Amgalant" emphasizes the ideas of peace, tranquility, and sanctity.

- Context: This temple was personally named by Khubilai Khan in 1279, the year of the unification of all of China. In the story, the temple serves as a symbol of spiritual authority and cultural heritage, tying the characters' experiences to the broader historical and religious context of the Mongol Empire.
20. Boortsog (Боорцог)
    - Meaning: Boortsog is a traditional Mongolian fried dough, often served as a snack or dessert. It is made from flour, butter, sugar, and milk, then shaped into small pieces and deep-fried until golden brown.
    - Context: In the story, boortsog is mentioned as part of a traditional meal, highlighting the character's connection to Mongolian culinary traditions. It is a common treat during celebrations or as an everyday snack, reflecting the hospitality and cultural practices of Mongolian households.
21. Borscht (Борщ):
    - Meaning: A traditional Eastern European soup made from beets, popular in Russia, Ukraine, and other Slavic countries.
    - Context: Reflects the cultural significance of food in the region.
22. Bulgan (Булган):
    - Meaning: A province (aimag) in northern Mongolia, as well as the name of its capital city.
    - Context: Represents a region in Mongolia, known for its scenic beauty and historical significance.
23. Buuz (Бууз):
    - Meaning: A traditional Mongolian steamed dumpling filled with meat, usually lamb or beef.
    - Context: A popular dish in Mongolian cuisine, often served during celebrations.

24. Catholic Burial Traditions (Католические похоронные традиции):
    - Meaning: Refers to the customs and rites followed by Catholics regarding death and burial, often involving specific rituals, prayers, and the consecration of burial grounds.
    - Context: Jim Edmund's stepfather followed strict Catholic traditions, which influenced his burial arrangements in Laeken Cemetery.
25. Chinggis Khaan (Чингис Хаан):
    - Meaning: The Mongolian name for Genghis Khan, the founder and Great Khan of the Mongol Empire.
    - Context: Represents the legacy and impact of Genghis Khan on world history.
26. Choir (Чойр):
    - Meaning: A town in Govisumber Province, Mongolia.
    - Context: Represents a specific location in Mongolia, potentially significant to the story.
27. Courchevel (Куршевель):
    - Meaning: A famous ski resort in the French Alps, known for luxury and attracting wealthy visitors, including Russian oligarchs.
    - Context: Associated with high-profile events and scandals involving Russian elites.
28. Dalai Eej (Далай Ээж)
    - Meaning: "Dalai Eej" translates to "Mother Ocean" in Mongolian, a term of reverence personifying the ocean as a nurturing, life-giving force.
    - Context: In the story, "Dalai Eej" is mentioned as the name of a market, evoking the idea of abundance and sustenance. The term reflects the cultural significance of the ocean in Mongolian tradition, symbolizing respect and reliance on natural forces.

29. Dalai Lama (Далай-лама):
    - Meaning: The spiritual leader of Tibetan Buddhism, often regarded as the reincarnation of Avalokiteshvara, the bodhisattva of compassion.
    - Context: A highly respected figure in Mongolian Buddhism as well.
30. Datsan (Дацан):
    - Meaning: A term for a Buddhist university or monastic college where monks study philosophy and other subjects.
    - Context: Places of learning and spiritual practice within Tibetan Buddhism.
31. Deel (Дээл)
    - Meaning: A deel is a traditional Mongolian garment worn by both men and women. It is a long, robe-like piece of clothing made from thick, durable fabric, often adorned with intricate patterns or embroidery. The deel is typically fastened with a belt or sash at the waist and can be worn in various styles depending on the occasion or region.
    - Context: In the story, a deel is worn by characters symbolizing their cultural identity and connection to Mongolian heritage. The garment represents the enduring traditions of Mongolia, often passed down through generations and adapted to different social and environmental contexts.
32. Demchigdonrov (Дэмчигдонров)
    - Meaning: Demchigdonrov, also known as De Wang (德王), was a Mongolian prince and political figure during the early 20th century. He was the leader of Inner Mongolia's independence movement and collaborated with Japanese forces during World War II to establish the short-lived puppet state of Mengjiang.
    - Context: In the story, a reference to Demchigdonrov evokes themes of nationalism, collaboration, and the complex history of Mongolia during the turbulent period

of the early 20th century. His name reflects on the struggles for Mongolian identity and autonomy, as well as the difficult choices faced by leaders in times of political upheaval.

33. Dhamma Pajjota (Дхамма Паджота):
    - Meaning: A Vipassana meditation center in Belgium.
    - Context: Connected to the character Adrian Calvin, who works at this center.

34. Doctor Sainnamar (Доктор Сайннамар)
    - Meaning: "Doctor Sainnamar" refers to a character in the story, where "Sainnamar" is a Mongolian name. The name "Sainnamar" could be derived from "Сайн" (Sain), meaning "good" or "virtuous," and "Намар" (Namar), meaning "autumn" in Mongolian.
    - Context: In the story, Doctor Sainnamar is a figure of authority and expertise involved in medical or scholarly activities. The name Sainnamar implies a personality that embodies wisdom, goodness, or a connection to the autumn season, reflecting the character's demeanor or life stage.

35. Donrovyn Namdag (Донровын Намдаг)
    - Meaning: Donrovyn Namdag was a renowned Mongolian writer, playwright, and poet, known for his contributions to modern Mongolian literature in the 20th century. He played a significant role in shaping Mongolian literary and cultural identity during a time of great political and social change in Mongolia.
    - Context: In the story, the reference to Donrovyn Namdag evokes themes of Mongolian cultural heritage, literature, and the struggles of intellectuals. His works often explored complex human emotions and the impact of societal transformations.

36. Dundgovi Aimag (Дундговь аймаг)
    - Meaning: A province located in central Mongolia, translating to "Middle Gobi." Known for its vast steppe

    landscapes and nomadic culture, it represents the harsh yet beautiful Mongolian environment.
  - Context: In the story, Dundgovi Aimag establishes a specific geographic and cultural setting, providing insight into the environment, lifestyle, or background of certain characters. It reflects the traditional Mongolian way of life, influencing the story's mood or themes.
37. Events in Mongolia in the Mid-1990s
  - Meaning: A period of significant transition following the democratic revolution of 1990, marked by political reform, economic hardship, and cultural revival.
  - Context: In the narrative, these events provide the backdrop for the protagonist's reflections on his Mongolian heritage. The social and political developments influence the characters' understanding of their identities and the broader historical context of their lives.
38. Erdenet (Эрдэнэт):
  - Meaning: A major city in northern Mongolia, known for its large copper and molybdenum mining industry.
  - Context: Represents Mongolia's industrial landscape.
39. Ereen (Эрээний):
  - Meaning: Refers to Ereenhot, a border town in China near Mongolia.
  - Context: Represents the connection and interaction between Mongolia and China.
40. Ferme ta gueule, ferme ta gueule
  - Meaning: A French phrase meaning "Shut up, shut up!" with "gueule" being a slang term for "mouth," more vulgar than the standard "bouche."
  - Context: In the story, this phrase is used where one character forcefully demands silence from another. The repetition intensifies the command, indicating the speaker's frustration or anger.
41. Finlandia:
  - Meaning: A brand of Finnish vodka.

- Context: Represents an international element in the story, highlighting the character's tastes or experiences.

42. Five-ruble shelf
    - Meaning: A cheaply made or inexpensive shelf, referring to mass-produced items that are affordable and accessible, often used for practical rather than aesthetic purposes.
    - Context: In the story, the "five-ruble shelf" is described as being cluttered with various artistic supplies, emphasizing its utilitarian function. The term evokes a sense of frugality or simplicity, as the shelf is likely not valued for its craftsmanship but for its affordability and usefulness.

43. Franz Kafka (Франц Кафка):
    - Meaning: A Czech writer known for his surreal and existential works, such as "The Metamorphosis" and "The Trial."
    - Context: Kafka's diaries are referenced, connecting to the story's themes of alienation and existential dread.

44. Gandan (Гандан):
    - Meaning: Short for Gandantegchinlen Monastery, a prominent Tibetan Buddhist monastery in Ulaanbaatar, Mongolia.
    - Context: A significant religious site in Mongolia, often a place of worship and pilgrimage.

45. Ger (Гэр):
    - Meaning: A traditional Mongolian yurt, a portable round tent covered with skins or felt.
    - Context: Represents the nomadic lifestyle and cultural heritage of Mongolia.

46. Gerege (Гэрэгэ):
    - Meaning: A diplomatic passport or tablet used in the Mongol Empire, often carried by envoys to signify their authority.
    - Context: Symbolizes the power and reach of the Mongol Empire, as well as diplomatic immunity.

47. Gerelsaikhan (Гэрэлсайхан)
    - Meaning: A Mongolian name meaning "Beautiful Light" or "Bright and Good."
    - Context: In the story, Gerelsaikhan is a character who becomes involved with Oyunaa, further complicating the emotional landscape. His relationship with Oyunaa highlights themes of infidelity and shifting dynamics in the characters' lives.
48. Gobi Desert (Говь):
    - Meaning: A vast desert region in Mongolia and northern China.
    - Context: Represents the harsh environment and natural beauty of Mongolia.
49. Gou Hua Painting (国画)
    - Meaning: Traditional Chinese painting, known as "guó huà" (国画), which involves brush and ink on paper or silk. It is characterized by delicate brushwork, subtle use of color, and poetic elements, focusing on landscapes, flowers, birds, and figures.
    - Context: In the story, the view of the Himalayas from Avid's hotel room is compared to a "go hua painting," emphasizing the serene and picturesque quality of the landscape, much like the idealized scenes often depicted in traditional Chinese art.
50. Guangping Leave
    - Meaning: A term referring to a significant or symbolic departure, specifically related to a historical or ceremonial context. The term "Guangping leave" likely alludes to an important event during the fall of the Yuan Dynasty when the rebel leader Zhu Yuanzhang captured the region of Guangping, signaling the decline of Mongol rule in China.
    - Context: In the story, "Guangping leave" is used to describe the departure of Zhu Yuanzhang after a pivotal victory, which foreshadowed the end of Togoontumur's reign over the Yuan Dynasty. This event is portrayed as

an ominous turning point, adding layers of historical weight and prophetic significance to the narrative.

51. Gvozd (Гвоздь)
    - Meaning: "Gvozd" is a Russian word that means "nail" (as in a metal nail used in construction or carpentry).
    - Context: In the story, "Gvozd" (Nails) is the name of Avid's rock music band in his youth.

52. Hudag (Худаг)
    - Meaning: In Mongolian, "hudag" refers to a well. It can also metaphorically refer to narrow alleys or lanes in urban settings, similar to the Chinese "hutong."
    - Context: In the story, "hudag" evokes a sense of traditional or older parts of a city, implying a connection to cultural heritage and daily life centered around communal water wells or narrow urban neighborhoods.

53. Hohhot (Хөх хот)
    - Meaning: Hohhot (also spelled Huhhot or Hohhut) is the capital city of the Inner Mongolia Autonomous Region in northern China. The name "Hohhot" comes from the Mongolian word "хөх хот" (khökh khot), which means "Blue City." The city is an important cultural, economic, and political center in the region.
    - Context: In the story, the reference to Hohhot indicates a connection to Mongolian culture, as the city is a hub for Mongolian ethnic identity within China.

54. Ingoda (Ингода)
    - Meaning: A river in southeastern Siberia, Russia, part of the Amur River basin, known for its natural beauty and role in local ecosystems.
    - Context: Mentioning the Ingoda River in the story may highlight the geographical and cultural connections between Siberia and Mongolia, or evoke the remote, natural landscape of Siberia relevant to the setting or background of certain characters.

55. Ikh Khuraldai (Их Хуралдай):
    - Meaning: The Great Assembly or council of Mongolian nobles that played a key role in decision-making in the Mongol Empire.
    - Context: Represents the political system and governance of the Mongol Empire.
56. Ikh Tenger State Residence (Их Тэнгэрийн Төрийн Ордон)
    - Meaning: The Ikh Tenger State Residence is a government-owned complex in Mongolia, located in the Ikh Tenger Valley near Ulaanbaatar. The name "Ikh Tenger" translates to "Great Sky" or "Great Heaven," reflecting the Mongolian reverence for the sky or heaven.
    - Context: The Ikh Tenger State Residence is used for official government functions, hosting important national and international meetings, and accommodating visiting dignitaries. In the story, a reference to the Ikh Tenger State Residence underscores the significance of a political event or highlight the involvement of high-ranking officials in the narrative.
57. Ikh Zasag (Их Засаг):
    - Meaning: The Great Yassa, the legal code established by Genghis Khan.
    - Context: Represents law, order, and governance in the Mongol Empire.
58. Irichka, Irichka! Kakimi sudibami! (Иричка, Иричка! Какими судьбами!)
    - Meaning: A Russian phrase meaning "Irichka, Irichka! By what fate do we meet!" often used to express surprise or curiosity about an unexpected encounter.
    - Context: In the story, this phrase is used during an unexpected meeting between characters, with the diminutive "Irichka" suggesting familiarity and affection. The phrase highlights a moment of serendipity or coincidence in the narrative.

59. Javzandulam (Жавзандулам)
    - Meaning: A Mongolian female name combining "Javzan," associated with the Buddhist term "Javzandamba," and "Dulam," meaning "kindness" or "gentleness." The name could be interpreted as "Holy Kindness" or "Blessed Gentle One."
    - Context: In the story, the name Javzandulam highlights the character's cultural or spiritual background, indicating a connection to Mongolian traditions, Buddhism, or a nurturing personality. The use of this name emphasizes the character's deep-rooted connection to Mongolian heritage.
60. Kanjur and Danjur (Канжур и Данжур):
    - Meaning: Collections of Tibetan Buddhist scriptures. The Kanjur is the translation of the Buddha's word, and the Danjur is the commentary on it.
    - Context: Ugandkhamala Bandid is described as having studied these scriptures.
61. Karakorum (Хархорум):
    - Meaning: The ancient capital of the Mongol Empire under Genghis Khan and his successors.
    - Context: Represents the historical and cultural heritage of the Mongol Empire.
62. Kasaya (Касая):
    - Meaning: A traditional Buddhist monk's robe, often saffron or maroon in color, symbolizing renunciation and humility.
    - Context: Represents the spiritual and ascetic life of a Buddhist monk, often seen in descriptions of religious characters or settings.
63. Khanddolgor (Ханддолгор)
    - Meaning: A Mongolian female name combining "Khand," derived from the Tibetan word for "goddess," and "Dolgor," meaning "tender" or "delicate." The name conveys grace, femininity, and spiritual purity.

- Context: In the story, Khanddolgor is a character whose name reflects a combination of strength and gentleness, embodying both divine qualities and a tender nature. The name often implies high moral standing and spiritual significance, consistent with Mongolian cultural values.
64. Khatanbaatar (Хатанбаатар):
    - Meaning: A title meaning "Heroic Lord" or "Heroic Warrior," often used to refer to national heroes.
    - Context: Symbolizes bravery and heroism in Mongolian history.
65. Khongor (Хонгор):
    - Meaning: A common name for a beloved person or animal, also a place name in Mongolia.
    - Context: Represents endearment and familiarity in Mongolian culture.
66. Kinokuniya Bookstore:
    - Meaning: A famous Japanese bookstore chain known for its extensive selection of books in multiple languages.
    - Context: Avid mentions purchasing books from this store, highlighting its significance as a literary hub.
67. Khatan (Хатан):
    - Meaning: A title for a queen or empress in Mongolian culture.
    - Context: Represents the status and power of women in the royal court.
68. Khatun (Хатун):
    - Meaning: A title for a queen or noblewoman in Mongolian and Turkic cultures.
    - Context: Represents the historical role and status of women in Mongolian society.
69. Khöömii (Хөөмий):
    - Meaning: A traditional Mongolian throat singing technique.
    - Context: Represents a unique aspect of Mongolian musical tradition.

70. Khulan (Хулан):
    - Meaning: A type of wild ass native to Mongolia, also a female given name in Mongolia.
    - Context: Represents the natural environment of Mongolia or may be used as a character's name.
71. Khurelchuluun (Хүрэлчулуун)
    - Meaning: A Mongolian name combining "Khurel" (bronze or copper) and "chuluun" (stone), symbolizing strength and resilience.
    - Context: The name Khurelchuluun reflects the character's strength and endurance, possibly representing their connection to Mongolian heritage and values. It might highlight qualities of toughness or durability in the character.
72. Kyat:
    - Meaning: The currency of Myanmar (Burma).
    - Context: The value of the desk clock is given in Kyat, indicating the setting is in Myanmar.
73. Kyakhta (Кяхта)
    - Meaning: A town in Buryatia, Russia, near the Mongolian border, historically significant as a trading post between Russia and China.
    - Context: In the story, Kyakhta is mentioned in relation to its historical importance in trade and cultural exchange. Its inclusion emphasizes themes of trade, historical connections, or the geopolitical significance of the border region.
74. Lady Sayadov (Burmese: ဒေါ်စရဒေါ်)
    - Meaning: A revered female meditation teacher in Burmese Buddhist tradition, with "Sayadov" being an honorific for highly respected figures.
    - Context: In the story, Lady Sayadov's portrait hangs in a meditation center, adding depth to the spiritual themes and highlighting the influence of Buddhist teachings on the characters.

75. Laeken Cemetery (Кладбище Лакен):
    - Meaning: A famous cemetery in Brussels, Belgium, known for being the burial site of royalty and notable figures.
    - Context: The location where the epilogue takes place, emphasizing its historical and cultural significance. Represents themes of death, memory, and legacy.
76. Lagshin (Лагшин):
    - Meaning: In Tibetan Buddhism, Lagshin refers to the physical form or body of an enlightened being or deity.
    - Context: Refers to the sacred aspects of the physical form in a spiritual context.
77. Mahamudra:
    - Meaning: A term from Tibetan Buddhism referring to the "great seal," a meditative practice focusing on the nature of mind and reality.
    - Context: A concept related to spiritual practice and enlightenment.
78. Mandal (Мандал):
    - Meaning: A term used in Tibetan Buddhism for a spiritual and ritual symbol representing the universe.
    - Context: Represents spiritual completeness and the cosmos.
79. Manzushir (Манзушир):
    - Meaning: A Buddhist monastery located in the Töv Province of Mongolia.
    - Context: Represents Mongolia's rich religious history and monastic traditions.
80. March 8 (International Women's Day)
    - Meaning: International Women's Day, celebrated on March 8th, is a significant public holiday in Mongolia dedicated to honoring and appreciating women.
    - Context: In the story, the mention of "Happy March 8!" reflects the cultural importance of this day in Mongolia. The holiday is widely recognized and celebrated across

the country, and its observance underscores the respect and value placed on women in Mongolian society.
81. Matrosskaya Tishina (Матросская тишина)
    - Meaning: A notorious prison in Moscow, Russia, known for holding high-profile political prisoners. The name translates to "Sailor's Silence."
    - Context: A reference to Matrosskaya Tishina in the story evokes the harsh conditions and political overtones associated with this prison. It implies involvement in serious legal or political issues, underscoring the gravity of a character's situation.
82. Mikroraion (Микрорайон)
    - Meaning: "Mikroraion" is a Russian term that translates to "microdistrict" or "residential neighborhood." It refers to a type of urban planning prevalent in the former Soviet Union and other Eastern Bloc countries, including Mongolia.
    - Context: In the story, the term "mikroraion" is used to describe the setting of a character's home or the environment in which certain events take place. The use of this term reflects the Soviet-influenced urban planning that shaped many cities in Mongolia.
83. MNT (Mongolian Tögrög, ₮)
    - Meaning: The official currency of Mongolia, the Tögrög, with the symbol ₮ and ISO code MNT.
    - Context: In the story, MNT denotes the currency used in financial transactions, such as a character asking for a loan of 900,000 MNT. It anchors the story in a Mongolian setting, reflecting the local monetary system.
84. Morin Khuur (Морин хуур):
    - Meaning: The Horsehead Fiddle, a traditional Mongolian string instrument.
    - Context: Represents Mongolian music and cultural expression.

85. Naadam (Наадам):
    - Meaning: A traditional festival in Mongolia, featuring the "Three Manly Games" of wrestling, horse racing, and archery.
    - Context: Represents Mongolian culture and national pride.
86. Naturmort (натюрморт)
    - Meaning: Derived from the French "nature morte," meaning "still life," it refers to a genre of art depicting inanimate objects, often arranged to highlight texture, light, and form.
    - Context: In the story, the items in Avid's hotel room—a brass teapot and two glazed bowls—are described as being "prepared for a naturmort." This emphasizes the static, carefully arranged appearance of the objects, evoking the artistic tradition of still life painting where everyday items are given aesthetic and symbolic significance.
87. Nikolai (Николай):
    - Meaning: A common Russian male name, but in this context, it refers to "Nikolai Vodka," a brand of vodka.
    - Context: Indicates the cultural or social environment where certain products or names are commonly recognized.
88. Noyon (Ноён):
    - Meaning: A title for a nobleman or lord in Mongolian society.
    - Context: Represents the aristocratic class and social hierarchy in Mongolia.
89. Ohotnichyi (Охотничий):
    - Meaning: "Hunter's" or "Hunting." This refers to a brand of cigarettes or a type of cigarette commonly associated with hunters in Russia.
    - Context: Symbolizes something rugged or connected to the outdoors.

90. Orosoo (Оросоо)
    - Meaning: "Orosoo" is a Mongolian female name. It is derived from the Mongolian word "Орос" (Oros), meaning "Russian," with "oo" added as a diminutive or affectionate suffix. The name indicates a cultural or familial connection to Russia.
    - Context: In the story, a character named Orosoo reflects cultural or personal ties between Mongolia and Russia. The use of this name suggests a background that involves Russian influence or heritage, highlighting the historical and social connections between the two countries.
91. Oyunaa (Оюунаа)
    - Meaning: A Mongolian female name derived from "oyun," meaning "wisdom" or "intellect," with the suffix "-aa" as a diminutive or affectionate form.
    - Context: In the story, Oyunaa is Avid's wife, with whom he has a strained and complex relationship. Despite the turmoil, Oyunaa's presence in Avid's life is significant, as their relationship plays a central role in exploring love, loss, and the search for meaning.
92. Oyunchimeg (Оюунчимэг)
    - Meaning: A Mongolian female name meaning "Adornment of Wisdom" or "Decoration of the Mind."
    - Context: In the story, Oyunchimeg is Avid's wife, whose marriage becomes strained over time, leading to emotional distance and eventual separation. Her character represents the challenges of maintaining love and connection in the face of life's hardships.
93. Padmasana (Падмасана):
    - Meaning: A cross-legged sitting posture used in meditation, also known as the Lotus position.
    - Context: Practiced by the meditators in the story.
94. Pavel Korchagin (Павел Корчагин):
    - Meaning: The protagonist of the Soviet novel "How the Steel Was Tempered" by Nikolai Ostrovsky.

- Context: Symbolizes resilience, dedication, or Soviet cultural influence.

95. Père Lachaise (Пер Лашез):
    - Meaning: The largest cemetery in Paris, France, known for being the resting place of many famous individuals, including artists, writers, and musicians.
    - Context: Laeken Cemetery is compared to Père Lachaise, highlighting its importance as a burial site for notable figures.

96. Rakh (Pax)
    - Meaning: In Mongolian folklore and ancient beliefs, "Rakh" refers to a mythical dragon that is believed to cause solar eclipses by swallowing the sun. This dragon is associated with the superstition that during a total solar eclipse, people would make loud noises, such as banging pots and pans, to scare away the dragon and restore sunlight.
    - Context: In the story, the mention of "Rakh" serves to illustrate traditional Mongolian beliefs surrounding solar eclipses.

97. Rodin's "The Thinker" (Мыслитель Родена):
    - Meaning: A famous bronze sculpture by Auguste Rodin, depicting a man deep in thought, symbolizing philosophy and contemplation.
    - Context: The statue is mentioned in connection with Aajim's reflections in the cemetery, symbolizing deep contemplation and existential thought.

98. Russkaya Dusha (Русская Душа)
    - Meaning: "Russkaya Dusha" translates to "Russian Soul," representing the spiritual and emotional depth, resilience, and compassion unique to Russian culture.
    - Context: In the story, this term conveys the profound emotional or philosophical reflections of a character with a Russian background, emphasizing the enigmatic and soulful nature of the situation or dialogue. The term

evokes a sense of identity and collective experience that is quintessentially Russian.

99. Samandabadra:
    - Meaning: Likely a misspelling or variation of "Samantabhadra," a bodhisattva in Mahayana Buddhism symbolizing universal benevolence and virtue.
    - Context: Relates to the spiritual or religious elements of the story.
100. Satyanara Goenka (Burmese: ဦးဂိုအင်ကာ):
    - Meaning: An Indian teacher of Vipassana meditation, instrumental in spreading the practice globally.
    - Context: In the story, Goenka's teachings highlight the global influence of Vipassana meditation, emphasizing the significance of mindfulness and meditation in the characters' spiritual journeys.
101. Saya Tetji (Burmese: ဆရာကြီး တက်ကြီး):
    - Meaning: A renowned Burmese meditation teacher known for transmitting the Vipassana tradition. "Saya" or "Sayagyi" means "respected teacher," and "Tetji" or "Thetgyi" was his name.
    - Context: In the story, Saya Tetji's presence symbolizes the deep-rooted tradition of Vipassana meditation, adding to the spiritual atmosphere and emphasizing mindfulness and the pursuit of inner peace.
102. Sayaaji U Ba Khin (Burmese: ဆရာကြီး ဦးဘခင်):
    - Meaning: A prominent Burmese meditation teacher who revived Vipassana meditation in the 20th century. "Sayaaji" is an honorific meaning "respected teacher," and "U" is a Burmese honorific for men.
    - Context: In the story, Sayaaji U Ba Khin's teachings play a subtle role in the spiritual atmosphere, reflecting the inner journeys of the characters seeking deeper understanding and peace through meditation.

103. Scriptures of the Kanjur and the Danjur
      - Meaning: The Kanjur (Sanskrit: काङ्ग्युर, Kāṅgyur) and the Danjur (Sanskrit: ताङ्ग्युर, Tāṅgyur) are two significant collections of Tibetan Buddhist scriptures, essential for understanding and practicing Tibetan Buddhism.
      - Context: In the story, the scriptures underscore the spiritual and scholarly significance of Tipitakadhara Ugandahama Bandid, highlighting his role as a revered teacher in the Buddhist tradition. The mention of these texts roots the narrative in the rich tradition of Tibetan Buddhism.
104. Secret History of the Mongols (Монголын нууц товчоо, Mongolyn nuuts tovchoo)
      - Meaning: The oldest surviving Mongolian literary work, an epic chronicle from the 13th century detailing the life of Genghis Khan and the early Mongol Empire.
      - Context: In the story, references to the "Secret History of the Mongols" evoke Mongolia's rich historical and cultural heritage, particularly the legacy of Genghis Khan, influencing the characters' identity and values.
105. Servalat:
      - Meaning: Likely a variation of "Cervelat," a type of smoked sausage popular in Europe.
      - Context: Represents European cuisine and may tie into a scene involving food or drink.
106. Shaman (Шаман):
      - Meaning: A spiritual healer and leader in indigenous and traditional religions, particularly in Siberia and Mongolia.
      - Context: Represents the spiritual traditions and practices of Mongolia and surrounding regions.
107. Soviet Bloc (Советский блок):
      - Meaning: The group of socialist states under the influence of the Soviet Union during the Cold War.

- Context: Represents the political and historical influence of the Soviet Union on Mongolia and other countries.
108. Soyombo (Соёмбо):
    - Meaning: A symbol in the Mongolian script, also found on the national flag of Mongolia, representing freedom and independence.
    - Context: Represents Mongolian identity and the values of freedom.
109. Tang (Танг):
    - Meaning: A traditional Mongolian fermented dairy product, usually made from mare's milk.
    - Context: In traditional Mongolian medicine, tang is valued for its probiotic properties and is believed to aid digestion and boost immunity. Its mention in the story emphasizes the cultural and medicinal importance of dairy in Mongolian life.
110. Tatiana nightclub:
    - Meaning: A fictional or real establishment named after a common Russian female name, often associated with elegance and tradition.
    - Context: The nightclub serves as a crucial setting for plot developments.
111. Tengri (Тэнгэр):
    - Meaning: The sky god in Mongolian and Turkic shamanistic beliefs.
    - Context: Represents the spiritual connection between the Mongolian people and the heavens.
112. The burning of Jordan Bruno to the story of the horrible bliss
    - Meaning: Refers to the execution of Giordano Bruno, an Italian philosopher burned at the stake in 1600 for heresy by the Roman Catholic Church. "The story of the horrible bliss" refers to the paradox of martyrdom, where suffering is seen as a path to divine reward or bliss.
    - Context: In the story, the narrator expresses disdain for the violent and dogmatic aspects of Christianity. The reference to Bruno's execution highlights the narrator's

skepticism towards religious history and its brutal consequences.

113. Tipitakadhara
    - Meaning: A title meaning "Bearer of the Tipitaka," combining "Tipitaka" (Sanskrit: त्रिपिटक, Tripiṭaka), the Buddhist scriptures, and "dhara" (Sanskrit: धार, Dhāra), given to a monk who has mastered the Buddhist scriptures, the Tipitaka.
    - Context: In the story, the character Tipitakadhara Ugandahama Bandid is a monk of great respect and scholarly accomplishments, representing spiritual authority and the pursuit of enlightenment.

114. Togon-Temur the Great Emperor of the Dai Yuan Dynasty (Тогоон-Төмөр)
    - Meaning: The last emperor of the Yuan Dynasty, also known as Toghon Temür, whose reign marked the end of Mongol rule in China and the retreat of the Yuan court to the Mongolian steppe, continuing as the Northern Yuan. His name, *Togon* (Тогоон), means "pot," and *Temur* (Төмөр) means "iron," translating to "Iron Pot." The spelling *Togon-Temur* is based on the *Britannica Encyclopedia*.
    - Context: Togon-Temur's reign symbolizes the decline of the Mongol Empire in China and the persistence of Mongol identity and power in the steppe as the Northern Yuan Dynasty. His leadership and legacy are referenced in the story to evoke themes of historical transition and resilience.
    - Context: In the novel, references to Togon-temur evoke themes of the rise and fall of empires, the transience of power, and the connections between Mongolian history and the protagonist's identity. As a historical figure, Togon-temur represents the significant legacy that influences the characters' understanding of their own place in history and the world.

115. Tržní kolonáda
- Meaning: "Tržní kolonáda" translates to "Market Colonnade," a historic wooden colonnade in Karlovy Vary, Czech Republic.
- Context: In the story, a reference to "Tržní kolonáda" evokes the cultural and architectural heritage of Central Europe, particularly the traditions of spa towns like Karlovy Vary. The setting highlights a character's experience or memory associated with the unique atmosphere of such a place.

114. Tsagaan Davaa (Цагаан Даваа)
- Meaning: "Tsagaan Davaa" translates to "White Pass" in Mongolian. "Tsagaan" means "white," and "Davaa" means "pass" or "mountain pass." The term is often used to describe mountain passes that are covered in snow or have a white, snowy appearance.
- Context: In the story, "Tsagaan Davaa" refers to a specific mountain pass or a symbolic location that characters traverse or reference. The mention of this pass evokes themes of journey, challenge, or transition, often associated with the harsh yet beautiful Mongolian landscape. The term also carries cultural significance, reflecting the traditional importance of natural landmarks in Mongolian geography and folklore.

115. Tsogzolmaa (Цогзолмаа)
- Meaning: A traditional Mongolian female name, possibly symbolizing brilliance or radiance.
- Context: In the story, Tsogzolmaa plays a significant role, tying into themes of family and heritage. Her presence impacts the protagonist's understanding of their identity and past.

116. The Thinker:
- Meaning: A famous bronze sculpture by Auguste Rodin, depicting a man in deep thought.
- Context: Symbolizes contemplation, philosophy, and perhaps the existential themes in the narrative.

117. Tsam Dance (Цам):
    - Meaning: A sacred dance performed in Tibetan Buddhism, often depicting various deities and religious concepts.
    - Context: Represents the rich cultural and religious traditions of Tibetan Buddhism.
118. Tugrug (Төгрөг)
    - Meaning: Tugrug, also spelled Tögrög, is the official currency of Mongolia. Its symbol is ₮, and its ISO currency code is MNT. The word "tugrug" translates to "circle" in Mongolian, referring to the round shape of coins.
    - Context: The Tugrug has been the official currency of Mongolia since 1925, replacing the Mongolian dollar. It is used in everyday transactions throughout Mongolia.
119. Tumen (Түмэн, Түмэт)
    - Meaning: A military unit of 10,000 soldiers in the Mongol army. During that time, the Mongol military was organized into hierarchical units: *Aravt* (10 soldiers), *Zuut* (100 soldiers), *Myangat* (1,000 soldiers), and *Tumen* (10,000 soldiers).
    - Context: The term reflects the highly organized and disciplined structure of the Mongol military, which was instrumental in their conquests and governance. It symbolizes the strength and unity of the Mongol forces
120. Tushita (Тушита):
    - Meaning: A heavenly realm in Buddhist cosmology where future Buddhas reside before their final rebirth.
    - Context: Symbolizes spiritual attainment and the continuity of consciousness beyond death.
121. UAZ 69:
    - Meaning: A type of Soviet/Russian off-road jeep vehicle, commonly used in military and rural areas. UAZ stands for "Ulyanovsky Avtomobilny Zavod" (Ulyanovsk Automobile Plant).

- Context: Represents a vehicle commonly used in the Soviet Union and post-Soviet states.

122. Ugandahama Bandid (Угандхамала Бандид):
    - Meaning: A title or honorific used within the story, likely signifying a learned person or high-ranking monk in Mongolian and Tibetan cultures. "Bandid" (Sanskrit: पण्डित, Paṇḍita) typically refers to a scholar or someone of high spiritual attainment.
    - Context: In the story, Ugandahama Bandid is a revered spiritual figure. His character symbolizes the transmission of ancient Buddhist wisdom and the pursuit of spiritual enlightenment, serving as a guide for other characters on their spiritual journeys.

123. Uyangaa (Уянгаа)
    - Meaning: A Mongolian female name meaning "melody" or "harmony." The name reflects gentleness and artistic beauty, often associated with someone who brings peace or joy, much like a pleasant song.
    - Context: In the story, Uyangaa is depicted as an artist with a sweet and innocent demeanor. Her name aligns with her personality and work, as she is described as a "happy artist" whose optimism is evident in her paintings. Avid considers taking her to Amsterdam, believing she would appreciate the city's rich artistic heritage.

124. Vincent van Gogh (Винсент Ван Гог):
    - Meaning: A famous Dutch post-impressionist painter known for his vivid and emotional works.
    - Context: Represents art, creativity, and possibly the inner turmoil of a character.

125. Vperyod s pesnei! (Вперёд с песней!):
    - Meaning: "Forward with a song!" This is a Russian phrase often used in a military or enthusiastic context, encouraging people to move forward with energy or spirit.
    - Context: Reflects the mood or atmosphere of a scene.

126. Xanadu-colored
    - Meaning: A color reminiscent of the mythical city of Xanadu, often associated with a greenish-gray or misty hue.
    - Context: In the story, this term describes the footbath and the window frame in Avid's hotel room, evoking a mystical, dream-like quality that contributes to the exotic and tranquil atmosphere of the setting.
127. Yassa (Ясса):
    - Meaning: The legal code established by Genghis Khan, also known as the Great Yassa or Great Law.\
    - Context: Symbolizes law, order, and the governance of the Mongol Empire.
128. Yesugei Baatar (Есүгэй Баатар):
    - Meaning: The father of Genghis Khan, a respected Mongol leader.
    - Context: Represents historical Mongolian figures and their importance in Mongolian culture and history.
129. Yurt (Юрт):
    - Meaning: A portable, round tent used by nomads in Central Asia, similar to the Mongolian ger.
    - Context: Represents the traditional nomadic lifestyle of Central Asian peoples.
130. Zanabazar (Занабазар):
    - Meaning: A prominent Mongolian religious leader, artist, and sculptor, known as the first Jebtsundamba Khutuktu.
    - Context: Represents the artistic and religious heritage of Mongolia.
131. Zud (Зуд):
    - Meaning: A natural disaster in Mongolia, characterized by harsh winter conditions that lead to the death of livestock.
    - Context: Represents the challenges of the Mongolian climate and its impact on the nomadic lifestyle.

www.ingramcontent.com/pod-product-compliance
Lightning Source LLC
LaVergne TN
LVHW040135080526
838202LV00042B/2914